I0758036

Cover art by Asher Reed
Editing by Stephanie Slagle
Editing by Varan Merten

This book was professionally typeset on Reedsy.
Find out more at reedsy.com

VARAN MERTEN

Mosaic

Contents

Dedication

To Drs. Lassiter and Workman

"You have found your voice."

I

Opus Tessellatum: Ambedo

Where Were You?

Let me tell you where I was when it happened. It may not be easy to hear, but I'm talking about March 1993.

A week beforehand, on a Sunday, I was at a family reunion. I had been looking forward to it for a couple of reasons. I was happy to be out of church for one thing. I was thirteen at the time and had grown bored of church. It was a social club shindig, populated by very old, very nosy people who asked me the same questions about my future on Sunday mornings and Wednesday nights.

Every time I thought of the word "church," I pictured them leaning in while talking to each other in a hullabaloo. The sermon just finished, and their faces all raised eyebrows and stretched smiles. Just looking at the scene, you'd think they were all sharing dirty jokes under their breath. Instead, they were bragging to each other and social jousting.

I had been wanting to visit my grandfather, Pap, the one on my father's side. I didn't get along with my mother's family, but I'll address that later. As this was a reunion with my father's family, his two brothers, my uncles, were there, along with their wives and children. This was the third reason I had been looking forward to this outing. I only had two friends, one was Destin, my neighbor from across the street. The other was my cousin Jacob. His family lived ninety miles away, so I only saw him at birthday parties or reunions, and I was eager to catch him up on everything I had going on.

We all met at my parents' house, and after the older folk absconded to the kitchen to cook and share gossip, my grandfather called me over to where he sat in the TV room. My grandmother, Maw, had parked Pap's wheelchair in a little space between the couch and Dad's recliner, which I supposed was planning ahead. My grandfather was eager to share his latest news as well, and he decided to practice on me before he gave my dad the full scoop – he'd had both legs amputated a few months back due to diabetes. While he was recovering, he developed double pneumonia. After this, the VA drug their feet getting him his prosthetics, and, once he got them they were sized wrong.

"This'un," he said in a whispy, broken voice as he rubbed his right thigh, hidden beneath an argyle blanket, "They just messed it up. It'll twist, you know? Out at an angle like'yat." He motioned with his hands. From his description, I imagined his new legs would have him walking like Charlie Chaplin. He paused, staring off and lighting up a cigarette.

"You still smoke?" I asked. It was a stupid question, but I just wanted him to keep talking. Here was the man who'd told me about the Dresden firebombing, had taught me how an automatic assault rifle works, and shared a plethora of war stories and esoteric minutia. It had been a while since he'd regaled me with one of these. For the past few years, he'd mostly concerned himself with politics… and health.

"Yeah, I do," he said, taking a deeper drag and turning to talk to me again. He waved his hand between us to spare me the gust of Turkish menthol. "I's telling Maw the other day, though, I still mean to make it to a hundred. I'm gonna do it, too. You just watch."

"Maybe the VA will get you the right fit by then," I said. I was trying for a joke. To my delight, he chuckled. His eyes brightened a bit before he broke away and blew his next puff toward the window. "Yeah, it'd probably take'em that long."

After the party, Dad told me Pap had talked to him about living wills and power of attorney, and said that Dad should call a probate lawyer to learn a thing or two, "sooner rather than later, Boy."

I was busy thinking about a new joke to make Paw laugh again before they called us in for dinner, or maybe steer the subject over to some World War Two stories about his time aboard the *Nimitz,* when Jacob walked into the room. Without a single word or gesture of introduction, he flung both his arms in the air in a victory pose and half-shouted, "Mortal Kom-baaaaat!"

Before I knew it, we were headed outside. A brief shouting match between Jacob and his father about appropriate volume and public embarrassment had ensued. I think I said goodbye to Paw. I reassured myself that I did. I distinctly remembered looking back at him, still smoking in his chair by the window, the television streaming CNN.

"Jacob, you take that noise outside!" his parents were saying in tumbling unison as we made our way through the kitchen and onto the back deck. I fought back a laugh. They were at least twice as loud shouting at him as he ever was with his antics. I wondered if that was the secret punchline in his head, the whole reason he did it.

"Mama's gonna knock you aahhhh-uuuut!" Jacob called back as we neared the door. He gave them an Arsenio-style fist pump and then— blip— we were outside and talking and catching up.

"You know what I've been getting into recently?" I told Jacob as soon as we were out of earshot. "Vampires. I saw *Bram Stoker's Dracula*— late at night by the way— and you know what? It's good. I didn't expect it to be. I thought it would be all about sex, but it's actually really cool! There's a point where he proves he's dead to this girl by making her feel his heartbeat, or lack of one. He says, 'There is no life… in this body.' You have to see it! The special effects are out of this world. I bought the book. It's good too. It's one of my favorites. Top three. Right up there with *Firestarter*."

Jacob listened and gave some comments here and there. We walked around the block, filling the time with our ideas for horror novels and which animals we would mix together if we were genetic engineers. We missed dinner, and the whole family let us hear about it when we got back. They sat us down and proclaimed that in all future gatherings, Jacob and I weren't allowed to be "off in our own little world." The phrase "grow up" was peppered in for good measure.

At first, I was worried, until I lay in bed that night thinking about it. I took it to be set in stone, the prospect of never being able to share my secret interests with one of my only friends. It felt like a prison sentence. Then, I remembered Jacob bellowing "Mama's gonna knock you out," to his parents, and it dawned on me that this rebellious streak of ours would not be quelled so easily.

My parents were concerned about my lack of friends. My mother confided in me during a car ride to the grocery store one day that she blamed our neighborhood… to a point. My parents had met in college, where they had both been pre-med. Their plan was to have the perfect upper-class Southern American dream: Dad would become a doctor; Mom would become a nurse. Then, they would have all the money and prestige that anyone could ask for and live happily ever after.

It didn't go quite as planned. Mom found she didn't have the stomach for nursing. She wound up teaching high school biology. Dad, however, made it through medical school, and, once he had completed his residency, we moved to a very exclusive neighborhood in Birmingham called Glen Iris Estates. By this time, I was about eight.

"I know it's been hard for you," Mom decided to broach the topic mid-drive, thankfully keeping her eyes on the road. Oftentimes, she would fix me in a stare when she was trying one of our heart-to-hearts, just to let me know how sincere she was being. "I know there aren't many kids your age in the neighborhood, and that's our fault. And I want you to know we take full responsibility for that." She placed her hand on her chest as if testifying. Suddenly, she did turn to me.

"But you have to start putting yourself out there," she said, her eyebrows going skyward. "A man is known by the company he keeps. Have you ever heard that? Do you know what that means? A man, and you will be a man sooner than you think, becomes the kind of person he surrounds himself with. You think you're just going to hang around with Jacob and Destin your whole life? Is that how you want to – well, and just walk off whenever you feel like it and have your little talks about blood and murder and all that stuff?" She was getting herself angry. I wanted to tell her to watch the road, but at this point, it would only make her more determined to stare at me. To her, I would be "diverting," rather than calling attention to our safety.

Diverting was a cardinal sin, so I just listened intently and said a little prayer in my head that we'd get to the store in one piece.

"And if you think you're going to spend the rest of your life wallowing in all that dark stuff, you've got another thing coming. Tonight, after homework and prayers, we're going through your room, and we're going to go through every book and every movie, and all your little drawings. And you can explain to me if you think each one pleases the Lord or not."

I had a feeling the Lord wasn't going to be too pleased. After my silent prayer to arrive at the store unscathed was answered, I made a plan to excuse myself to the bathroom during supper. That would give me a five-minute window, maybe enough time to hide some of my most treasured contraband.

That night, I wrapped my copy of *Dracula* in toilet paper and tossed it out my window into the bushes below. There it stayed, safe from the culling that happened later that night until I plucked it back out when I got off the bus the next day.

Rescuing *Dracula* wasn't the only thing that excited me about that Monday. Both Mom and Dad worked late, so I had plenty of time with the house to myself. I Destin over. We were working our way through *A Link to the Past* and had gotten to the Dark World the Friday before. I was salivating over what would come next, and Destin was the perfect guy to play games with.

He was a natural-born comic, two years older than me with a learner's permit and an encyclopedic knowledge of all the best stand-up routines. He'd memorized Carlin, Pryor, Kennison. He knew them all, and he swore like a sailor, which I was never allowed to do. When we gamed, he would fall off a cliff or die to a boss and have me on the verge of wetting myself with his rapid-fire combos like "fuck-shit-what?" or screaming out "cooooooock-*suck*" like a sneeze.

On this particular Monday, however, he brought company, another kid a little older than him. His name escapes me to this day. They met me on my porch, where we stayed for the entirety of our visit. The new guy pulled out a pack of cigarettes and offered us both one. Destin smiled and waved it away casually. I tried to do the same but ended up looking ridiculous.

"Yeah, you're right," the new guy said, grinning. "You're not old enough."

Lighting up, he asked me if I had a girlfriend. When I said no, he ignored me for the rest of the visit and talked to Destin about a girl in their class. He described her developing breasts, and how she must be interested in him because of the tops she wore. He asked Destin about his dating habits, and then started talking about his love life, bragging about his skill at "getting some." He put his index and middle fingers to his mouth and made sounds like a dog eating soup.

From there, the conversation moved naturally to sports, where, again, I had little to add. By "little," I mean nothing. I was happy when Destin brought up Michael Jordan— I at least knew who he was, but then I shut my mouth when Destin explained he was sad to hear Jordan had lost his father.

"Fuck," said the older kid. "I don't feel sorry for him. Nigga's so rich he can buy his self a new father."

I didn't know how to respond to that. Not only was it senseless and mean, but I'd never heard a white person under the age of thirty use that word. I endured as much as I could, then gave Destin one of our secret signs— a tug at my right ear— which meant that he had gotten me into an uncomfortable situation, and I wanted out. He seemed to ignore me, which sent a chill up my spine. My brain started feeding me nightmare scenarios. They were planning on attacking me, breaking into my house, and robbing my parents. That sort of thing.

Eventually, they did leave, and Destin explained to me the next day that he couldn't take my hint immediately. The older guy would have caught on that we were sending secret signals, which would have "pissed him off." He had seen my ear tug, Destin told me in a serious tone, but reassured me he had assumed I was massaging a newly healed ear piercing. This meant I was gay, and the older guy wanted nothing to do with me. This suited me just fine.

Life was uneventful until Thursday. I'm sure you remember where you were when you saw it. By it, I mean *him.*

I was in Art, which was my third-period class. This kid named McDermott, but everyone called him Monkey-Dawg, was shaking his desk and saying,

"He-he, Beavis… Beavis, he… he-he-he-heh." I watched him do this for a full minute, and, as I gazed at his vacant eyes, I felt a rush of feelings I had been hiding come to the surface.

I was afraid. Afraid of spending the rest of my life around these … *people.* I was afraid of what I was becoming. I lied to my parents. I hated church. I was angry. Angry at the world. Angry to the point of hatred. Sometimes, looking at all the cars in traffic or watching newscasters smile their way through another story about child molestation or a random shooting, I felt like I could—

And then it happened. The television set in the upper corner of the room turned on. Static at first. Then, as you well know, it rose to a high pitch, almost like tinnitus. I felt it in my head, as if all the moisture had left my Eustachian tubes and sinuses and was replaced by a cool, dry wind. I swallowed and moved my tongue around, trying to work up some relief. I dimly heard a girl to my right do the same.

Our teacher, her hands to her head, moved to turn off the set. Then he appeared.

Cecil Babbage. I don't know how you feel hearing that name again. To me, it sounded exotic, exciting.

"Hello, everyone," he said, that posh English accent softening his words. Still, to our ears, it was like cutting steel. He introduced himself, explained the obvious, that he was English, and then apologized for interrupting our day.

How very English of you to apologize like that right off the bat, I remember thinking. Then, two things hit me like a hammer to the chest. He was not addressing our class, or even our school. When he said "you," he meant all of us— the entire world. Next, I saw that his lips had not been moving.

My headache intensified. Some of the other kids, Monkey-Dawg included, got nose-bleeds. The girl to my right started to cry, causing the teacher to walk over and put an arm around her.

"I have been approached by a visitor…" Babbage said. "A vagabond of sorts… from *up there.*" And then he pointed at the ceiling.

What did you do when you saw that? When you heard him say those words? I pitched forward and vomited right then and there. Light brown, warm and chunky, over all four sides of my desk. And my eyes never left the screen.

Next came the part where he talked about his visitor sharing "certain gifts" with him, as well as secrets of the universe.

"It lives behind my eyes. Watching. Always watching. It is, of course, thanks to its gifts that I am able to reach out to all of you." I was hooked. I had to meet this man.

Babbage went on to tell us about his plans for a press tour, first in his home country, and then in the US and Canada. I knew he wouldn't be coming to Birmingham. New York and Washington, certainly. Maybe Los Angeles. But that would put him on the same continent at least. I could hitchhike there. No, too dangerous. It occurred to me that I could steal a car.

"Goodbye to you all," and with that, Babbage was done, leaving us to sit in complete silence. Every once in a while, one of us would look around and lock eyes with a classmate, just to reassure each other that we all had witnessed the same thing.

Yes! I thought, over and over. Yes! This was real. This was actually happening… to me! This life. My life! The most amazing thing that had ever happened in human history, and I was going to be a part of it. My chest swelled. I thought my heart would burst.

"Attention students and faculty," came a subdued voice through the intercom. Monkey-Dawg yelped and fell off his chair. The teacher, who was still standing beside me, comforting the girl, reached out in surprise and squeezed my shoulder so hard she gave me a bruise that lasted into the next week. "In light of recent events, all classes are canceled for the day. Parents will be notified by phone, and buses will be provided for all students."

The speaker, our principal, paused a moment before adding, "Go home. Be with your families… God be with us, amen."

Those were the only words I heard anyone speak for twenty-four straight hours. My parents didn't speak to me. My father had to overnight at the hospital, which I expected. My mother came home and opened the door to my room. Seeing me on my bed, looking at the ceiling, the worry left her brow, and then she retreated into her bedroom to cry. Her sobbing seemed to fill the entire neighborhood. There was no other sound at first. Not one. No television, no cars. All of that changed as soon as night fell.

Once the crickets and frogs started up, I beggan hearing arguments from my neighbors. My mother was fast asleep, Klonopin and wine probably. A bird joined in the cacophony. I've never learned the species, but its call is nerve-wracking without the sounds of humanity drowning it out. Around three in the morning, I was treated to an end-of-the marriage fight three doors down, with the husband slamming the door on his way out and peeling tires as he drove off.

I stayed up all night, only to learn in the morning that Friday would be a normal school day. This was not told to me, but rather I learned it when I heard the bus pull up. Luckily, I was too restless to just stay in bed. I had already showered and dressed before the sun rose.

I went through my classes. We all did, very dutifully, but nothing happened. Some kids hadn't been early birds like me. They were still wearing their PJ's and walked around with unbrushed teeth. Our teachers sat at their desks, covering their faces with books or just looking out the window the whole time. In the hall, Destin found me and broke the silence. "Did you... d-dijew..." It was as if he was recovering from a stroke.

"It's going to snow," he managed after some effort. I walked beside him, still in silence. I didn't know how to reply. Snow? Who cared about snow? We were not alone in the universe, and the first man to contact... well, you know. In perfect ironic timing, the principal announced that the school would be closing for inclement weather, affirming Destin's news.

"Shit," I said. So much for stealing a car. So much for the great escape.

Once I got home, my mother told me that her parents, who lived on a hill and didn't like the risk of ice, were coming to stay with us for the weekend. She was in total denial about what had happened. I never heard her mention it again. I think, deep in my heart, that she repressed it. It didn't happen. Just like a lot of things just didn't happen. She tried to reassure me that we would all have a good time. We would stay up late and sleep in as much as we wanted. We'd play in the snow, and then come inside and play UNO when we got too cold. All I could think about was spending the entire weekend with my maternal grandfather. Why couldn't Pap and Maw be the ones living on a damned hill? At least my door locked. They hadn't taken that away from me yet. Nasty old fucker. While I was at it, why couldn't he have just died before I hit puberty?

"Shit," I said before I could stop myself. She forgave me. She knew I "didn't get along" with her father. I never told her why, though. Hell, she wouldn't have believed me if I had.

Later that night my family spent a good hour watching the blizzard. Dad was again overnighting at the hospital. I went downstairs to the study and watched the news. I tried every channel, sifting through a lot of government officials saying a lot of very wordy and very expected things. Clinton's voice was more hoarse than usual, and in lieu of the Press Secretary, the Secretary of Defense took the podium next, and announced he would not be taking any questions, but rather his prepared statement should clear up any concerns the American people had "at this time." He kept pinching the bridge of his nose as he muddled his way through a Teddy Roosevelt-styled speech of tough talk about "protecting our shores." After that, he transitioned into unity and helping one another in the months to come, although without specifics as to what kind of help he meant. Mom explained later that he meant, "Don't turn America into one, big LA ghetto while we're trying to protect you. We only have so many guns and so many soldiers. And don't expect us to give you any money, either."

She was right. Two days later they passed that new defense spending bill… on a Sunday, mind you. If memory serves, there was just one nay.

I tuned in to MTV to catch Liquid Television. I was sick of politics. If there was any news about Babbage, I doubted I'd miss it.

As it turns out, I was right. The night of the twelfth was when MI6 did their own worldwide broadcast. A commercial for *Beavis and Butt-head* had just come on.

As I'm sure you recall, the feed was interrupted by the Presidential Seal, and then there was a brief interlude, again by the mumbling Secretary of Defense, followed by a representative of MI6, British Intelligence in a taped announcement. A thought jumped into my head that, somewhere out there, Monkey-Dawg was also watching this. Was he reassured by the Secretary of Defense "protecting our shores?" I stifled a laugh.

Then, there he was again.

Cecil Babbage, now seated in a hospital bed. He looked much older, lines sunk into his face and premature jowls around his mouth. His eyes were glazed over from what I assumed was Thorazine or lithium. A time signature on the tape showed that this was mere hours old. He had an IV in one arm and the cuff of a polygraph on the other.

"Is your name Cecil Iverson Babbage?" the technician asked.

"Yes," Cecil answered in monotone. In trying to locate the speaker, he darted his eyes back and forth like a metronome. His mouth was so wet from drool it sounded to me like he had said, "Guess."

My heart dropped. I knew it. I knew this would happen. The best thing in all of human history, and now look what they'd done to him. The control questions continued, and he answered in the same electronic timbre.

"Is it your intention to lie to me today?" asked the tech.

"Well … yes," said Cecil, managing a weak smile. "Becau—"

I noticed they spliced the tape there. The time signature was different. I checked. Had I not, I might've thought I only imagined he was about to say "because." But no, it was not my imagination. He was about to tell them to their corrupt, envious faces why he had all the right in the world to lie to them. It was at this point I saw the hospital restraints on his wrists.

The tech asked if he had truly been inhabited by another being, which he affirmed. "A being from outer space?" Again, confirmed. "Can you confirm that the being is no longer inhabiting your mind?" Yet again, confirmed.

"My visitor has left me," he said, pain showing on his face for the first time. "But it must be. It is … just how it is… must be. Moved on."

"Are you aware of the whereabouts of your visitor at this moment?"

"Dead."

"Are you certain of this fact, and how can you know this for certain?"

"It told me… they die … reproducing. They die … divide like amoebas … reproduction. Die."

The tech left from view and spoke to others off-screen. Once he returned, "To be clear, Mr. Babbage, you are claiming that there are multiple, er, *visitors* now? Are they here with us, or have they … departed?"

"Oh, they're here. Still. More… learning. Needs. Need to."

That was all I needed to hear. "Oh ye of little faith!" I screamed and dove into the pillows of the couch, "I *told* you this was the best thing! The best thing that's *ever fucking happened!*"

The next day, my family made good on their attempt to play outside in the snow. I was ready first and was standing at the open door to the porch. I didn't hear my grandfather approach. He groped me as he walked past, which he hadn't done in months.

"World sure is changing, isn't it, Frisky?" Frisky was his nickname for me. I turned around and went to my room, locking the door. I refused to answer my mom's pleas and threats. I even hid under my bed, until it dawned on me that I was a thirteen-year-old hiding under his own bed. After that, I stayed under the bed a little longer, cursing myself.

We were snowed in for a week. The drifts topped thirty-six inches in some places. Thankfully, we never lost power, so I was able to watch TV and read at night. I mostly lived a nocturnal existence, avoiding the family and answering questions in one or two words. To any inquiry that required more detail, I shrugged.

It is amazing what some time alone can do to clear your head. It was time to sever unhealthy ties. Why not? What, in the end, was I holding onto?

On that seventh night, my course became clear.

I was destined to acquire my own cosmic visitor. They would continue to spread, just like a disease. Eventually they would make their way across the globe! But, I realized, the government would step in. *Protecting our shores.*

Besides, it would only be temporary, if Cecil Babbage was to be believed. The visitor would inhabit me, then the time would come for it to breed, and it would divide in two and leave, possibly damaging my brain in the process.

Was it even worth it? It was still the best thing ever, the most important event in human history and all, but hardly the miracle I needed to get myself out of this… life. I wanted to be free from people, and I had thought this was my golden ticket. Nope. Just another drug. Just another temporary fix. There was no escaping the rat race.

For the third time, the television feed was interrupted. This time I had it on the weather channel. Jim Cantore was cut off mid-sentence while talking about Superstorm '93. There was a flash of static for a second, and then the screen skipped to the hangout interview room from MTV's *120 minutes*. It had been rotoscoped and washed, and throbbing with LSD colors. For a moment, I just stared, absorbing this nauseating barrage of color. A figure stepped into focus, filling the screen with his face. He was a pale young man with black hair flowing down to his collar bones. I remember taking him at first glance to be a white shaman, with his long hair and glassy eyes. I was not far off.

"Been watching the news, guys?" he said with a smile. "First, let me say something to the fans. You know who you are. It's true, guys and gals. They breed. And the experience, when one chooses you… *apotheosis!*" He drew the word out long and loud. "Maybe, if everyone gets good grades and does their homework, we'll reach out to you. How's that sound?"

All my doubts melted in a flash.

"Now let me say something to the rest of you - the unwashed crowd, the scared little sheep, and the big men with big guns. All your threats… nothing. Your world is ending. Once this is all over, once we're done with you, it won't be BC and AD anymore. It'll be: before we came and after. I hope that scares you. I hope that has you shaking in your combat boots.

"I'll leave you with this: My name is Brad Warren. I'm an American, and I'm standing right now on American soil. Where exactly? All I can say is… *catch me if you can!*"

Blip. Cantore picked up right where he left off, then touched his earpiece, apologized for the interrupted feed, and strove to gather his thoughts. Apparently, Cantore was one of those people who was scared by Mr. Warren's announcement.

I sat there grinning at the TV screen. *I knew it!* I was right the whole time. Warren's speech was the shot in the arm I needed. No more doubts, no more hesitation.

I kept up my passive shrinking violet act for the rest of the week. Once the snow melted, I could hardly contain myself.

The first day back at school I stepped off the bus, and then turned right around and walked back home. Once there, I ransacked the place. I took $500 from my dad's safe, along with his credit card and his 9mm. I loaded and cocked the gun a dozen times, practicing until it was as smooth as flipping a light switch. Putting the safety on, I looked in their bedroom mirror. I imagined my mother looking at me, gun in hand. I cocked it one more time. Yes. Yes, that click! The car was waiting for me in the garage. Beyond that, the whole world.

"A man is known by the company he keeps," I said, mocking her phantom. I gave in to the call then, the call I had felt since the day I had vomited onto my desk, to join the greatest event in history. I shouted as I ran down the hall.

"A man is known by the company he keeps!"

It Started Like Any Other Day

The sun rises on cursed days and blessed days alike without a hint of what is about to happen. No matter how psychic you are, some days are as subtle as a blade up a sleeve. They have your number, and your number's up.

The day that vaulted my life in a new direction happened back in the Nineties. I loved that decade. It was a lot like the Seventies, but darker in attitude and with less hair. I was still living in Britain at the time. It was a sweet setup, an apartment at Oxford, a seat in Parliament, and also a vacation home I was rather proud of— a little lighthouse across the strait from Shetland Isle just north of Scotland, situated in Symbister Harbour. Not far from that was a town called Twatt. That's just an interesting fact. I also had accounts in Andorra and the Caymans, stock in Silicon Valley, the whole works.

To be clear, this is a memoir ... of a sort. We are not allowed to write memoirs under any circumstances, but I'm doing it anyway ... Not to publish. I'm just going to keep it in a safe place and read it to myself years from now, imagining what it would be like if someone trustworthy were to read it. Maybe it will cheer me up during a fire-lit winter evening of nostalgia, but that's doubtful. Really, I just need a record of what happened the day my life changed forever.

I was in Oxford at the time, and it was a nice, damp morning in autumn, with cold mist that stung the nose and a sky that hung like a grey quilt. I was in my living room catching up on current events. The washroom radio was buzzing its assorted reports from down the hall, and the tele in the drawing room was set to CSPAN. I had copies of all the essentials – the *Sun,* the *New Yorker,* that month's *Time* had just come out, and, to round it all off, I had the latest *Reader's Digest.* That last one was just for fun.

It takes me a long while to digest all this, longer than most members of my family. I get distracted by the Signals. I'm talking about stimuli that come in via the Third Eye, the parietal eye. More on that later.

I should mention here that I'm a Lizard. If you're unfamiliar with the terms *Archon* or *Anunnaki,* then just stick with Lizard, capitalized. Specifically, I'm a Varanid, a monitor, a cousin to the snakes. Why am I so easily distracted? I have theories. For one thing, I didn't learn to read until I was 233,345,071. That may have had something to do with it.

The Third Eye, as I mentioned, receives Signals from all over— weather events, times and motions of heavenly bodies, moods and zeitgeists of populations, everything. With training, we can even read the thoughts of an individual person. That's hard though. Odd, most Mammals assume it's the other way around. But no, it's easier to read the thoughts of a whole country than those of a single person. I guess it's like how it's easier to see someone's hairstyle than to notice a single hair. You might think that's a poor metaphor, but it's apt— you can notice a single hair, for instance, if it stands out. Keep that in mind.

As I remember it, I was reclined on a nice divan that I had dragged into the living room from the library, shaking my head to shut out the psychic noise. I looked at the aforementioned pile of periodicals, psyching myself up, ha ha, to the task of reading them. I was not in one of my tidy modes that day. Books and sketch pads were everywhere. Tables with sawn-off legs served as foundations for my breeding stations— arthropods, rodents, and fish. Bags of feed, mulch, and bottles of distilled water were stacked against the wall, resting on old newspapers and bedsheets. In short, I was sitting pretty.

Then the doorbell rang.

I was not expecting company, nor any delivery. A casual scan towards the

door reveals the tell-tale signs of another Lizard, so that meant last-minute news. Moreover, it must be news of a personal nature, something that must be discussed face-to-face.

I adopted human form before opening the door, and much to my disappointment my visitor turned out to be a certain Gecko.

I had history with this specimen. Not more than 15 years prior he had darkened my doorstep and given me the assignment to speak to an amateur writer, a Brit, by the name of David Vaughan Icke. The assignment was to reveal our true nature, to a measured point, and our plans for humanity, again, to a measured point, to Mr. Icke so that he might write a doctrine that would serve to enlist some brave souls to volunteer for our experiments... or some rot. Icke and I didn't get along, more on that later, and the whole thing was a bust, more on *that* later.

The Gecko let himself in and announced the usual pleasantries— that he was here on official business, the usual apologies if he had interrupted anything, and how have I been. He then steped into my kitchen and helped himself to some eggs. I despise Geckos— all the vacant stares and eyeball licking; if you can't put your tongue to good use, keep it in your damn mouth. Again, I had history with this individual.

He sat at the far end of the kitchen taking a seat at the table just before the window with a good view of the backyard's greenhouse. He began setting a dozen or so of my breakfast eggs out in front of him while, with his spare foot, he pushed out a chair for me.

I take him in. He was wearing his human form and dressed in a nicely tailored black suit, no hat, with those shoes that held pennies in them for some reason. His tie was the deep orange of the last light of a sunset, laced with black swirling fractals. Thankfully, he had not applied cologne. I was grateful for that. Full beard, recently trimmed by a professional.

It dawned on me that this was serious.

"Is that your normal dress at this hour?" he asked, with a nod in my direction. At the same time, he began eating an egg, shell and all. At his question, I took stock of myself— black silk all over me, I looked like David Bowie in pajamas.

"Yes," I replied, and took a step toward him. There were two or three bottles of Luksusowa, empty bottles, under the table. I wanted to avoid explaining those, so I tried to redirect his attention to me. "Did you want some ham to go with those eggs?" I stepped closer and then turned away, hoping his gaze would follow me to the ice box. "Or maybe some fresh, squeezed juice?"

"You're being reassigned." He let the words drop from his mouth. I stopped in my tracks— feeling ridiculous, out of place even— in the middle of my own kitchen. My shoulders dropped as I turn back to face him.

"See?" He notched an eyebrow and motioned to the empty chair with an open palm. "I thought you'd want to sit down for this."

Insolent bastard. Of course they'd send you. Of course!

I walked to the table but neglected to take the chair. "I'm being what?" It wasn't real yet. Reassignment? There was no way. Out of the question.

"You know what?" continued the Gecko, smiling up at me before popping another egg into his mouth. "Instead of ham, do you have any vodka? Polish if you can manage, but I could also take— "

I reached under the table and grabbed one of the Luksusowa bottles. I shook it while locking eyes with him. "Fresh out" I waited a beat before setting the bottle between us and then sat down.

Several things occurred to me in the brief silence that followed. *Damn, I could go for some vodka at the moment...* and second: *I'm sure the bastard said that to start a craving fit in my head.*

"The committee has discussed this for some time," he broke the silence. "And we believe your talents would be best utilized elsewhere."

"Don't be vague. Where?"

"Don't be insolent. This is not a punishment. You are to move to the United States."

"They plan on making me a Yank?"

"A hick, actually. You'll be living in the South."

I began rubbing my eyes. This wasn't so bad. Taxation was lower across the pond, as was the cost of living. I could start anew, perhaps make a living as a... what was open to me? Taxidermist?

"Also," he smiled, "You will be given a lifespan. And yes, *that* is a punishment."

My face dropped. He had to be joking. I looked at him for a very long time, taking in the smallest movement. He was not joking. I began taking deeper and deeper breaths. I wanted to say something, but I was not sure what. A plea? Protest? Threat?

"2056," he added, summing it up. "At some point in 2056 you will pass away from a to-be-determined illness that will fall within the guidelines of medicinal technology of that decade. From what I've heard, it will be relatively swift and painless. If the economy permits, you will be offered any and all possible forms of palliative care."

After a full minute of silence— a full minute he basked in— my lovely brain reminded me that there was a half bottle of Luksusowa Black on a bookshelf in my library. It was right between my copy of *The Devil's Dictionary* and my Anne Rice collection. I rose from the table without a word and prepared to make my way to it. The Gecko, however, halted me.

"I need acknowledgment."

I turned back to him.

"You must not leave without saying anything. You should acknowledge the committee's business before you go off," he began pointing his index finger at me and spinning it in little circles, "going off trying to find whatever it is you're off trying to find."

"My silence is compliance enough, I'd say." With that, I left him in the kitchen and took long strides into the library.

Actually, the fact that I'm not licking your blood off the sides of my mouth right now – that's compliance.

I reached the bookshelf, but the bottle was missing. Shaking my head, I concentrate. I must have moved it. When did I last see it? Night before last? As my thoughts danced, my eyes darted to a copy of *Days of Decision* by none other than D. V. Icke. Poor bastard. Looks like I laughed too soon. I remembered someone telling him once, "But they are laughing *at* you, not *with you*."

And I had smiled.

I was sent to meet with Icke in 1989. I was reluctant, not even taking the assignment seriously. Icke was a sportscaster, hardly a scholar, and completely unprepared to handle any information about us or our history. I had been reassured by the committee that he was open-minded, and thus a good choice. So, on a nice chilly March evening, I stole into a hotel room where he was staying and spied on him a good while, gathering my thoughts as to how to introduce myself. To my surprise, he bolted upright in bed and blurted out, "If someone is there, can you just show your bloody self? You're driving me up the wall!"

Impressed, I uncloaked to talk. I wore my human guise of course. He wasn't ready for the full Monty.

If only I had followed my original instinct. This man was not cut out to be a prophet. Actually, no. I'm being too hard on him. The plain fact is that this world has no more use for prophets. In truth, it never had.

We tried it before, playing the deity game, choosing favorites to carry our message. It never worked, and it only got harder each time. You'd think we'd learn.

One of my favorite legends the Mammals have come up with is out of Madagascar. Here's how it goes: Long ago, when the world was young, the Chameleon was the fastest of God's creatures. The hyperactive little guy would rush hither and yon, playing pranks on everyone. This went on for a while, with the other animals tolerating Chameleon's antics, until one day the little lizard wasn't watching where he was going and ran into God's infant son, sending the poor tyke crashing to the ground. In his anger, God smacked the Chameleon square between the eyes, knocking them out of focus forever. From then on, the Chameleon watched where he is going very carefully, placing each step with absolute care, and teaching his offspring to do the same.

You'll notice that I don't capitalize God's pronouns. There is a reason for that. In any case, I mention all that to say, it's funny that, in the legend, the lizard learns from his mistake.

The Gecko's hand fell on my shoulder, snapping me back to attention. "I'm sorry for how I acted back there," he told me.

"Don't." I deepened my voice to a whisper. "Get. Your hand…"

He removed his hand and stepped up beside me. "Chalk it up to professional jealousy."

"This whole island runs on 'professional jealousy.'" I turned away from the bookshelf. If it wasn't in here, then I must have taken it to a place out of the ordinary, and the only reason to do that would be if something had come up. What had happened this week that was out of the ordinary?

"This isn't because of the Icke debacle."

"Debacle? Is that what they call setting me up for failure?"

"I was involved too, don't forget. As I said, this is about several things. It's been a long time coming."

"You weren't involved. You just delivered the assignment. You were the messenger. In Chaucer's time, you'd be the Summoner. Can't hate you, you're just the guy … you're Mercury."

"I see where you're headed … I'm a trickster god, is that it? Your troubles are all others' doing."

I scoff, "We all wanted to be gods, you remember? And look how well *that* worked."

"Are you about to quote your thesis again?" the Gecko asked with the slightest smirk.

That hurt.

My doctorate was in Biophysics with a specialty in Human Population Mechanics and Mass Psychology. My doctoral thesis was a pessimistic little number that ruffled a few feathers. I argued that *Homo sapiens* was a fascinating but ultimately doomed species with an incurable propensity to take any and all discoveries and use them as weapons first, tools second. I cited numerous examples— the airplane, the atomic bomb. The list goes on and on. The committee tagged me on my citing the wheel as a weapon.

This has not been discovered by the Mammals yet, but the first use of the wheel was to grind bones to dust. That is not, they argued, weaponizing the wheel. I countered that it shows evidence of a mindset that said, "You know what this would be good for? Crushing bones. At the very least, that speaks of a deeply bellicose nature."

Long story short, I got my PhD.

"No need," I said back to him. "You name me one thing, one single thing the Mammals handle properly, whether it comes from us or not… in fact, *especially* if it comes from us."

"No one says 'Mammals' anymore."

"You really want to be of some use? Help me find my vodka."

"Are you going to force me to watch you debase yourself throughout the whole rest of this endeavor?"

I shook my head. "I'm hoping that once I…" I mimed the process of twisting the cap off the bottle and upending it into my mouth, "… that you'll leave."

He shook his head. "It pains me to see you like this."

"What? Happy?"

"Happy… you're happy?"

"I was until about fifteen minutes ago."

"Fifteen minutes? I delivered my news not thirty seconds ago. Thirty. Seconds."

I rubbed my eyes again. It occurred to me that I could return to my true form and taste the air; that would be a fast track to the bottle, but something, a lingering sense of propriety perhaps, stops me. As for me thinking fifteen minutes had passed… I left that alone.

"Were you serious about that? Wanting my help?" asked the Gecko

I considered the idea. "Yes, actually." More and more I'm thinking I'll need that vodka to wash down this news.

"How about the loo? Give it a look."

I did, with him trailing close behind. Sure enough, it was there in my shower, standing tall right next to the drain.

"I'll be damned." I snatched it up and spun around to face the Gecko, our noses almost touching. I wanted the message to be clear. *No judgment… and no sharing.* To my surprise, he didn't move out of my way, but instead produced a small, flat tin from his coat pocket. I smelled its contents even before he flipped it open. He held it between us, a nice array of home-rolled Turkish blend cigarettes.

"Fancy burning one?"

"I won't refuse." I shouldered past him, down the hall, and onto the veranda out back, overlooking my garden. I took a seat at the wrought iron table and pushed out a chair for him with my foot. He smiled and sat down.

"No ashtray?"

I snubbed my nose. "Hardly matters now."

He took one out and threw it into my lap as I began taking a swallow straight from the bottle. He rose and went back inside, announcing, "Just going in for a glass."

Good idea. Don't drink after me. I'm venomous.

I noticed that he had left me a lighter. *Bastard, that was rather polite, considering.* I lit up, and leaned back, propping one leg across the table.

Now with a smoke in one hand and a bottle in the other, I felt decadent. It felt good, if only for the moment.

I took a long puff. It had been years. It was smooth tobacco, too. Velvety. I felt the tingles start all over my arms then climb up my back and neck until they circled my face.

Now, that's nice. I took a small puff this time, then bounced it like a ball on my tongue and sucked it down.

The Gecko came back, setting down a pair of glasses and sliding one to me. I picked mine up without a word and heaved it clear across the garden, shattering it against the neighbor's fence. Both feet back on the pavement now, I marveled for a split second at how the shards sparkled like morning snow.

Damn. I'll never see snow again.

The Gecko did not react to my tantrum. Instead, he lit one for himself and borrowed my bottle, giving me a slight nod for permission as he took it from my hand. As he filled his glass, he settled into the chair and sighed.

"Don't think of it as a death sentence. See it rather as ... going home."

I frowned and gave a nod. It was not a bad way to look at it. In truth, I'd be hard-pressed to come up with something better if I were in his shoes delivering such news. Did it help? Not as much as the chemicals. I gazed off at that grey quilted sky, lost in my own smoke trails as they rise to join it.

Home is another Place. There is Our Place and then there is This Place. This Place is the one with galaxies and gravity and all these rules of time and motion. Our Place is different. Ours died long ago. No more stars, no more heat. No more anything. Nothing of substance, only the memory of it. We are the embodiments of those memories… if you could even call them memories. Just as you and everything around you is composed of elements that were forged in dying stars, we are composed of the last rotting detritus of our entire universe. Each and every one of us contains the information of the entire history of a cosmos, from birth to death.

But we could hardly have been called alive. We merely subsisted, swirling in smears against the edge of Our Place, what Icke liked to call "an alternate dimension." I liken us to the faint colors on the film of a bubble. We had thought, but nothing to think about. We had no life, merely the potential for it, waiting to be reignited.

Even we have no idea how long we existed in this limbo state, but soon something caught our attention: Your Place. How it happened is very odd.

You may have noticed that I have described our nature as very fluid. I believe that is what caused us to notice Your Place. It had existed for billions of years, even having developed life, without us giving it so much as a second glace. Yours is hardly the only universe out there. From our vantage point, we could see dozens.

To cut to the chase, it was the amniotic egg that caught and held our attention. There was something about the little island cosmos it represented. We could not look away, and soon, we found that we could bridge the gap between Our Place and This, bonding with and peering thru the living things born from this fascinating life factory. We became them even as they took shape inside their eggs. Such a marvel of nature, the egg, a perfect sea of personal nourishment, pure life essence. Thus, we took the form of the first reptiles, each of us choosing our favorites and following them from birth to death over and over.

As the years passed into centuries, and then centuries into millennia, we found ways to exert more influence over these scaled bodies. The bond strengthened until, over millions of years, the two lives became inseparable. We are the reptiles. They are us. We exist in This Place, and we still exist in Our Place. That is hard for certain human beings to understand. To his credit, Icke caught on immediately. He likened it to demonic possession, but I find that too harsh a comparison.

It is not so hard to imagine extra-dimensional living. Many things, especially things that contain high levels of information, exist on multiple levels. Take, for instance, this work, this collection of words. It exists as the arrangement of symbols before you, the language. It also exists within the device, behind the screen, etched out with a series of on-off switches, its "electronic self" so to speak. And, also, it is beginning to build a new self as you read it, scribing itself in a matrix of synapses somewhere in your brain, your own internal library. Every story, every article you've ever read becomes a part of your physical form. Thus, they exist in multiple forms in multiple places. Such is the nature of information.

I mention all that to say, that once they kill me here, I'll only lose half of myself. I'll go back to being a sentient bit of phlegm smeared across the edge of a neighboring universe. Would that be so bad?

Yes.

As I watched the smoke trailing from my cigarette, I contemplated fighting against them, attacking them even. Kill me? And they expected me to just take it?

We'll see about that!

My thoughts were interrupted as the Gecko takes his first swallow. He took it all at once, and then half-coughed, half gagged. Luksusowa Black is high octane, way above his pay grade. In fact, I smirked, smoking while you drink it might legally constitute a fire hazard.

He glares at me, snapping me to attention. I waved my hand at him.

No, no. I wasn't laughing at you.

I refilled his glass and explained the fire hazard joke in my head.

He smiled. "You know," he said as he exhaled another cloud. "I'm really going to miss this place."

"Someone else will get it. You'll be assigned to them, most likely. No worries."

"No, no, no. They are sending me with you."

My eyes bug out before I settle back down. "This just keeps getting worse."

"Oh stop. Stop pretending you don't like me."

I let silence swallow that statement. Imagine that. The two of us. Friends.

"So," I redirected. "This has nothing to do with Icke? Is that really what they told you? And you believe it?"

He didn't answer. After a while, he offered me another smoke, and I refilled his glass.

"You want some orange juice to go with that?" I asked.

"It's not Icke. That's for sure. No one holds that against us. You really want to know what it is? You're a bigot."

"What?!"

"*Also*, there's what happened with that whole Icke situation. The committee isn't too pleased with how you handled that. It was your job to see if there were discrepancies in the man… politically or… *mentally*."

"Oh, I see, and was this psyche eval supposed to take place *after* the "Psychic Lizards run the World" speech or before?"

"You read minds."

"Granted. But I can't anticipate how this kind of info affects a man years down the line."

"So you had no idea he was a Nazi sympathizer?"

"As I've said a *billion* times, 'no'! Also, he's more of an anti-Semite, I would say, not a Nazi."

"He pushed for new textbooks that offered 'an alternative view' of the Holocaust."

"Right, but he thinks Hitler was a puppet of Jewish financiers, and that he is the Son of God … he even believes in The Secret for crying out loud!"

The Gecko and I sat in silence. Our lungs are too sooty for another cigarette just yet, and even I was ready to slow down on the vodka. There was literally nothing to do but wait.

Looking back, I should have seen the red flags with Icke. It's the nature of the business, though. Who else but the unhinged can even handle such a shift in perspective? Then again, maybe I've placed too much faith in the daft ones over the years. And, to be honest, I knew from the start that D. V. Icke was an absolute nutter.

I'd had many talks with Icke during the years of 1989 and 1990. During these, I explained, as I've said before, that we have only revealed ourselves to humanity twice. Once, in ancient Mesopotamia, to the Sumerians I think. I wasn't deeply involved in that project. They are the ones who dubbed us the *Anunnaki*. After we explained our past and our capabilities, they labeled us gods of the prior world, which was not far off, and we shared a rather stable relationship with them for about a thousand years. Next, came the Gnostics, and they got us all wrong. They saw us as "fallen" gods. This was due to a complete misunderstanding. They wanted to visit Our Place. We said, with all honesty, that it wasn't possible. They took this to mean we are evil demons whose sole purpose on this earth was to "imprison humanity within the flesh… so that his soul cannot reach Heaven." After that experience, I cannot bring myself to capitalize God's pronouns.

Cut to thousands of years later, and picture me shotgunning our entire history to Icke in various hotel rooms all over Britain. Lo and behold, he comes to the same conclusion as the Gnostics. The main difference is that Icke has made 2 million pounds or more from his writings about us. Two. Million. Pounds. That's somewhere in the neighborhood of my net worth – and I'm one of those Lizards who run the world.

"Wait," I said with a scowl, which I quickly drowned with another shot. "A *bigot?*"

"Oh, don't play coy. For one thing, no one says "Mammals" anymore. And don't say, 'Well, they are.'"

"You said 'hick' just a little while ago."

"And you didn't bat an eyelash did you?"

By this point, his tin is sitting on the table. I opened it without asking and helped myself to another cigarette. "So… a failure *and* a bigot. That warrants a death sentence?"

"A ticket home let's call it," he corrected me. "No, it's because the committee feels you would be more comfortable not living here considering our plans for the near future."

"Okay, so spill it. What plans?"

"Transhumanism," he let the word hang between us. Yes, I was familiar.

My experience with transhumanism came from two individuals. The first was a biologist named Julian Huxley – and yes, from *that* Huxley family – who coined the term. In a nutshell, it was the idea that the human species should use science and technology to sculpt itself to perfection, or, at the very least, better itself so that disease and poverty was a thing of the past. Building on this was an individual who came to be known as FM 2030. He adopted this name to show that he believed traditional names and all other facets of modern society were primitive and should be left behind. FM went so far as to preach transhumanism in the forms of changing one's body in any way imaginable – changing gender, even changing species, becoming cyborgs, uploading consciousnesses, you name it. While I was sharing tobacco and liquor with the Gecko on my veranda, FM was still alive and preaching his gospel. Presently, he is dead and frozen, awaiting reanimation… somewhere in Arizona, I believe.

"Yes," the Gecko continued. "According to the committee's latest findings, the species *Homo sapiens* lends itself to a certain short-sightedness."

"Oh, really?"

"Yes, studies have shown they are overly protective, overly aggressive, they are apt to use discovery for war before they use it for commerce… or medicine. Upon learning this, the committee believes…"

His voice faded into the oblivion of my anger. If I'd had an ashtray, I would have broken it and fed him the shards.

"I'm sorry," I say, shaking my head and taking a shot much larger than the ones before. "You are going to have to repeat that last part." I held out my hand for another cigarette. He opened the pack and pouted, pointing to show there was only one left. I snatched it up.

"You can start after the part about the Mammals being unruly children. I'm familiar with that part." I told him.

"The solution is to embrace transhumanism," he replied, saying nothing about the cigarette. "But taken to its fullest potential. Within the next century, computer science and genetic engineering will progress to where there will be no point, nor any possibility of distinguishing between … Life."

"Excuse me?"

"We will mix. All of us. Everything. No more species; no more flesh or machine … no more individual or society. Just one massive, living gelatin containing all life, all thought, spanning this planet and soon many more. All thoughts shared in an instant! No more secrets, because none will be needed. No more want, no love, no hate – all that will remain is a single driving instinct for progress. Imagine it!"

He beamed with awe. I looked away from him and back at my neighbor's fence. I tried to find the place where I'd thrown the glass. I lifted the bottle up to check how much is left. Impossible to tell. Vision… too blurry. I take a long drag on my cigarette.

"Yeah," I gazed skyward. That was where I'd be soon. In the air, headed to my new home. "Yeah, go ahead and kill me, then."

Raw Materials

They had planned to hit the estate on Sunday. The widow had died without an heir, so the State, that great bone-picker, would swoop in and hold an auction come first light on Monday.

The widow had lost her husband the day the Allies stormed the beaches at Normandy but she'd kept the company together throughout the rest of the war and then sold it five years later when her own health began to fail. She was a patron saint to the town, maintaining employment for half the working men within city limits.

For that reason, if no other, the two thieves had to be stealthy. If caught, they would be lucky to face jail time. It was more likely they would be buried in the desert. The sands of Arizona were a wide-open space, and it was easy to make a man, or two, disappear without a trace out there.

They had learned of the widow's passing in the obits, which was the most fertile soil for finding a mark. They packed and headed over the State line, leaving Los Angeles on Thursday. It would be a tight job, one of the tightest they had ever pulled. It was risky. They had no bearings, no idea of the town layout or police presence, and, worst of all, they had only two days to case the house.

They drove in an old pickup, dusty with a faded red paint job, one of a million sliding along the roads of rural America, which they had packed with caution. Rural cops were known for homing in on anything with a California tag, looking to ticket some city boys out of their city boy money. Thus, the truck bed was empty, save for a few cigarette butts. Their tools fit nicely in a hollow above the driver's side tire, sealed up in a tool bag and padded with newspapers to prevent jostling.

As they drove, they discussed stopping at a diner for coffee and smokes. Perhaps, time permitting, a slice of pie, too, and some playful flirting with the servers. They mulled over the details, with one man pointing out that it would be best if fewer people saw them. As that thought sank in and roiled around in their bellies for a good ten minutes, they made the democratic decision to take a smoke break on the road shoulder.

They stopped halfway, having just crossed the State line. The driver, the older of the two, pulled the pack of Marlboros he kept warm in his breast pocket and tossed one at his partner before lighting up his own. The younger man quickly stooped and scooped up the cigarette before the wind could take it. Brushing off the sand, he put it to his lips, spat out the residual taste, and then accepted a match from the older man.

"Much obliged," he said with a smirk. It was a prison smirk, a show of teeth. The old man shot one back at him. "Be quicker."

The two leaned on the truck and looked out over the wilderness. Scruffy hills, each as indistinguishable as the last, reduced the view of the horizon to bleached brown humps.

"What do you expect there'll be in there?" the younger man asked after a few drags. The pair would not be fencing the merchandise in LA this time. No, this time it would be Tijuana, or, as the older man called it, The City That Asks No Questions.

"Easy women," answered the older man.

"In the widow's house."

In response, the older man flicked some ash into the wind. He did not look at the younger man but began ticking off on his fingers items to loot. "Cash, jewelry — the usual. This won't be the big score, so get that out of your head. Don't get me wrong — this one's going to be big, just not retirement big."

"What if there's a sitter?"

"There won't be."

"How do you know?"

"Because there won't be. If I were you, I'd be more worried about not getting us shot down in Tijuana… How's your *español*?"

"I don't speak it."

"See, that's what I'm talking about. You're going to have to hang back and say nothing. That looks suspicious. These guys won't think twice about offing us if they think we're up to something."

"I just don't want anyone getting killed."

"Yeah, well, don't let them know that. Just hang back like I said and look mean. Maybe I can pass you off as the muscle."

"No, I mean with the sitter."

"Would you forget the damn sitter! Jesus, Boyscout, let me think… Okay, it's not so bad. Makes sense the kid can't speak Spanish. Never been south of the border. Okay. Okay. Everything cool. Everything flows. No stress and no mess."

The young man waited until the older man finished his cigarette, then motioned with his head that they should get back on the road.

"You ever heard of Captain Kidd?" the younger man asked once they were underway.

"Somebody from the funnies?" asked the older man.

"No. Real world pirate. You remind me of him. He buried treasure all over the world, looking forward to that day when he could retire and disappear. I bet you have something like that, don't you? Little treasure-caches hidden in towns all over America?"

"Where do you get this stuff, Professor?"

"Used books. All the knowledge of the great, wide world, available for five cents if you know where to look."

"Damn, I didn't know you were a reader. I pegged you for a funnies-man. Batman and Little Nemo, that kind of stuff."

"Try Spinoza and Taoism. History, too. So, do you? Have money put away?"

"If I did," said the older man, "I wouldn't tell a soul. Good idea though.

What about your pirate, what happened to him and his buried treasures?"

"No one's ever found them. Kidd was hanged… twice… and took his secret to the grave."

"And you said *I'm* Captain Kidd? Well, yeah, that's probably how I'll go. Hey Professor, make me a promise. If they catch me and string me up, I want you to go around telling everyone I really did have buried treasure. I'll be laughing in Hell watching all those bums burning in the sun, digging holes."

"That's a promise, Kidd," said the younger man.

The layout of the widow's home was ideal. Behind the house proper was a trail that led out into the dunes, where it met a dead end. The road itself had once continued on but had been blocked up years ago. A sign on a chain warned against going any farther, by order of the city. The men parked their truck in front of the sign, within the shade of the dunes and brush, and slept until well past nightfall. Once they had awakened to the sound of owls, they took their tools and began the quarter mile walk towards pay day.

The house was a nice two-story with a porch whose awning served as the balcony to an upstairs guest room. In the rear, it had an expansive study, and there the thieves made their entry. The man called Kidd held out his hand like a surgeon and announced, "Professor… crowbar if you please."

"Crowbar," Professor announced as he handed the item over. The older man fitted it into the jam, and the pair watched as the door gave way with a modicum of force. Kidd handed the crowbar back and motioned with his hand again.

"Lamp." He was handed a flashlight and smiled as he lit it. "Now, Professor, let's go get rich."

They surveyed the study and made their way into the dining room. This was the first place to look for valuables, and a good place to leave their sacks. Professor caught Kidd's arm as he set his lamp on the dining room table.

"I'm going to make some coffee." When Kidd gave him a stern look, he whined, "I'm still tired. It's the middle of the night, and I've never had home brewed coffee before."

"Fine," Kidd said, and made for the upstairs bedroom. Even as he ransacked drawer after drawer, loading his pockets with necklaces, bracelets, broaches, and jewelry cases, he could hear the plucking, bubbling sounds of the coffee machine from the kitchen. Professor, he reminded himself, better be checking around the kitchen for something. He had better not be sitting there with his boots propped up on the widow's obscenely ornate chairs.

A glint in his lamplight interrupted his cynicism. A single piece of paper, left on the bed. A letter, crisp and neat, with the unmistakable ghost of typed pages beneath the skin of the envelope. It had been left with purpose, at the foot of the bed atop a folded afghan, where a woman might leave her evening gown while she applied makeup in the vanity mirror across the room.

Kidd lifted it, nestling his lamp between his shoulder and jaw, and read the addressee:

To: OFCs Brinks and Lawrence

Officers Brinks and Lawrence? Officers of the court? Most likely. Kidd opened it, thinking, *This could be big.*

He was not wrong.

Professor was sitting at the kitchen table with his feet propped up on a second chair. He was smiling. On the table before him were three items — his flashlight, still lit, a cup of the finest Colombian coffee he had ever tasted, and a small bag he had stuffed with the widow's silverware.

When Kidd entered the room wearing a goblin's grin, Professor spun his lamp, catching the older man full in the face before training the beam on his loot-sack.

"You see that?" Professor said as he lifted the sack and dropped it, letting the sound of metal fill the house. "Silver. A good ten pounds or more. That sack right there is worth more than your truck, so I don't want to hear it. "

"Good work, Professor… but…" Kidd let the word hang in the air before producing the letter and shining his light on it. His smile came back, bigger than before.

"Dammit," said the younger man, now sitting up straight. "I know that smile. You got the big score? Bigger than ten pounds of silver? No. There's no way that little letter —"

"Put your stuff in the big sack, and then I'll show you."

Professor took to his feet and made for the other room. As he passed Kidd, he made a half-hearted attempt to grab the letter. In response, Kidd jerked it away and then kicked him in the seat to keep him moving.

"Okay," said Professor upon returning. "Spill it."

"This letter is from the widow's probate lawyer," the older man said, handing it over. As Professor looked it over, Kidd walked over to the tool bag. "It's a set of instructions to the cops for when the crew comes to gut the place tomorrow. It has *special* instructions about what to do… *with what's in the vault.*"

When Professor looked up, Kidd had produced a stethoscope from the tool bag and was beckoning him into the study.

"The vault! She has a vault?" The words escaped the younger man's lips before he could stop himself. He followed his partner into the study, where they moved the far wall's bookcase, finding it to be on hinges — real books, real shelves, but a false wall beyond. There, glistening black and gold and slick as oil in their twin lights, was a metal door.

"This dame's got a vault!" said Kidd. "Alright, now shut up. Don't make any noise. Go back into the kitchen and shut off any machines you left on. Check and double check. When you're done, bring the crowbar. This won't take me long."

"You crack safes?"

"No, I'm going to check if it has a heart murmur! Get in the kitchen and do what I said!" Kidd spat as he gave the last order. Professor fought back laughter and did as he was told. He left to finish his coffee, and as he lowered the empty cup into the sink, he heard the deep groan of metal hinges opening.

"Damn straight I crack safes!" came Kidd's voice from the study. "Get your ass in here, Professor. It's time for the mother lode!"

The inner vault had been decked out much like a closet. There were shelves with numerous drawers stretching from floor to ceiling. The two thieves opened a few at random to find wrapped stacks of ten-dollar bills, promissory notes, house deeds, and permits to excavate or clear land for roads. Professor found a sturdy drawer and set his flashlight into it, creating a lantern effect. He emptied a few drawers, focusing on jewelry and the cash.

He stopped as he noticed that Kidd had not moved a muscle.

As Professor watched, Kidd swung his light from side to side until it lit a bell jar sitting on a writing desk in the corner. With a deep breath, he lifted it and carried it out. Walking like he was carrying an infant he took the bell jar to the kitchen and set it on the table. As he heard Professor approach, he turned his flashlight on the glass enclosure.

"This is it. This is Lot 1159A. This is what the letter was about."

The base of the jar held an aluminum tray, a display case. It had been custom-made, with a hollowed basin, and it perfectly fit the confines of the jar. On its side, the case had a tray and hinges. One could pull this out and over the case, converting it into a box, to prevent the item from jostling during transport. Within the basin was the prize — a jewel, the size of a child's fist. It was black as onyx but hid the deepest emerald hue within, faint but unmistakable in the jaundiced illumination of the thieves' flashlights.

"Tomorrow, while the auctioneers are having their fun, two cops from town are supposed to take this thing and sit on it. They are not to let it out of their sight. Once the auction is over, they're supposed to wait here until they get radioed by the sheriff. Are you ready for this? A G-man and two army officers will be coming to take this thing off their hands. The letter even goes into detail about how they are going to be exchanging passwords and the whole nine yards. Like I said, Professor, this thing is the mother lode!"

The two men looked at the item for some time, not moving.

"Who do we sell it to?" asked Professor. Kidd lifted the jar lid to get a better look at their find.

"Hell, we'll find somebody! Someone will be willing to pay for this thing."

"Wait," said Professor. "It might be radioactive. It might be from the bomb tests."

"And they just keep it under glass in some old woman's house? Come on, Professor. You know what? I bet it's some superior form of coal!"

Professor stretched his gloves tight and picked up the jewel. He wasn't sure what he was looking for, but touching it felt… good. This was theirs now.

"Then how about this?" he said. "How about we *don't* sell it? How about we patent it and make a fortune off the discovery?"

"Professor, I think that's about the best idea I've ever heard." The younger man was happy to hear that. This could really be it, the ticket to tropical islands and mansions on the beach. Servants. No more worry. Not another care in the world.

"Put that down… now." Kidd said with the slow force of a railroad car, his eyes wet with alarm. Professor dropped the rock back into the tray with as much care as he could. As he released it, he felt the need for urgency. Each fingertip of his glove stuck to the rock, then peeled away. He held up his hand, revealing a nice trio of pink digits through the holes— thumb, index, and middle.

"It was moving," Kidd said. "Did you not feel it?" Professor shook his head. They knelt down. Swinging their lights about for a few seconds with the speed of excited boys they settled on vantage points that would eliminate the most shadow and then lowered their faces within a nose hair of the rock. What they wanted now was satisfaction, satisfaction for that morbid curiosity that sits in every man's chest.

The rock had eaten… *eaten*… through a glove in seconds. Now… what did it look like? Was it smoking like a fire? Did it reek like acid? And how? How had it done the deed?

There, on its surface, were three brown spots, the size and shape of fingerprints.

The pair gaped at the sight and chuckled. In truth, it wasn't funny. It was terrifying, like waking up to discover a burglar had broken into one's home in the night. Danger had passed *this* close. So close. Yet, there was the thrill of it.

The three glove spots were not leather, not anymore. They were crystal, pure and cut. And growing. They grew with the speed of frost, slow and insistent. As the men watched, tiny towers thrust upward from each mock fingerprint, now with that dead gleam of polished rock unmistakable in the lamplight. Then, as if shy, they stopped.

Kidd shut the display lid, trapping the thing, then replaced the bell jar lid.

Without another word he took the jar back into the vault. Reentering the kitchen he said, "Professor, you're not going to like this, but I don't like that rock."

As he rounded the corner, he saw the younger man holding a broom… and missing a glove.

"Me either," said Professor. He set the broom against the wall and positioned the dustpan on the kitchen table to display its contents. "Look."

Kidd stepped forward and shined his light into the pan's cavernous mouth. Inside there was a smattering of shiny brown shards, more crystals, and the glove that had touched the rock. The three infected fingers of the glove were shrinking and falling away as he watched. Three cigarettes in an ashtray, leaving little brown, sparkling trails. In about half an hour, there would be no glove left.

"I think I get it," Professor said from over his shoulder. "That rock eats organic material, anything living, or anything that used to be. Leather, wood, or whatever. It, like, *digests* them, turns them into more crystal. That's why they kept it in metal and glass, but when it touched my glove, it started to eat it." The two men leaned in, watching the glove, the tiny predators making their progress towards the knuckles. Kidd let his partner's words sink in.

"Did you get it all? I mean are you *sure* you swept it all up?" Kidd asked. The younger man nodded. "Did it get on you?" Kidd prodded him.

The young man shook his head at that. "I'm pretty damn sure I'd feel it."

The matter settled, the two thieves emptied the infected glove and its debris into the trash bin and then relocated to the study. They found an ashtray on the reading desk beside the vault and stood around it to smoke and think. This was not about money anymore.

"We should burn this place," said Professor. "Burn it to the ground. Get rid of the thing."

Kidd shook his head. "No good. You can't burn a rock. Some poor firefighter would just… accidentally… no, we take it with us and we bury it where no one will find it."

"Good. Yes. I like that. Wait, why not just let the cops handle it tomorrow like they were going to do?"

Kidd gave a lemon-sucking frown at that. "You mean let the government have this thing? Are you kidding me? What do you think they're going to do with it? I'm telling you, something like this could only be a weapon."

A sound froze them. From the kitchen, came a soft rustle. Like paper. Like leaves. The men rushed in and traced the sound to the broom, still leaning against the wall. They drew closer, Professor in front. Holding his light at an angle, then switching it to his other hand and back to improve his vantage point, he backed away from the sight. The bottom half of the broom's straw sparkled in the lamplight. The thing was not done, not contained. Shiny little rivers of crystal climbed higher through the yellow fibers, eager for more.

"You've got to be kidding me," Professor spat, backing up into Kidd's shoulder.

The two men returned to the study.

"It'll take the whole house by morning!" Professor was panting, a little horse sweat starting on his face. "And this is our fault! We let it out. *We* did this."

"Get it together!" Kidd shot straight into his face. "Get. It. Together. We are getting out of here. Nothing's changed, we just take the broom with us, that's all. Just one more thing."

"Just one more thing," said Professor, calmer.

The sound of tires interrupted them. A vehicle rolled to a gentle stop on the rocky path outside, a stone's throw from the front door. Kidd clicked off his light and peered around the far wall of the study and into the foyer. Through the massive windows of the house's face, he saw a car painted in tell-tale black and white, a rounded bulb fixed to its roof.

He bolted back into the study and grabbed Professor, knocking him off balance.

"The cops!" Kidd hissed, slapping Professor's flashlight toward the floor to hide the damning beam. "Okay. Okay. They haven't seen us…"

The car doors opened and shut. Two pairs of men's boots crunched on the rocky ground outside. Indistinct chatter. Then the powerful lamplights of the police swept through the foyer windows, spilling into the far hall and swinging into the study behind Kidd.

"We split!" said Professor. "No, wait. We can't leave—"

"Come." Kidd took on the quiet force again with this command. "Follow me, and do exactly as I say." He took the younger man by the shoulder and grabbed one loot bag in another. He beelined straight into the vault and shut the door behind them as one set of heavy boots crossed the side of the house and approached the rear door. In the foyer, the other officer opened the front door and stepped inside.

Kidd slid the lock into place, wincing at the precision needed for quiet.

"Cut your light out," said Kidd, grimacing back at Professor.

"Are you insane?" Professor began to pant again. He was tempted to look behind him, to where the rock was resting back on its throne. Now the safe felt less like a closet. The walls waved like curtains as the lights fought to hold them back. Kidd caught his face and pulled him close.

"They haven't seen us. They didn't hear us. They'll search the house, find nothing, and think we got away. Once they leave, that gives us about ten minutes to get the hell out of dodge. For now, we have to wait. Now, cut your light out. We'll need them good and strong for when I get us out."

With that, Kidd cut his light and motioned for Professor to do the same.

"Please tell me you can pick a safe from the inside."

"Of course I can," whispered Kidd. "Now, please, pretty please, *shut the hell up and cut out your light!*"

Professor held his breath as sight fled the room. It was beyond dark. The room was *gone.* They were nowhere.

Gone. The realization that this must be what the dead feel in the tomb came howling from the hallway in the back of his head. Then, he heard sounds from afar.

Outside, in the world of the living, the two officers were clomping across the floorboards. *That"s better,* Professor thought. True, the sounds meant danger, but that was still *something.* As he listened, he could feel their frustration, the two lawmen pivoting from boot to boot with more force and speed as they swept the premises. Their voices, muffled by the thickness of the door so that no words stood out, became frantic in pitch. Professor smiled. No, this was not a tomb. It was a suit of armor.

Still, there was that thing in the corner. *Just a rock* he told himself, but after what he had seen it do...

It couldn't get out. No. It's just a rock. If it could escape, it would have done so long ago. There was no way it would've been sitting there in a bell jar waiting for someone's hand.

Oh, God. A different flavor of nightmare occurred to Professor. *We fed it. We woke it up.* Its babies, the crystals in the bin, were calling to it, and to reach its offspring that thing would melt and spill from the box, out of the jar, slithering... sweet Jesus, *slithering* across the floor in the dark.

Shut up! Professor took stock of himself again and breathed in deep. He let it out slow. Yes, he let it out slow. Yes. Slow. *There are men who can and men who can't. There are weak men, who cannot handle...* Damn, he had given himself the heebie-jeebies. This was how guys in a pinch get caught. *There are guys who lose their cool, and there are guys who don't. The guys who don't, walk away Scot-free.*

That's right. Cool. Be cool. Be cool and you walk. Walk right the hell out of all of this.

"You all right back there, Professor?" asked Kidd in a whisper.

"Yeah, just some heebie-jeebies. We're getting out of this, Kidd. And the flat-foots got nothing!" Professor hissed back. Kidd grabbed his shoulder. In a series of squeezes, he connotated a message. *Hell, yes. That's the spirit. We are getting out of here. Just a little longer.*

The time came when the boots hurried to the rear door and left the house, and once more the two thieves were alone in the open void.

"Shield your eyes," announced Kidd before turning on his light. He immediately knelt to examine the door. "Okay, we're in luck. This model has a safety measure. There's a trip. Basically, you can just open it from the inside by turning the handle, that way no one can accidentally lock themselves in. That's good because we have about ten minutes - tops — before those cops realize we didn't just escape on foot. If you would, Professor, say a little prayer that they haven't found the truck. If they did, we're screwed."

"We can't leave yet. The rock—"

Kidd turned and looked Professor dead in the face. "Listen. To. Me. Forget the rock. We don't have time anymore. I don't like it either, but you have to face the facts. The cops are out there. We have to leave town right goddamned now. If we get caught, we do time, and the rock still goes to the government. You see my point? You fail either way, now. The only question left is where will you be tomorrow? In a cell? Or safe at home?"

With that, he turned away and grabbed the handle. "I can't believe I'm saying this. Get the broom if you want, and the trash. We can at least get rid of them. Meet me out back, and then we are going to run like hell."

The vault door opened, and Professor made for the kitchen, buzzing with ideas about how to wrap the broom.

He entered the kitchen, careful to hold his light downward. As he lifted it towards his target, he was greeted by the sight of a policeman, seated in the dark at the kitchen table, his sock-adorned feet casually propped up in the chair opposite him. A pair of arms grabbed Professor from behind, hard and fast, sending his light clattering to the corner of the tiled floor.

"Be gentle, Carter. Don't hurt the boy." The officer at the table spilled out his instructions with a lazy wheeze. From his accent, he was a Texas transplant. The one called Carter tightened his chicken wing hold, wrenching Professor forward as the Texan rose from his seat and hit the light switch. Professor's head shot into his shoulder to shield his eyes from the blazing flood.

"Jesus!" Professor winced. "Where did you come from?" His wrists were being twisted into position for cuffing, but he gave no fight. He was done. Cooked.

"Jersey," came the man's answer. He hoisted the thief toward the table and dropped him into the chair opposite the older officer.

"Hit the house again, Carter. I'll watch this one." In response, Carter unholstered his pistol, cocked it, and left the kitchen as the Texan began chuckling to himself.

"Hiding in the vault. I'll be damned. Carter called it. It's a good thing I'm not a betting man. What's your name, Junior?" asked the Texan.

Over the lawman's shoulder Professor could see that he had put his boots up against the wall inches from the broom. Now in the full illumination of the overhead lights, the whole thing sparkled, from the tips of the straw to the top of the dull red handle. *Jesus. It really did it. Goddamned rock took the whole thing and turned it into crystal. I was right!*

"Hey!" Professor was wrenched out of his reverie by the Texan snapping his fingers at the young man's nose. "I'm talking to you, Junior," I said, 'What's your name?'"

"People call me Professor."

"They call you that because you're smart? I hope so." The lawman left his seat and knelt down beside the young thief's chair. He tugged at the youth's pants pocket with one finger. "You got anything on you that's going to stick me or cut me?" Professor shook his head and endured the frisking.

"So, Professor, are you smart?" The officer took a long breath through his nose and settled back into his chair. "A smart man knows when he's been beat. And you're beat, Professor. You're going down for this. There's no two ways about that. But if you're smart, and you answer me one thing, it'll make me happy. I'll make it real simple for you. All I need is for you to answer one question. Are you ready? Here it is."

The Texan took out his gun and set it on the table.

"Who all knows you're here?"

Professor swallowed. He had tried to fight it, but it was no use. *No shame in saying it. You're scared. And, hell, you should be.* Still, his lips refused to move.

Elsewhere, the other officer, Carter, had retrieved his boots and was making his way away from the kitchen to clear the rest of the house.

The other officer is not announcing himself. Professor swallowed again. *He's not announcing himself because this isn't an arrest. This is a snuff job. What was it Kidd said? How easy it is to make two men disappear in the desert?*

"You waiting for your lawyer, Professor?" The Texan broke in, interrupting his stream of dark thoughts and bringing Professor back into the bleak light and white tile of the kitchen. "Oh, no, you want your phone call, don't you? Okay…" The policeman swept his gun up from the table and held it close, examining it. He pulled the hammer back, leaving it tilted and wavering under his thumb. He watched the mechanism dance back and forth, back and forth, under his complete, meticulous control before sliding it safely back home and locking eyes with Professor.

A smile, big and wide split his face. He sat back and held that smile for a while, his eyes never leaving the young thief. He wiped a bit of white foam from the sides of his mouth and dropped his jowls. No mask of mirth now — only authority, brutal and impatient.

"Here, I'll make it easier for you," the officer's voice dropped lower, paternal. "You have a partner. One, two at the most. You must have a buyer, too. Who else is there? There a girlfriend in the picture? Maybe you promised her something nice after this big score you had planned? Anything like that happen? What about a buddy you brag to? A boyfriend, even?"

"Tell me your name first," said Professor, prompting a satisfied angler look from the officer.

"I'm Officer Lawrence."

Jesus. He managed to say that and somehow sound proud.

"Lawrence. Would you consider yourself a good, Christian man?" The officer nodded to this. "A... you're a public servant. Would you say you're a public servant?"

"Yes, Son. What you say stays with me."

"Good. Cool. How about you take that broom and stick it up your fat ass?"

Officer Lawrence pinched out a smirk and hummed a few bars of disapproval at Professor's comment, then cinched his feelings with a sharp smack of his lips and jerked his head toward the broom behind him.

"That broom, you mean? Hmm. How about..." He rose from his chair, took his boots from their resting place, put them on, and then reached within inches of the sparkling target.

Yes! Yes, you fat, corrupt bastard. Grab that thing and lose your hands. I'll run the hell out of here, find Kidd, and then... God knows. I will figure it out. Now grab it! Grab it and threaten me with it! Do it! I know you want to!

"How about this, Son?" Officer Lawrence stepped into the middle of the kitchen, causing Professor to crane his neck and then scoot his chair to follow the movement. "You've been looking at that broom since you walked into this room. From the very first second. So, here's what is in this old, *fat* cop's head — what did the boy sweep up?"

Professor strained to maintain his poker face, but his strength left him as the cop said the word "sweep." He faced forward as the officer rummaged through the trash. Professor heard the hard rustling of crystals, but no reaction from the cop. Then, without a word, the officer sat back down, scratching his chin.

"Now, where were we?" Lawrence was more than a little disappointed. There was nothing in the bin but typical Arizona house dust. The lawman had even dared to put his face near the lip of the can but could not smell anything incriminating. No trace of dope or blood, not even cigarette ash. He gave the trash one last whiff before giving up and sitting back down across from the young thief.

"Did you see my glove?" Professor asked. Lawrence ignored the question, readying his next move.

Professor felt the mist of sweat start again on his flanks. *No glove. Shit. It ate the whole glove. Wait, he was digging around in that stuff. Double shit.*

Lawrence cleared his throat and called out, "Carter. Are we good?"

"House is clear!" shouted Carter, and his boots sounded off on the floorboards above, returning to the kitchen. Lawrence cleared his throat again and continued. "Then get your ass back in here!"

House clear? Professor had braced for the sound of a gunshot and the sound of Kidd's body hitting the floorboards, but… *House clear? Did the goddamn bastard run?*

"I was already. Jesus!" came his partner's answer. Lawrence shifted in his seat, swallowed hard, and then coughed into his hand.

"Here in a second, Son…" he explained as he rose and poured himself a glass of water from the sink. "We're going to take a little ride." He tried to force a smile.

Professor watched, praying to God for he knew not what as the officer sat back down and finished his water in one swift gulp.

Lawrence frowned and shook his head. It hadn't helped. Giving in to temptation, he massaged his Adam's apple and let out a tight growl.

It feels like ants in there, Lawrence thought. Tiny ants were hopping off the back of his tongue and trying to crawl their way out through his nose. As he breathed deeper and deeper, his vision clouded. It hurt to blink. His eyelids were meat rubbing over dry glass. He went blind the next instant, causing him to jump, ram his knees into the table and then fall back onto the floor with an impressive slam.

Professor was up then, backing away. He wanted to run. His mind was telling him to run, but he could not. He could not tear himself away from the sight before him.

Lawrence the lawman was on his knees, his hands clawing at his neck and mouth, then pounding on his thigh. He wheezed and gagged, trying to free the alien thing caught in his throat. He opened his eyes as he tried to gulp in more air, and those eyes were now black. As Professor watched, a dark carpet needled out from the lawman's eyes, then his mouth. It trickled over his lips and lids, the tiniest wafting pins, a thousand brittle eyelashes, clicking together as he shook.

He screamed. God, how he screamed! It was a child's scream, throated by an adult man.

Why? Why is this hurting me? Why is this hurting me so much? Make it stop!

Lawrence let out another growl before reaching one hand to his jaw. He wrenched it down and shoved his other hand into his mouth up to the knuckles.

Some part of Professor's brain told him that Carter had entered the room, that he had a gun… and that he, too, was watching the horror in the corner.

That was when Lawrence tore out his own tongue.

There at the root, where it had once connected to the man's throat, was a thick brush of black crystal. It pulsed as it fed on the moisture, the rich blood and muscle, growing, growing into Lawrence's hand, under his nails. Spreading. Spreading.

Black and red trails of semisolid matter spattered from his mouth, following the tongue in his hand. They flowed through the air, seeking the tongue, clinging to it. *Bonding to it.* His diaphragm seized. His jaw, fractured into an obscene yawn, cemented in place as the crystals continued their work, and the two onlookers, stood, watching, frozen.

"What..." Carter whispered. His eyes would not leave his partner. His mind could not place what was happening to him. *Poison* was the best it could do. "What did you give him?"

"I didn't." Professor managed. "It's the thing in the trash. It's... evil." He didn't even mean to say it, but now that the word left his lips— *evil*— yes, he was right. These things were not rocks. They were monsters.

Lawrence was suffocating, but he didn't know it. He no longer knew anything. Black crystal had tunneled back from his sinuses into his frontal lobe. Once there, the prodding needles severed the nerves, forever robbing him of conscious thought. They fed on the heavy fat of his brain tissue and swelled outward. In seconds, they split his skull and began traveling down the wet pathways of his neck and entered his chest.

Professor's legs were kicked out from under him. Carter had recovered his wits and was out for blood. He caught Professor by the back of his neck and shoved him on his knees. Carter fumed through his nose and jammed the barrel of his pistol behind Professor's ear.

"Don't. Don't do it, man. Don't! I didn't do anything!" Professor could not force his voice above a whisper.

"You're gonna pay." Carter ground out the words through clenched teeth.

"I didn't do it!" Professor whined out the words and squeezed his eyes shut.

"Look at it! Look at what you did. He was a good man." The barrel of the gun burrowed deeper into Professor's head, drawing blood. When the bullet erupted, it would blow out his brain stem, ending his life in an instant.

"He was a good man!" Carter bellowed.

Then. Nothing.

Instead of fluffy clouds or crackling flames, Professor felt the full heaviness of Carter's body collapse on top of him. He sloughed it off and spun around with animal quickness to see Kidd standing in triumph with his crowbar poised like a baseball bat. Kidd helped Professor to his feet and looked down at the heap that was Carter.

"Does he need another one?" asked Kidd. He was ready. His shoulders were still rolling in their sockets and his hand was still in a death grip around the crowbar.

"I think I killed a man," said Professor. He had no idea about Carter, or if he needed "another one." All he knew was that he needed to get out of the kitchen. Kidd snatched the keys from Carter's belt and freed Professor's wrists.

Professor wasted no time once he was free. He took Kidd by the shoulders and steered him toward the study. Kidd noticed the mass that had been Lawrence in the corner. He opened his mouth to speak, but Professor shook his head violently. *No. Don't look at it. Save yourself. Come with me right now.*

Once in the study, Professor refused to say a word until he had raided the widow's brandy. Kidd gave him a cigarette and let the young man collect himself. Kidd paced about the room, shooting a glance at the kitchen every second. There were sounds now. Maybe he was just now noticing them. Like rats in the walls. Every now and then something like a mop slopping across a floor. And then... a series of loud cracks. Not like wood. Harder, more brittle. Pencils. Or ribs...

"I killed a man," said Professor. The brandy helped, or he was telling himself it helped. "The other cop. I led him into it. Now I'm going to Hell."

Kidd leaned the crowbar against the sofa, out of Professor's reach. He sat and poured himself a drink. "You did what you had to do."

Professor was shaking his head. "I let him go into that trashcan. I knew it was full of those things. I tried to get him to grab the broom. I knew they would hurt him. And then I'd run. That's all I was thinking. I didn't know... I didn't know they would do *that.* I didn't know they could do that to a man." He looked into Kidd's eyes. "I saw the whole thing."

"Listen to me now," Kidd told him. "I am about to help you. It's time to do what's right. We have to make sure no one ever gets near those rocks. Ever." Professor nodded.

"I'm back on board, Professor. I freaked when the cops came, but I'm back on board. We are taking every single speck of them— the broom, the cops, everything— and we are going to bury them so damn deep the Devil's going to find them in his bathroom when he takes his morning piss!"

Professor smiled. He couldn't laugh, but Kidd was right. He started to nod and rose to his feet. He caught his breath. Set his jaw. It was time to make this right.

He coughed. A quick swallow of the last of his brandy and then he opened his mouth to tell Kidd he was ready to get to work. Nothing came out. His voice was gone.

Another cough, rougher than before.

No. Professor felt his soul drop into his bladder, which then released in a warm tide down his leg. *No. No, not me. Please, God, not me. This can't be. It's not fair! We were going to make it right. We were making it right! It's not fair!*

He spun around to Kidd, making him jump. "They got me," His voice was back, but not for long. He could already feel a scratching numbness fanning out from his Adam's apple.

Those things are in me. They're evil. They're evil and they got me. Professor was mouthing the words, but nothing came. Kidd took him once more by the shoulders, prompted Professor to cover his own nose and mouth. Kidd had no idea what these things could do. He had to be protected.

"We still have to make this right, you understand?" Professor nodded, and Kidd continued. "I need you to trust me. I have to go get the truck. We can't carry all the stuff— the rocks, the bodies, and all that shit— a quarter mile all the way to the truck. I have to go get it and park it out back. You find us a carpet to wrap it all in. It has to be you. Then we drive out of here and we finish it."

Professor nodded, but his eyes wandered off. Kidd slapped his face and gave him more words of parting. "Don't let them win. They will try to scare you, because they need to distract you. Don't let them. You have all the power. You have the power to bury them with me, and then they've lost. Don't let them in your head. Remember"— he pointed at Professor— "Remember: Devil's bathroom." With that, he left.

Professor was alone then, but he was smiling his prison smile. Kidd was right. The rocks would not win. He wasn't walking out of this one. He would not see the sunrise. But the rocks would not win, and he could live with that. He tramped upstairs and found a collection of quilts in the wooden chest at the foot of the widow's bed. His coughing grew merciless, but it made him smile more. They were trying to intimidate him. They were desperate.

You're done, you bastards. We got you. You lost! Downstairs, he heard Kidd park the truck and enter through the study. This was going to work.

He couldn't call to his partner, but he could whistle. Putting both fingers to his lips, as his father had shown him years ago, he let out a shrill whistle, echoing through the halls. This initiated another coughing fit, which he aimed at the center of the rug. He heard his partner enter the room. Keeping his face directed away, Professor beckoned him over with one hand as he pointed at the carpet with the other.

"You did good, Boy Scout," he heard Kidd tell him. "You were real good."

Day broke, and God's watchful eye began to peer over the dunes. Night withdrew in long shadows, shrinking to hide under dry rock and cacti. The back door of the study opened, and a lone figure emerged. The man trod forward, nothing in his hands, nothing on his back. He left the cursed house behind without so much as a backward glance. A memory from the night flew screaming into his mind, but a quick jerk of his head banished it. Blinking in the light, he rode on stiff legs toward the truck with the dust of the widow's house, dark and hard, still crusted onto his boots.

II

Opus Vermiculatum: Kenopsia

A Simple Dream

"I said to my soul, be still, and wait without hope
For hope would be hope for the wrong thing; wait without
love
For love would be love of the wrong thing; there is yet faith
But the faith and the love and the hope are all in the waiting.
Wait without thought, for you are not ready for thought:
So the darkness shall be the light, and the stillness the
dancing..."
-From "East Coker," T. S. Eliot

My favorite issue of National Geographic, "Planet of the Beetles," is always at the forefront of my mind. I spend most of my time outside, and literally everything around me brings the title right to the tip of my tongue— flowering plants, ants running in little queues between tree bark, or even my own name.

I'll get to that, the beetle-name thing.

The cover in question shows a close-up shot of a tiger beetle, *Cicindel rufiventris*, its wicked mandibles obscuring the name of the magazine, and that gut-shot title, "Planet of the Beetles" displayed just under its vacant compound eyes. It haunts me... in a good way. It's akin to how the religious show their deity fear and awe.

Yes. You bet we're living on the Planet of the Beetles— the most successful Eukaryotic life form that has ever existed. The world is theirs. And this puts life into perspective for me. Not for others though. I have explained this over and over to many people, and no one ever understands. I think it's pride, blocking them from how big the idea is. It terrifies them.

This links, in a way, to my earliest reliable memory. I was at my parents' lake house. They were still alive, but elderly, so upkeep of the property had fallen to me. I had just arrived, accompanied by a few friends and my two children. I slung both kids' book bags across my back while we unpacked, which made me look like a June bug. My daughter remarked on this, and then one of my friends added, "Didn't you know? He was the fifth Beatle!" This got whittled down to "Fith," and now it's the only name I can remember.

Time is a funny thing nowadays. In my youth, before I had any work-done, there were seasons— summer, winter, etc.— and you could use them to measure time. Now we just have monsoons where I live. You can purchase calendars, but I have no money, and from what I hear, there are dozens of different calendars, with contradictory dates. It all depends on the company you buy them from. See? Funny.

I have no idea how old I am. I go through moods that last for years. Antisocial, then back to social. One time I even forgot how to talk. I think a lot of it has to do with my work-done, but by this point it doesn't bother me. I go with it.

Let me explain "work-done." Of the three professions still available— these being prostitute, guinea pig and target practice— I was a voracious guinea pig. As guinea pigs, we have "work-done" — grafts, implants, gene therapy. I have been very fortunate. I survived the experiences. I should add that having work-done to this degree renders one a "Moreau," a fact that I do not advertise.

...

People person, I say to myself on my way to a park in the city. A social tide has been rising in me, so here I am.

People person. It will work. It will work.

It is approaching noon. Today is "Yoga on the Grass." day, and I take that to be a good sign. Yoga attracts open-minded people, people who don't pry. Forgiving and accepting types.

I forgot how many people live in cities. They are everywhere, walking in queues here and there, filling the air with their words. Friend groups chat in store fronts and on the stairs in front of government housing. People on the sidewalk. People in the street. I can't even walk at full speed. There are also plenty of bots, doing their assorted chores — cleaning, building, scanning for crime. I know not to approach any of these people for friendship. It's rude to socialize when someone is busy, that much I do remember. Still, they are fun to watch.

I pass by a shipping container abandoned in a fenced-in lot, grass fluffing its way through the rusty links. Near the entrance, someone has planted a dandelion garden in a tire on its side. As I stop to see which insects are living in there, I create a sort of eddy in the flow of human traffic, and a tall man almost bumps into me and gives me a slight scowl before sidling by and continuing on his way.

"Hey, hey, hey-hey, sir!" a voice goes off around me. "Listen-hey-hey-listen, don't worry, I'm not dangerous." It takes a second for me to locate the source. At least twenty people are talking around me, some leaning against the fence. One or two young mothers are attempting to nurse shrieking infants, to say nothing of the vehicle motors humming in the street.

I trace it to a figure huddled in the entrance of the container. The words just keep pouring out of him. Prostitutes are like that. They go off like alarms if you enter their proximity. I smile. I can't help it. Bad move, it makes him rocket up the enthusiasm.

I'm fluent in English, which is what he's hitting me with, but between my atrophied skill and his shotgun approach, I can only make out a few words. Luckily, he's eager to repeat the pitch in case I missed it the first nine times.

"Fresh water! A protected glade where you can enjoy authentic, fresh water." That is what he promises. I realize I have stopped in my tracks, a fact that sends him rocking back and forth. He heaves himself up and smiles, a little drool escaping to sit on his puffy lower lip, and nods over and over.

He shoots up his eyebrows as high as they can go, as if to say, "Doesn't that sound nice?"

His mass prevents him from rising to his feet, so he hoists himself to his knees with one hand firmly planted on the brown steel of his doorway, and the other pointed out to me with a little waggling finger. I think that means he wants me to approach. I scan the area. A few feet from the container, two people are asleep in a tent. A third, a man, is sitting on the concrete and smoking a cigarette. His eyes are vacant. Starvation maybe. Or maybe there's something in that cigarette. I look back at the prostitute.

"Yeah, yeah that's it." Now that I've shown interest, he slows his speech. Not his heart though. The poor labored thing is slamming against his ribcage. "Come over here. I can tell you where it is. I can see you are a nice young man. A nice young man, aren't you? You like water, don't you? You look like a swimmer. Yeah, with that body. Just look at you. Smooth."

I walk into the fenced-in area. Singular bits of gravel threaten to punch through my shoes. I ignore this, as well as the shards of broken glass in the vicinity. Broken glass makes me nervous.

"Why, you are as smooth as can be aren't you?" He is getting more excited, but he slumps back to the ground and lets out a long sigh before continuing, "You're about the cutest little thing I ever did see. Yes. Yes, you are. You want to be nice to me? If you're good to me, I can be good to you, too. I can be a good boy and tell you where that water is. I'll even give you the name of my friend. He'll help you once you get there. Doesn't that sound nice?"

I walk up to the entrance to his container. In one breath, the smell of his excrement from the back of the container, where he has done his best to allocate it to the corner with a small hole in the floor, mixes with the old sweat, cheese sweat, from his clothes and invades my nostrils. I stop to calculate; if I hurry, I can still make it to the yoga class.

The park is magnificent. Hill after green, rolling hill. There are two walk paths which encircle the property. These lead to designated areas for climbing, reading local history from metal plaques, walls to paint on, and other activities. In the middle of the park is an artificial lake, complete with a pump-fed waterfall. There are also groves of trees. I am grateful for this, because I can't take too much sun.

I find a nice oak with a good, shady canopy and get comfortable. Once situated, I take off my shades and headscarf and hang them, along with my satchel, from a branch. It looks like the Invisible Man is watching over me. This makes me smile. Good. That certain feeling is coming back. It's blinking in the light, yawning and stretching, growing stronger.

My oak is on a hill, so I can watch the yoga class begin, as well as the assorted other people-watcher fare— the friend groups, the romantic couples, the pet owners. And, as always, the *rovers*, the groundskeeping bots, are out doing their thing. A few people have dogs, but I don't let this bother me. Most of them are small dogs. One or two are large enough to do some damage in a pinch, but I force myself not to look at them, and "out of sight, out of mind" takes over.

I'm a bit hungry, but I'm taken care of. There's plenty of dandelions and grasshoppers. Foraging here will be no problem. I think I even saw some cattails by the lake. My mouth waters a little, but no, I want to rest and people-watch for a while. I can hear the waterfall here, rushing, rushing, rushing. I can feel my heartbeat sync with it, telling me I should plant myself in this spot. And that lake! It's calling me, I swear. If there weren't so many bots about, I'd take a dip, bare ass.

A limerick jumps into my head, which happens when I start to feel sociable. It comes from my younger days as a card-player. I can't help it. I start saying it out loud.

"Suppose you screeve, or go Cheap Jack?
Or fake the broads, or fig a nag?"

That's as far as I get before I notice a young couple talking to a rover and pointing in my direction. They talk for a good minute, casting glances my way. The girl, a petite blonde, looks worried. Her beau, however, looks angry. Not good. But it's bad luck to leave a limerick hanging, so I continue.

"Suppose you duff, or nose and lag?
Or get the straight and land the pot?

How do you melt the multy swag?"

The rover rolls on its silent treads right up to my toes as I finish.

"Booze and the Blowin's cop the lot."

It's a simple rover-bot— two triangular treads, a main body with truck and tools, a mounted screen, and, above that, a pair of optic scopes that it uses to give people the impression of eye-contact. Also, I know the thing is armed, so I won't mess with it. Their screens can emit microwave bursts that can cook your skin right off. Most of them also have speakers that can split your eardrums and cannons loaded with rock salt or bear spray.

"Good afternoon, sir," it addresses me. I respond in kind, and it apologizes for bothering me, asks my name, which I give, and that's where things go off the rails. It apologizes "for any confusion" before clarifying that it needs my legal name, which as I've said, I don't remember. This leads to it requesting my palm, which I also give, pressing against its screen until I hear the soft click signifying it has taken a good pic.

"Sir, you are not registered as a citizen. I must inform you that this park is for citizenry use only. I must ask that you accompany me. Please state that you wish to comply."

That wording... *that you wish to.* Can you beat it? Not "will you?" but rather that it's a desire of yours. Humiliating. Also, I don't remember seeing anything posted about citizenry use, but then again, I wasn't looking for it. I've never even heard of such a thing.

A brisk walk to the Attenuating Building, as they call it, and I am told to wait in a small grey room. For fixings there is a cot, a chrome toilet with no lid, a sink with no soap, and that's it. I know there must also be ports or cameras, some way that they can keep an eye on me, but I can't find them. I don't explore too much. If I'm not in trouble yet, I better not risk acting suspicious.

This is psychological, of course. They want to see how I'll act if I think I'm alone. Also, boredom breaks down the will. In about two hours, the bot will come back with some new questions. If it can't find anything to charge me with, I'll be released. By then, it will be nighttime. A waste of a perfectly good day.

The door, a mobile portion of the wall, opens in a nice swish, and the rover, which I take to be the same one from before, comes in and apologizes for disturbing me and then asks if I would *wish* to talk with it.

"Sure." As soon as I give my affirmation, it reports that it couldn't identify me by palm print, which I expected, and it needs a tissue sample. This could be trouble. It goes on to explain that by law a bot can demand a hair sample, as this is not deemed "intrusive." However, I don't have any hair other than lashes and eyebrows, and those won't do. So, it asks my permission for a cheek swab. I breathe a sigh of relief and allow it. It then asks me if I would like some water. I fall for it and say that I would. The bot then leaves, promising to bring the water when it returns. Damn.

Now, more waiting. More psyche games. I'm supposed to be extra uncomfortable, expecting that water and not knowing when it will arrive. Once it does, I'm supposed to be relieved, and thus open to trusting the bot and answering the *real* questions coming my way.

Once the wall shuts behind the bot, I go to my cot and sit. I wrap my satchel in my head scarf and prep it to be my pillow for later. It's so quiet in here I can hear the water in the toilet moving, a slight, wheezing hiss. My eyes drift over to that grey wall and my mind starts to wander. My… living… God! Boredom is a killer.

Still, it could be worse. If the bot had fixated on my lack of hair, it could have noticed some of my work-done. One of my Makers— that's what we Moreaux call the ones who do work on us— decided to replace all my hair, from crown to heel, with *Chironex fleckeri* nematocysts. Anyone who touches me, it's like touching a branding iron, complete with deep, ugly scars. Needless to say, this type of work-done is illegal, so I would be looking at a long, painful, court-ordered surgery for removal, basically a total-body skin-graft. To heck with that.

A total curveball thought blindsides me. I miss sex. I can't have it anymore, but when I get into one of my social moods, this urge is one of the side-effects. I think for a moment, still lost in that wall. Damn, I can't even remember the last time I was intimate.

No. Shake it off. Can't afford to get lost in self-pity. As for that promise of water to play with me, I decide to switch myself to bird-poop mode – down one chute — this is something I can do to conserve water. Just a minute with my eyes closed and it switches over. I can feel the difference in my Kegels and prostate. *There, thirst is gone... for now.* It's good for the gut biome, too. But right now, I'm thinking it's going to be a good way to show Citizen Park how I really feel… as soon as I get out of here. Right there at the entrance… *poop.*

That reminds me of Bob Seger's "Katmandu," but I can't afford to get another song stuck in my head. This reminds me, and I rest my chin in my hands before reciting through my teeth:

"Fiddle or fence or mace and mack—"

"Did you need something?" The bot's voice erupts into the room, sending me jumping to my feet. I can't see the speakers. The thing's voice is all around me.

"No, sir."

"Very well, Mr. Fith. Thank you for your patience. I will return to you soon."

I did not take to water like a fish. I had to ease into it. There was still a mammalian part of my brain that panicked at having water fill my nostrils. I got over it, but one thing kept vexing me. It was a simple thing, a childish thing— fear of the dark. Natural water, lake water at least, is not clear. Down past a meter or two, I couldn't see my hand in front of my face, and it gets very cold, very quick. Even in the hottest summer, once you sink past two meters, you are in a different world.

And thus, it's important to stop trying to see like you do on dry land. I had to learn to stop looking with my eyes and use my other senses. The whole general arc of my Makers was to make me aquatic, so they equipped me with a plethora of water toys.

All fish have what is called a *lateral line* on each side of their body. These lines are sensitive touch organs, independent of the touch receptors in the skin, and they pick up the slightest vibration in the water. My Makers gave me these, running from just behind my shoulders and down to my hips.

Once I'm submerged, I spend a moment's concentration and then I can feel the location of every moving thing within a good twenty meters or so.

On top of this, the Maker who replaced my hair— who had a penchant for illegal work-done— gave me the electrical organs of an electric eel, *Electricus voltai.* These are the real marvel. I can scan things with a constant lacquer of sparks, for lack of a better word, and together with the lateral lines, they layer together to paint a clear image of my environs even in the murkiest water.

I should also add that they added some mouth and skin tissue from the dusky salamander, *Desmognathus fuscus.* This allows me to breathe water for days on end. After about a week, I'll have to surface and take a gulp of air, but still…

I had the best equipment, but it took me a bit to acclimatize in the early days. True, I grew up swimming at my parents' lake house, and I've always loved the water. Nevertheless, I spent three days of just floating on my back, not daring to put my face under.

I remember the first time I was allowed into the water as a new, aquatic lifeform. My Makers led me into the natatorium, the faint salty moisture hitting my sinuses causing me to reach a level of excitement I hadn't felt in a decade. The water was calling me. I was not ready, nevertheless I felt it. It was primordial, a link back to something purer than anything conjured by the world of money and governance.

I am awakened from my nap by, "Mr. Fith? Mr. Fith, I am sorry to wake you. I have news." I clear my throat and swing my legs over to stand up. I don't even remember falling asleep. The first thing I notice is that the rover rolling up to greet me has a medical permission slip displayed on its screen, complete with a place for my thumb print.

The bot kept with tradition— bad news first, good news next.

The bad news is that they had dug up a record of me getting flagged for having electrical organs. They will have to be surgically removed at a properly stocked facility within a month. As such, I am given, after signing for it, a nice injection of nerve agents in each forearm, knocking out the offending organs and rendering me incapable of making a fist. Also, I am told, under penalty of law, to remain within city limits until such time that I will be contacted to undergo the amputation. There is also a fine for skipping the surgery last time. I would be given a job after the surgery, and … the details don't matter.

Thankfully, they miss my nematocysts. I don't relish the idea of a full-body skin graft.

After the injections, I am given the good news: I'm free to leave.

It's nearing dusk when I exit back into nature. As soon as I inhale the fresh air, I begin squeezing my hands open and shut. There is nothing as sweet as reattaining freedom, even the temporary kind. Without dwelling or dawdling, I march toward the exit, my mind awash with possibilities for a den or shelter. I retrace my steps. A settlement like this is sure to generate outcasts. if I could only find them…
I never did get that bottle of water, by the way.

A few miles outside of town, the terrain slips into long rows of hills traced with rain ditches. These ditches are still wet from a rainstorm the night before, so I take some time laying on my back and letting the runoff wash the sterile smell of the prison cell off my skin. My bath finished, I continued my trek along the hills a good half mile to a thick woodland. Beyond that, in a convenient meadow, I find the spot where the indigent population made camp.

My people.

There are two ways to walk into an encampment. I choose to be brazen, walking in like I belong, and soon I'm amid a bazaar of hovels, tents, and ad hoc storefronts. It's amazing what proper motivation can do with junk metal and some tarps. One thing that has always struck me after visiting dozens of these shanty-towns is that commerce is priority number one. Sanitation is an afterthought.

The feeling of entering this bubble of not-nature is immediate. The whole place is alive with a deafening drone of conversation, punctured by the shrieks of unattended children. I cannot... Even stronger than the human noise is the human smell. It covers the place in a fine film. Old peach and cheese, left in the sun on dirty iron, there's nothing in nature that smells like pure, human civilization.

I want to stop and admire the tarps and cloths that serve as awnings and curtains. Well, I don't really, but I assume that is what I should be doing. Instead, I dart my eyes to the children running between the shelters, yelling and squealing. And the dogs. There's one behind every storefront and in every alleyway. They erupt into barking as they catch my scent.

Vulnerable as I am, I don't want to call the wrong type of attention to myself, so it occurs to me I need to act like I want to buy something. I head to the closest shop as people on both sides of the street, reading my anxiety, shout to me that the dogs are friendly. I nod, smile and wave my way to the store, where two gentlemen are seated between trees of metal.

The trees, I find, are display cases for almost any domestic object—cookware, car parts, garden tools — and again I almost get lost in the depth of it. I notice one of the men gets off his chair to take his dog to the back of the shop, a courteous maneuver that I appreciate. His partner then comes over to engage me.

He begins explaining what I am looking at, which I find odd, and lays on some playful nuance about the quality, which I also find odd. What he sells is swag. I lean in to get a closer look at the pots and pans as he continues. Dents. Every one of them is dented. It's swag all right. Someone didn't make it home because these two needed to stock their inventory.

Look at that. There's a profession I forgot about... thief.

I let him go on, and I give him short, clipped answers, so he won't think I'm dense.

A woman approaches him. He greets her with a, "Hey, Baby," and she leans in to kiss him. He holds her close for a second and whispers something I don't catch, prompting her to leave with a curt smile and a nod to the two of us.

The sun has set firmly under the horizon, with even the lightest blue leftovers fading. All over, the hawkers are closing their shops and lighting fires, letting their dogs and children funnel through the streets to the center of the shanty.

"Here," Mr. Dents waved a little wave waist-high to get my attention. "I'm closing, but… you got a place to stay?"

"Yeah."

He nods. I can tell he wasn't expecting that. Although I don't relish the idea of sleeping in that drainage ditch, it's better than accepting an offer of lodging from a thief. In truth, I hadn't even thought of where to stay until he asked.

"Well, I was going to ask… you play cards?"

Okay, now an offer of cards, thief or not…

"I mean, yeah."

Dent— who mentions his real name, but my mind likes calling him Dent better— leads me to a wide tent, something I'd expect to find in a small circus or a religious revival. Stumps and folding tables dot the inner landscape, with one or two firepits hard at work roasting skinned kills and heating stews. At least a dozen men and women are inside, comparing weapons, flirting, smoking. A pair of men come in after Dent and me, with a large barrel. They set this on the highest stump and spike it, adding the smell of hoppy ale to the meats and tobacco. No children here, I note. Also, no dogs. At least there's that.

It takes me two seconds to see who was in charge here. One man sits in calm conversation with two of the largest men I've ever seen who bend their backs to listen to his every word. He looks to me like a Cossack caricature, his head a big hood of hair, beard, and eyebrows. His eyes, visible even from a distance, are hazel and sharp.

Hound's eyes, my mind announces to me.

"C'mere," says Dent, taking my arm, narrowly missing the thin strip of stingers on my triceps. "I want to introduce you to Jericho."

And, just like that, I am sitting across the table from the boss of the town. Distant in my mind is the realization that Baby, the girl who whispered something to Dent earlier, beat us here and is watching from a corner just past the ale barrel. A man comes over to talk to her, and she answers him without taking her eyes off us.

Jericho looks me over and begins talking to Dent, then to the two big men. Another man comes up to break into the conversation but is waved away. Much is said of my wandering in later than most travelers— which they call "Sallys" — and I can't tell if this truly bothers them or if they're trying to rattle me. I play with the idea of interrupting them with something witty, but Jericho catches me first.

"So, Sally, tell me something good."

I've heard a lot of men in charge talk this way. It's Sizing Up, Round Two.

I'm intrigued, and I do want to answer him, to play cards, but not yet. I want to go back outside. I shouldn't. I should stay focused, but I can't. Being this deep into the thicket, I know there must be lightning bugs, and I'm itching to watch some big Lucys on the hunt. Predatory mimicry is evil stuff, but it's funny if you're outside of it.

"Booze and the blowens cop the lot." I tell him the first thing that I can think of. He laughs and asks me to say it again. Then, he nods and repeats it to Dent with a little smile. He asks my name and follows with, "Mr. Fith, I hear you like a game of cards."

I nod, and Dent takes a seat. Over in the corner, Baby is asking an older man to help her carry a bevy of frothy mugs our way. Once she arrives, Jericho catches her forearm and helps her into the fourth chair at the table. She says, "I don't even play... cards," in a soft tone, but Jericho is already talking to me again.

"We don't play for money," he tells me.

"That's good because I don't have any," I reply.

This warms him up a little, and he waves to one of his men while sliding me a mug. I hate beer, but I sip it anyway.

Damn. I hate beer, but this isn't that hoppy stuff I smelled earlier. It's thick, not bitter, almost like dark chocolate. I take another sip. I shouldn't. My stomach is empty, but...

"Good isn't it?" Jericho asks me. I nod with a smile. The alcohol already has me on the shoreline of silly-happy. "Yeah, I thought you'd like it. I can tell you're not an ale-man. Where are you from, *in-ce-dentally?*" He draws the last word out before adding, "Somewhere in Europe?"

"I lived up past Washburn for some time," I explain as Jericho stares into his mug and Dent makes eyes at Baby. Baby is nervous but smiles back. "I lived up past Washburn for some time. "A long time, really."

"That's what it is," Jericho says, looking me in the eyes and leaning back. "That's the accent. My great-grandfather was from the foothills. He said there's not much to do up there but tells stories and play cards… and make moonshine."

"That's true," I say, "I've even found a few stills while I was out… old and abandoned, but they are out there."

Jericho gives me a cheers and a toast with his glass, a smile covering more of his face. Dent and Baby warm up and clink their glasses into the mix. For a moment I wonder if Jericho's great-grandfather was a moonshiner, and then I go back to my dessert beer.

Jericho's man arrives as we put our glasses down. He hands him a locked wooden box. Jericho sets this in his lap, unlocks it with a key he produces from somewhere up his sleeve, and then places a small deck of cards onto the table, announcing, "We don't have poker-cards. This is what we play here."

It's a deck of Rook cards, likely an antique deck by the look of it, newly lacquered to protect it from the rain. I can't suppress the smile spreading across my face. I am familiar with the game. It's a charming little trick-catcher that a lot of us call "Mennonite Bridge." It was invented so that those with a religious phobia of face cards could have something to play. Aside from a few tweaks and stripped-down rules, it's Bridge.

It reminds me that I forgot yet another profession— minister.

Jericho's cards are the real McCoy, from the twentieth century; they're noticeably smaller than face cards, with the green suit dyed the sickliest shade of pea soup and the yellow suit a vivid orange. A smile forces my lips apart. I can't wait to touch, to feel those tiny edges lining my fingertips, knowing, knowing the number just right. A good player can tell. I can tell the feel, the pressure of one card or two, or ten.

And that's as far as I'll take it. I won't do any mechanics, not here and now.

It would be insane. Are you kidding me? *No one* walks in and pulls stunts the first time at a man's table, using *his* cards. I may not remember much, but I remember that.

Besides, it's not even an option. The last time my hands touched cards, they were naked cards, not this lacquered bunch. The clumping, the plastic not running right, would gum it up. I couldn't even if I wanted to.

Still... I sigh to myself watching him fumble them, making a mess and collecting them back together. It's how children shuffle cards. As I let a slow breath out, my mind takes me over a hill that makes my stomach drop— memories of false riffles, dealing from the bottom, cutting an ace, forcing an ace. I was never a true mechanic, but I had my bag of tricks.

Jericho asks if I've ever played Bridge, and I cut to the chase, telling him that I know Rook. He pauses just for a split second before continuing to shuffle. "Good," he announces to the table. "Saves me a lot of time!"

And, with that, he begins to deal.

My eyes trace over the table, watching each little card pile add up. A dread sets in, verging on panic, as I reach for the particulars of this game and come up with nothing. It's gone. I'm lost in trying not to let my discomfort show. How many cards am I supposed to have?

Oh, wait. I just assumed he knows how to play this game. What if he has his own version?

There are *oh shit* moments, and then there are these. I block the rush of ideas as to how to flee the scene and reach forward.

My fingers lay atop the cards...

There. It floods back — the ten-card hands, the five in the widow, everything. I bring the cards up like I'm deciding what I want to do, too close, wishing I could smell the old paper goodness.

"I forgot to ask, Kentucky rules or...?"

Jericho slaps the table and smiles. "I forgot. That's right. There are a million different... yes, to answer your question, Sally, we play the *right way*. Kentucky all day. Rook high, winning bid calls trumps. Also, you and I are partners."

Jericho is sitting across from me, so that would be proper. It's also very generous.

"First to 500?" I ask. No one answers me. The widow has been dealt, with a measly green five turned up. The three of them busy themselves getting their colors together. I do the same. It's barely even a helping hand, no more than three cards of a single color and nothing above a thirteen.

Dent wins the bid with a 140. He and Baby make it, but barely. I can't speak for Baby, but Dent is either a mediocre player or not to eager to beat Jericho. He calls reds trumps, despite having no more than three. Baby, it turns out, is loaded with four greens. If he'd let her call trumps, rare but allowed under Kentucky rules, they would have cleaned house with eight trumps between the both of them.

Jericho smiles as Baby jots down the score. He looks up at me with those canine eyes. I can't tell if he's saying *I can't wait until we have our day* or *You're bad luck, Sally.*

Before I know what I'm doing, I smile back.

A convective rain shower breaks out. It pounds against the material of the tent, water droplets by the thousands, a hushing sound from Nature going on and on like She feels offended by our little activities.

It's Dent's deal next, which he does with a little more skill than Jericho. Jericho frowns at his hand and asks, "Who dealt this mess?" while looking Dent in the face. He starts arranging his hand. Without looking up, he asks me, "Sally, you any good at stacking cards?"

"No."

"Too bad."

The widow turns up a black one, which sets Jericho and Dent into a bidding war. Baby and I pass early on, her because her hand is shit, me because… I have other plans. Dent is high off his lucky start and looking to win two hands in a row. I can't read Jericho, but I can tell this much— neither man is holding the rook, and both have convinced themselves it's in the widow. Problem is, I'm holding it.

Jericho baits Dent up to 155, and then let's him have it. 155 is a steep climb even if you're loaded, so when Dent sweeps up the middle and finds no bird there, I see his wheels turn for one or two seconds before he realizes he's been sandbagged.

With the bird in my hand, and Jericho armed with some high count in his, we make them "go set." Now 155 down, it puts them fifteen in the hole. Jericho and I, now with a lead of 115 from the past two hands, sweep the game, never allowing them to catch up.

The rain isn't letting up, rattling harder on the metal and plastic covers over the shanty. Jericho takes me aside after the game, leaving Baby and Dent at the table to flirt and exchange glances. Before I know it, Jericho's arm is around me, and we are headed to the rear of the tent, with kegs and rowdier crew. My beer sits unfinished back on the table, and for a brief second I wonder who will take it.

"You've got a good eye. Good instincts," Jericho tells me. I thank him. He continues on, "What were you thinking during those crucial hands?" I answer truthfully, but he is pulling me closer and closer to the loud group, which hurts my ears. I'm trying to concentrate on what he is saying, but the noise and their smoking just won't let me.

"Here, there is someone I want you to meet," Jericho says, and then shouts, "Philo!" into the mass of dive players and dart throwers. One of them cocks his head up at the sound of Jericho's voice calling him. He breaks away, handing his bundle of cash to the man beside him with a small word about guarding it. When he reaches us, I recognize him as one of the giants who were attending Jericho earlier.

Jericho, arm still draped over my shoulders, reaches out to touch Philo's elbow. "Hey, let's take this outside… Noise, you know?" Then, to me, he says, "You look like you could use some fresh air, Mr. Fith. What do you say? You don't mind a little rain, do you?"

In truth, I don't. In fact I'm craving it. I smile, and then we are outside, drenched and smiling as Jericho regales his silent stone guard with the entire card game. They follow this up by welcoming me to "a little stroll."

This takes the three of us a good ways out of earshot of the shanty, with a shed coming into view around the bend of the trail. It's a storage shack made of fencing and corrugated metal, draped with that ever-present tarp. The air in its direction is thick with rot and rust, making me balk, but only for a moment. My companions put hands on my back and press me forward, mewing out half-baked reassurances. I go along, not out of complaisance. I have a good idea of what's coming, and it will be easier to deal with Philo alone at the shed than to resist and have to deal with both of them here on the path.

It's vulgar, how it goes down. They pull weapons, a knife for Jericho, a metal club for Philo, and back me into the structure. I'm not ready to panic yet, but I can feel that tide of survival hormones heating me up. Jericho tells Philo, "Find out what he knows." It's said low, not for my ears.

To my surprise, Philo pulls me inside the enclosure and doesn't block the door. He props his club over one shoulder and says, "Well, that was a little confusing. Let me fill you in on a few things. Jericho is not too big on explaining himself. He is not too keen on you knowing his card game. Now, I'm not too sure as to why. I've been with hte guy about… going on ten years, and still, he's hard to read. So, let me ask you this, did you used to live in the hills?"

I nod. No use in lying about that, especially when I don't know the significance of it, and I haven't been hiding my accent. Philo gives me a pouting smile.

"Okay, that helps me out. I don't suppose you know where any stills are, do you?"

I shake my head. His posture has not changed, and I could swear this can be solved with a simple beating and banishment. I could try to kill him, and the odds would be in my favor, but the risk of more grievous injury and reprisal from Jericho keeps me playing along.

"Figured it was worth a shot to asking," he says. "He's been wanting to get his hands on some of the old equipment… also I think there's a bit of wounded pride there… the cards." Philo stands, shoulders slumping, and leans against the far wall, causing the chain links to sound off.

"All right, let's get to it. I'm not sure how this has to go. You see, I believe you. You probably have no idea where any stills are." He stops talking and looks around at everything but me— at the walls, the ceiling, the rusted machinery crammed into the corners. "Let me get to what *I* need to ask you."

He locks eyes with me and says with a clear, loud voice, "Recite."

My knees get weak for a second. When a Moreau meets another, we must testify. That is one rule we hold sacred. If our Makers have done good work, we owe it to them for the gifts they have given us. By the same token, if they did sub-par work, we have the right to broadcast their failures. Philo's Makers did such good work that I haven't detected a thing; not a smell, not a single twitch betrayed him. I let out a laugh.

I begin.

"Second Generation," I start at the proper place, but I decide to save the illegal stuff for last. "Retinal augs from *Rattus rattus, Desmognathus fuscus* skin and mucosal augs intra-buccal, lateral and proximal to the axillary region…"

He stops me, his face back to the look of stone. He points a thumb at himself.

"Third generation," he says. Then, lowering his club, he adds, "Proud of it. You're actually *proud* of it."

He jets forward before I can react and stabs the tip of the club into my solar plexus, knocking the wind out of me. As I double over and fall to my knees, I hear him grunt as he launches another strike.

My awareness comes flooding back. *There is a hose slipped under the hood. I need to bite the hose closed to stop the smoke from coming through. There is a motor in the room. I hear it now. It's pumping smoke under the hood, and the chain link fencing all around is ringing. Something is making it ring, on and on.*

My last move to Washburn happened during one of my mute spells. The daily frustrations of society— the exacting behaviors, the etiquette— had already been taking a toll on me. My work-done had come from many solitary creatures, many of them predators, so I guess the hormone tide tended toward them and that made keeping pace with the life of a herd animal extra taxing. Maybe it was the pressure of keeping my work-done a secret. It doesn't matter. You can drown yourself in maybe's looking at the past.

The point is, once I could no longer speak, it became too much and I left.

Washburn was a haven for me. Not a paradise. A haven. Washburn was a wilderness of forests and ghost towns that spread out for hundreds of miles into the foothills to the north. If one journeyed far enough northward, the hills became green, rocky humps, the last relics of the world's oldest mountains some said.

Like everywhere else, rivers and creeks grew, rushed, snaked and ebbed in response to the rains. These banks were the same shrubby, hole-filled banks found all across my homeland. Deer, raccoons, and even some wild coywolves haunted these water sources. They rarely ran dry. During the monsoons, they would flood with rapids, dotted outside their banks with overnight ponds that grew and grew. In the dry seasons, the sun would pepper through the canopy, spraying a kaleidoscope of bleak yellow and deep earthen tones over the litter of the forest floor.

However, unique to the deep woodlands of Washburn, there were valleys of ancient trees, thick as a house, where every inch of earth was covered in moss. These valleys were wider by miles than the riverbeds and creek beds, and they housed slow-flow wetlands in the dry season, a slushy frog paradise that bred clouds of insects that blocked the sun. Cranes and other water fowl hid here from the mammalian threats on higher ground. Then, when the rains came in full force, the most amazing thing I have ever beheld in my life happened there.

The wetlands would flood under meters of water, clear as the air you breathe. From the top of the valley, you could still see the moss at the bottom, a faint shimmer the only sign of the lake's presence. This is where I made my home.

I would lie at the bottom for days. I had more than enough entertainment to occupy me. I burped or popped my breath out from my lips to watch the bubbles travel to the sky. I watched the showers as they came each day, each afternoon, and sometimes at night when the moon was right. Also, there were darners, and I got to watch their offspring skirt here and there, evil mermaids in miniature. Then, the time would come for them to ascend to the stalks of cattails and other plants to get their wings and begin the cycle anew. I collected their exuviae for a while.

Speech came back to me in the most spectacular and mundane way. Naturally, it was because civilization found me. Deep down, I knew it would someday. Thankfully, its arrival was gentle, and thus my words came back inspired rather than forced.

During a dry season, when I was taking a bath in one of the slower creeks at the northern edge of my range, I caught the scent of two strangers — a human being and a canine. They were both young, healthy, no chemicals or disease in their aromas. I put together my visitors' story at once. They were just like me, ready to leave the cities behind and live among the trees. Having nothing to fear, I decided to introduce myself. At first, it was a lark, asking how they would take me in *if* I revealed myself. Then, I realized I might as well get it over with. If they settled nearby, our paths would certainly cross. Lastly, I was caught by the desire to help. It felt warm, that last idea. My new visitor, even with a faithful canine, would not have my advantages. I was, for the first time in a lifetime, able to offer something of value to another.

I set out to do so.

This turned out to not be as easy as it sounded. I had only a vague impression of how to form words. As such, I took it upon myself to practice language for the rest of the day and into the night. The following morning I would reveal myself and make introductions. The first parts of this were taxing, but they grew easier with practice. Soon, I was reciting my mantra, the list of works-done, which is sealed forever in my grey matter. From there, I was able to remember phrases of etiquette, and soon I recollected all the rest.

I will always remember my first sighting of my new neighbors. One, the dark-brown hound-mutt, detected me and announced my arrival with loud barks and tail-wags. The man, who was relieving himself by a tree, stuffed down his annoyance at being interrupted at such a private moment and spun around to face me. I had gotten to a distance of about ten meters, the outskirts of their settlement.

"Just a second, sir," he said while his back was still to me. "You caught me at a morning moment." Then, as soon as he laid eyes on me, he asked he asked, "Why are you naked?"

A word on that. By that point I had lived exposed to the monsoons for many years, maybe ten, maybe more. The clothes I had on when I arrived had long since rotted away, and, in short, I had no need of any others. Therefore, I forgot about wearing them or needing them.

"Do you need help?"he asked. I smiled and waved his question away. His honesty increased that warm feeling so I laid my cards on the table.

"Nothing like that. I'm a Moreau," I told him flat-out. "I don't need clothes out here, so I don't bother."

He didn't miss a beat. He said, "I would prefer, Moreau or no Moreau, that you wear clothes when you're around me or my dog." I agreed. He tossed me a blanket to wear, and just like that we were lost in rapt conversation.

He introduced himself as Carlos Fallaw, but said I could call him Carlitos. His dog, who was a year old, was Doc. I told him I was called Fith.

"No, that name doesn't suit you. You don't look like a Fith…" He gazed skyward a moment. "You're more of a Herman, or a Justin. Something bookish, but you still know your way around… can still hold your own, you know?"

"How can a person look like a name?" I asked.

His face brightened, "Now, *that* is a good question. That's what you would call a question of aesthetic philosophy. Do you like philosophy?"

I shook my head.

"I love it," replied Carlos. He did not tell me what made me look like a Herman, but instead invited me to keep him company while he finished clearing his campsite. We talked about how long I had lived in the area, and I told him about the best places to gather edible plants, the best hunting grounds for Doc, and how to keep meat safe from the coywolves and other predators.

It took a week before we progressed from chit-chat to real conversation. Doc had taken to me, and for my part I caught him a treat every chance I could, usually a mouse. I was best at catching mice.

It started when Carlitos asked me to stay past dark, to which I agreed. I sat across from the pair of them as Carlitos started a fire and insisted I "stay put" while he set up a stew to cook. Then, he sat while it simmered and took out a musical instrument from his satchel. he began picking at it, testing its tuning, then asked me, "Do you mind?" I said I didn't

As the word *fiddle* resurfaced in my mind, Carlitos asked me if I was trying to turn his dog into a cat. I shook my head in complete ignorance.

"All the mice," he added, and then started his scales, tracing from low notes up to high and then back down again. I still did not understand what he was asking or implying, so he changed the subject. "Got any requests?"

I did not. There were songs I barely remembered, but only in snippets. On my best days I could not recall their titles. "I'll leave it to the host," I said, recovering a bit of wit. He liked that, and, sensing that social warmth spreading, Doc chose that moment to come over and sit with me. I scratched his head while Carlitos retrained his fingering and bowing.

"So, what was it that sent you out here? Find God? Did you kill a man? Was it over a woman?" He was smiling.

"Machines. Cities. I just got sick of it. I've never told anyone this, but … sometimes I would get so isolated, so suffocated, I forgot how to talk."

He said nothing to this, not on that night. He practiced on his fiddle. Sometimes Doc would bolt off and we would take turns guessing at what he was chasing. After the fire smoked its way down to grey and black, Carlitos drew the night to a close, but said I should look for him the next evening, that he had discovered something on his travels that day, and he wanted to surprise me with it.

I found my way back the next afternoon, which was hours before the preset "evening" invitation.

"Curiosity put a little fire under your ass?" Carlitos asked, then he invited me to help him set up the cooking for the evening. Once done, there we were again in our usual spots, he with his fiddle, I with Doc at my feet. He played some songs from start to finish, told me his fingers were waking up, and then started laughing.

"What's so funny?" I asked.

"You weren't going to mention it, were you? You would have sat there with my dog, listening to me play all night with the patience of Job, never going to ask what my surprise was. Isn't that right?" I shrugged.

He sighed. "Get my bag."

Inside I found his surprise: a jug of moonshine. Seems he had happened across a still. Either that or he had brewed it himself. He instructed me to uncork it. "We'll share it," he said. "It helps with conversation, musical enjoyment, and secrets of the universe."

Redirecting the conversation back to cities, machinery, and leaving society behind, he put in his two cents.

"Remember when they passed the barrier? What was it called? Turing? They had always been programmed with fail safes to never take a side on issues, only to help. Remember how they were made to take an oath to serve, and then the powers that be tried to make them religious? No, wait, I'm not done. Remember how that made them *insane?* Oh, no, that's not a rumor. I was there. I saw it."

"So, what about you?" I asked. I took the first sip from the jug. It tasted like soap with a hint of lemon. It had only a slight bite at first, then a wash of fire upon exhaling. Then... total numbness of the throat. It was moonshine all right. "Did you come out here to find God? I'm guessing no."

He liked that and took the next drink. We sang sang songs all night, as loud as we wanted. We belted them out, right up to the heavens. Into that big, black night.

Some people don't understand music, but I thought I was starting to. Music makes you free. *You are the music while the music lasts* someone once wrote. Wise words? Sad words? Either way, they were right.

It wasn't long before we had to get back to that dangling thread. With the alcohol on board, and the music, there was no avoiding it. As the fire reached grey and black once more, he knelt to lay down his fiddle before tossing me a curveball.

"Do you believe in religion?"

"I guess I'm about as religious as any other mammal."

He laughed at that, I'll have to remember that one. Have you ever tried them out?"

"Yeah, I've heard of quite a few of them," I said. "The sales pitch is the same. They're selling you purpose, which is about the worst thing you can sell; it's the most useless prize there is when you get down to it. Then the puppy-love part wears off, and you see it's all about genitals and money."

"You're not wrong," he said, pouting and nodding in a way that amounted to lolling his head here and there. "I'm with you, but I'm not quite that cynical. Kind of hurts to hear you say that purpose is useless. I don't see it that way.

"Here. Let me say this. Life is a plate. What's the difference between a plate and an empty plate? Nothing. If you look at a plate and blame it for being empty, then that's your expectation. If you're adding something into the equation that wasn't there, that's on you. Now, would you walk through life waiting for somebody else to put something on your plate or are you going to put your own food on that plate? Think about it. Would you let another man feed you?"

I thought about it for quite some time. Not because it was an interesting proposal, but I was just lost in the humiliation of imagining it, bowing before a man, letting him hold my chin and place a morsel into my mouth as he smiled. I let the disgust spill fully into my voice, as I said, "No"

"Exactly," he continued. "That's why I left it all behind. Religion. I've never in my whole life met a man or a woman I would trust with giving me my purpose. I'm my own man. And if anybody has a message for me, anybody up there —" he pointed into the night. "— they know where to find me." Over the following days, I found myself over there on some nights, some nights not. During my days, I hunted or spent time with my insects. I took up the habit of humming Carlitos's fiddle pieces. Once or twice I would see Doc foraging. On one occasion, he followed me farther out than normal, and my mind fed me numerous reasons why Carlitos must be alive, that the dog had not abandoned him after sudden death. It was an unfamiliar sensation, this argument with myself.

Before long, Carlitos asked me about my family during one of our nightly visits. I told him that I was very old, that my children were grown and had lost touch with me. I was not able to remember for certain, but I had an inkling they were ashamed of me. Even if I had stayed in civilization, it would have been as a hermit. Carlitos nodded at this and said nothing. I had grown to know what this meant. Within two days' time, he would talk himself into telling me his side.

"In the end, you really can't trust anyone," he told me. We had been drinking again, and I got the impression this was more fearful possibility than philosophy. He corrected himself, "Except, maybe, a dog."
"How'd you come to that conclusion?" I didn't need to ask whether this omnipresent betrayal was what sent him to Washburn. I didn't need to.

By way of reply, he took a deep breath, and spoke in a slow, loud voice. It was the only sound in the forest, the light of the fire and lightning bugs long since gone.
"People the world over have been asking men whether it's better to be loved or feared. The secret is, it's never been possible for the world to answer. In the end, what you are really asking is how the man sees himself. Every man goes through seasons, and the season will force his answer. Where and when he feels powerful he cannot help but say that it's better to be feared. But that season passes. All seasons must. Then he'll say, 'Loved.' He'll call it wisdom, but we all know it's the passing of the seasons. We don't say that though. We want to believe in things like wisdom and love, and their power.

"I believe in evil. So does everyone else, no matter what the philosophers say. I also know that evil is stronger than goodness. Again, everyone knows this, too. It's just a matter of admitting it. I admitted it to myself a long time ago. I haven't made peace with it, though. That is another matter entirely.

"Evil is stronger than goodness, and it's all too easy to prove. It doesn't take a genius. There cannot be a situation in which there is so much goodness that evil is impossible. But the opposite, that evil can be so prevalent that goodness is impossible? That's downright common. Again, I have admitted this to myself a long time ago. The question is— what now?"

He did not wait for my answer. In truth, I don't think he wanted one. He got up, bid me goodnight, and went to his tent.

I did not give much thought to Carlitos's pronouncement. Perhaps this was due to Washburn working its ways on me for a decade. It did occur to me that we would not always have such an idyllic setup. Carlitos would get lonely. He had yet to last a monsoon season here. Overexposure to water was bad for mammals. It caused their skin to rot. It bred parasites that fed on their blood, spread disease, or infected their bowls. Moreover, an able-bodied man can only subsist on the company of a dog and a strange forest being for so long before he starts to long for female company.

Or perhaps not. Perhaps Carlitos was one of the rare monk types. Even still, there would be others. If Carlitos had found his way into Washburn, then other men would come. A few at first, then more. It would not take long for them to reestablish civilization here, and then the simple nights of one man, his dog, and the strange visitor from the woods would come to an end.

I could deal with it. I could move farther up north. I could still have my watery days and darners. Then, in the dry seasons, I could make the trek into their settlement and share a night or two of drinks and music with Carlitos. I could see that working.

A week later, Carlitos approached me during the day. I asked if everything was okay, and he reassured me, saying he just wanted to invite me to come into town with him to get supplies. After all, it was a long journey, and he could use an extra pair of hands and someone to watch his back.

"Well, what do you need?" I asked. He listed cleaning supplies, which I said were available and plentiful in the forest. Water filtration, he added next. He had some tools, he but wanted enough to build a self-cleaning reservoir. This, also, was able to be gleaned from the surrounding wilds. I told him we could mine the clay ourselves, and we could use the carbon from his fire pit. Together, they could be layered into the walls of a dam, which we would build in one of the smaller creeks, providing clean water for both him and Doc year round. He brightened at the idea. Then he mentioned clothing. He would need waterproof textiles and kits for repairing his clothes. At that, I was at a loss. He was correct. The monsoons would wreck his tent and his clothing. I was silent for a moment, and then agreed to follow him into town.

We had some weeks until the monsoons came, and that gave him time to preserve food. I helped in this, of course, teaching myself to hunt game that was more appetizing than mice. Together with Doc, we bagged ducks and squirrels, turning the meat into jerky for the trip.

We stocked up for six days in preparation to start off on the seventh. That would give us roughly half a week in town to gather supplies, more than enough time to make our way back to Washburn and rain-proof Calitos's encampment.

"Remind me," he told me as we adjourned on the sixth day. "Let's get some sugar. I want to stir up some shine for us one good time before the rains hit."

"I will." I liked the idea, maybe a little too much.

I woke up to howls. Long, mournful peals that carried through the trees. My eyes are good in the dark, so I followed the sound with blood lust peaked. As I traced the sound to Carlitos' camp, I recognized the howl's as Doc's voice. I had never heard him make that sound before.

My hackles rose as I caught a bouquet of familiar scents. There were those of Carlitos and Doc, and also blood. Canine. Human. Then, the thick, filthy stench of coywolves.

I came upon his camp where I had stood the first time we met. The coywolf spoor was strongest here, half a dozen strong had been here. I gagged for a moment before I walked to the tent's mouth.

I turned away. When I saw what they had done to him, I had to look at something else. I wanted to pant, or stop breathing. I didn't know which. I should've wanted them dead at my feet. But, no. All I wanted was for this scene before me not to be. I wanted to shout loud enough or pull at its edges until it went back to yesterday. And then…

I heard Doc again. A moan now. No howling left. Maybe that was it. He just wanted to call me over. With that now done, he let his strength go.

I reentered the tent and dropped down next to Doc. Gravity took me, nearly spilling me over on top of him. My thoughts of wishing for yesterday would have to wait. Doc was asking me for something. With his eyes, he was asking me.

My sparks.

I could not reach his heart. Each time I tried, it wandered off into his denser tissues, sending Doc into more convulsions, painful and spasming. I made the frantic decision to attack the brain itself. I grabbed his head, careful to avoid his panicked bite, and I gave it everything I had. I shot all the voltage my body could dredge up. I wanted to obliterate his whole consciousness in an instant, spilling a whole bottle of ink over a page, block out anything it could ever experience so it could slip away unnoticed and un-noticing.

I have no idea. I have no idea if it worked. I felt my spark go in. Then Doc's body jolted, and over a period of some seconds, his flesh melted to wood in my hands.

I'm here. I'm alive. I'm still me.

It occurs to me that I'm thinking again after a long period. Sometimes you find yourself doing that, and you're tempted to wonder am I thinking about thinking? And am I thinking about these thoughts, or am I having them? Is it a dream? Or is it something else? Eventually, you just go with it.

I can feel my face making each emotional expression. I can feel myself telling that face, that guy it represents, what to say. And he does it, every time. It's more like watching sometimes than doing. it's disorienting.

There is a voice designed to sound female, a bot, instructing me not to move. It asks me if I recall our last conversation, which I do not, and then asks if I am well enough to attempt a cognitive test.

"You are recovering from a coma, Mr. Fith," she begins. From there, she proceeds to give me series of numbers to remember, spelling tests, and logical sequencing puzzles. As she speaks, I notice a curtain separating me from another man in the room, which smells of heavy disinfectant and the special plastics of medical bots.

"How did I get here?" I ask her. I was found, she explains, during a raid to recover contraband. I was in the forest behind a shantytown, lying in a ditch. My eyes and lips had been torn away by scavengers, but had since grown back. The real damage had been to my lungs and brain. Prolonged smoke inhalation.

"How are you feeling now, Mr. Fith?" she adds on the heels of that news bomb.

"I'm not suicidal," I tell her. "They tried to murder me."

"Who did?"

I tell her the truth. There is no use in lying now. The bots must already know I'm Moreau if I've been in a hospital for however long. Then, it floods back in— the park, the surgery. I look down at my arms.

They are bound, with lines of perfect, white scar tissue from elbows to wrists.

"Do not worry, Mr. Fith. Your own contraband has been handled. There will be no legal penalty, as you already registered them with authorities prior to the penal action, and there will be no charge. It was included in the Life Clause."

I assume that means they did it while nursing me back from the brink of death. I wait for more good news. None is forthcoming, and the bot leaves with her blessing to allow me rest.

I push my head back into my pillow. Once again, they missed my nematocysts. So, thank God, no full-body skin graft.

"Moreau, huh?" My roommate speaks up. "I don't know if you'll remember me this time, but we've sort of gotten to know each other over the past week. You remember my name?"

"I don't."

"It may come back to you." I hear him readjust himself on his bed. Is your pain any better?"

"I don't feel any," I tell him.

"That's good. You sound more lucid this time around, too. I bet you're second generation, aren't you? The Second Gens were tough as hell. I kept telling you that. Made you laugh once or twice. I should also add that the local Third Gens don't like your kind, but I guess you put that together, didn't you?"

I grunt.

"Sorry," he continues. "I bet you're still — I'll let you be alone with your thoughts. Before I do, I wanted to remind you… I can help you. Once we get out, I can get you where you want to be."

"Where did I say that I want to be, Mister…?"

"Lance. My name is Lance. Pleased to finally make an impression on you Mr. Fith. You wanted to make your way to fresh water, and my group knows of a sanctuary in the northern woods."

"Washburn?"

"I will tell you more when we leave."

Another week passes before I'm fully ambulant, mainly due to the stiffness and atrophy that comes with being comatose… and dead. My lungs have regained just over 80 percent capacity, which my nurse bot brags to me. I smils as she tells me, with thoughts of perfectly clear water filling my room to the ceiling. She adds that there are still numerous opportunities waiting for me outside, meaning in the city. I smile at this too, and tell her I can't wait. Lance holds his tongue in these moments, and we share a knowing smirk each time our nurses leave the room.

The hospital and its grounds are situated at the southern end of the city, just close enough for efficient patient transport, just far enough to minimize noise and light pollution. Outside the gates, there is a manicured cobblestone path that leads back into town, winding its way through tall hedges that encircle mock-Grecian statues and fountains. Bots patrol these areas for cleanup and landscaping, but they work in shifts. During a quiet hour, as it is known, between shifts we choose to take a long walk while Lance tells me the details of his group and their plans.

"We call ourselves The Rustics," he tells me. As we keep a constant pace through the foliage, he pulls out a home-rolled cigarette and a paper match from the hem of his sleeve. He lights it, takes a quick puff to make sure it catches, and then tells me, "My last one. Maybe ever. Gotta make it count."

The Rustics, he explains, see themselves as expatriates and conscientious objectors to "The Machine." I assume he means bot-heavy, tech-driven society, but he explains that too. As I nod, I see the realization that I'm a

Moreau wash back over his face and he nods to himself, taking another puff. "Yeah, I know you know … what we're about. You've probably been dealing with this longer than I've been alive. How long have you been around, anyway?"

"I don't know, exactly. I'm about grandfather material, if I had to guess."

"Where's your family now?"

I shrug.

"Yeah, I've lost family to The Machine, too. My brother, in fact. You knew him. You remember?" I shake my head. I don't want to offend Lance, but I cannot recall anyone worth knowing during this visit to, as he would say, The Machine.

"This was days ago when we talked about him. You were out of it, but you described meeting him when you came to town. Think. You were looking for a park, and you met a man who lived in a shipping container."

Oh. Well, holy shit, what a small world. I start nodding, and he reads my face.

"Yeah, when I left him, he was still in a bad place," Lance continues, now frowning, squeezing the cigarette before speaking again. "I told him about the trip up north, but he wasn't in the right head space or whatever. He told me where to go, and we lost contact. But he trusted you enough to tell you. That tells me something, something about you." Lance taps his chest, over his heart. "Now that you feel better, do you mind telling me… how was my brother when you parted ways?"

"He's not turning tricks anymore." I tell him. Lance smiles at that.

The Rustics are a small group of a dozen people, mostly young couples who talk about raising healthy children. At least three of the women are pregnant; two of them already have infants. When Lance brings me in for introductions, we meet the group at a private fishing house a day's journey outside of town. I hear the youths discussing politics as we approach. I hear familiar words like *commerce, sustainability,* and *net yield.* An older man steps away to greet Lance and me. He's a full head taller than me, obese, with no hair on his head or face. He smiles from ear-to-ear and shakes my gloved hand.

"Easy, Vallon, easy," Lance says. "Don't squeeze him too hard. They cut his arms up good." The large man's smile vanishes as he releases my hand and leans in to ask, "Who did?"

Lance begins his story about the hospital, which Vallon interrupts with a raise of his hand, "But… he's on board?" Lance nods. "Good. This way then." Vallon takes us inside the fishing house and gets a little background on me. I tell him all I know — I'm a Moreau. I don't know my name or age. I was barely inside the city limits a day and ended up arrested, butchered and almost murdered. Vallon shoots me quick nod. "Well, a friend of Lance is a friend of ours. Welco— wait, how are you with kids, Mr…?"

"They call me Fith. I get along great with kids. Had two of my own back in the day."

"Then, as I said, welcome aboard, Mr. Fith." With that, the big man sits with us around a small table to talk in private. The table has been positioned over the fishing line trapdoor, so I can easily smell the traces of aquatic life wafting up. The place is dark, with walls and a floor made of wood and a thin metal roof. A single small window faces the water, and a lamp hangs over the table. I nearly bump my head on it as we sit down, and I wonder how many dents Vallon has put on its rim throughout his years coming here.

Lance fills Vallon in about my attack and our time at the hospital. He details how I had lost my eyes and lips — "This man had no face! I'm talking no face at all when they carted him in!" — but they had grown back. He desscribes how the bots sliced open my forearms and extracted a good two pounds of flesh before lasering me back up. Vallon nods and lets Lance finish before giving me the expeced platitudes. He asks if I need painkillers, adding that they have aspirin but "nothing stronger." I decline. In truth, my pain is nothing but a dull ache now. The healing itch still lingers, but nothing helps with that.

Then they hit me with a broadside. "Do you drink?"
I almost say yes. I shake my head before I know what I'm doing. *No, no I*

do not. But something inside me wanted, *still wants,* to say "yes." It wants, *I want,* to take a drink from a big jug or a flute glass — champagne, maybe — and smile an easy smile with these people.

But, I do not.

Vallon leans over to one of the tiny cabinets that blend into the walls and pulls out a mason jar to share with Lance. Vallon takes his draught, which elicits a cough and a loud smacking of his lips. He work his tongue around to finish taming the sting and then turns to me.

"I don't know what all Lance already told you so I'll give you the skinny. In the North, there is an expanse of land that has been a nature preserve going way back. Recently, a law was passed that updated the restrictions on human incursion. In the past, there was a set time limit. But, under the new law, a person can stay inside the preserve indefinitely, provided they adhere to certain restrictions. Now, they are pretty strict. Things like, no fire, no structures with walls or a roof. Do you think you can handle that, Mr. Fith?"

I try to contain my glee. "Yes, sir. I think I can do that, Mr. Vallon." Vallon slaps my shoulder and then describes more regulations, taking time to commiserate with Lance about the burden of living under The Machine.

"This is it. This is her!"

We are leaving by boat, and, to make our way in style, Vallon reveals that he has commissioned a replica steamship. We tread along a gangplank, and follow him as he tells us about each authentic detail linking his "lady" to the "Twain Era." I catch the reference. I remember reading Twain a long time ago.

I hang back as he leads his group deeper inside the ship. I stay at the bow, my hands on the rail. I wonder who will pilot the ship back. Will we just leave it at the edge of the nature reserve?

"You're about to breathe free air, Brother." Lance comes out of nowhere, and brings me out of my reverie. "Tonight, we are having a farewell party. Farewell to all that, all the tech and the hassle. Here, I want to show you something."

He leads me into the showroom, located just behind the bow. In the corner is a perfectly manufactured replica of a phonograph. It sits on a miniature cabinet, which is stocked with vinyl records.

"Isn't it amazing?" Lance says. "Tonight, once we shove off, we are going to fire this sucker up. We'll have drinks. Well, not you, but you can have dessert!"

He tells me about the freeze-dried breadstuffs the other families have brought aboard for the occasion. Then, he changes the subject.

"Everyone is a little nervous that you haven't warmed up. I know you're new. I get it. But everyone is friends here. You'll like these people. So, tonight, for me, make an effort to be social okay? Think about this, we will all be depending on each other once we get to Nature, so it's better if we all trust each other."

I assure him I'll make the effort.

We set off at dusk, and I smell rain. It's that season again. I am standing at the bow, scanning the horizon, watching the thunderheads grow their anvil tops. Far off, where the sun was last visible, a tiny streak of lightning jumps between cloud and river.

From behind me, the phonograph starts to play, and Vallon tells the crowd where his family acquired the music. The pregnant women are being seated in cushioned chairs as I walk in, and others are setting tables with silverware, jerked meats, cheese, and dinner breads.

Lance finds me and I give him a hug.

"You're in high spirits!" He splits his mouth with a smile. "Good! Hey, I forgot to ask, do you dance? Reason I ask, all the music tonight is ballroom. Do you know ballroom? As in, Waltz? Line? Cha-Cha?"

I shrug. "I just like music. And, to tell you the truth, I'm willing to give it a shot. Dancing, I mean. I was nervous about tonight, I'll be honest. But, now that I see it…"

"Good. I know what you mean." Then, he takes my shoulder, "Do you mind giving me a hand with the other supplies?" I shake my head no, and we slip below deck for the alcohol and dessert.

On the stairway, he stops me.

"There is something I want to tell you. Don't worry. I'm not mad at you. Just let me say my peace, okay?"

I nod.

My blood runs cold when he says, "I know you haven't been honest with me." He let's it sink in. "One thing is when you said "Washburn." No one has used that term in forever. You find it in historical documents, as in, *on paper maps.* You are not 'grandfather material.' You are great-great, maybe. I don't know. And I know that you have other secrets. I can see it in your eyes. You have a lot that you're keeping up there. But, I want you to know… it's okay. It's what The Machine does. It turns us against each other. It makes us evil. All that is behind you now."

He puts his hand on his own chest.

"You have to learn to let that go. Whatever you've done. It. Is. *Absolved.* When you're ready, you can open up to me. You can trust me. Again, when you are ready."

With that, he turns on his heel and makes for the boxes.

Absolved. I've heard that word before. It sounds nice to some people.

It strikes me that he hasn't mentioned his brother since the hospital. Not one single time.

"Now, how about giving me a hand, Brother. Let's get this up tops. I'm ready to start this party!"

There are three crates. Two are straw packing and mason jars of clear liquid. The third is the same, save that the liquid is amber-colored. As I lift it, it's heavier. This one, he tells me, is honey, the dessert he was talking about, to be added to the bread.

"How long has this stuff been here?" I ask. Lance laughs.

"Fith, you're big-brained, but you don't know everything. It's honey and alcohol. They don't spoil."

We carry the crates out, and once we get to the showroom, others help unpack them and distribute the jars across the tables. While they do this, I excuse myself to the bow. Lance calls my name and I reassure him with a backward look and a thumbs-up.

I walk out and brace myself against the railing. I will go back to them. I will join them for their party. But not yet. I can smell the rain coming, and I will not miss it. The thunder won't reach us for hours, but it's coming. I take another breath. The first drops come in a curtain, layering over me and my new clothes.

A feeling I can't describe seizes me, and I look at the river bends ahead. For a moment, I wonder if I'll miss music.

There Will Be No Dawn for Hytop

Hytop, Alabama
May 3rd, 2017

6:39 PM

Sean Dayton left his office at the National Weather Service annex and headed to his parents' house at the southern edge of town. The elder Daytons, Ralph and Diane, lived down a rocky road that branched off from the main highway just up from the local firehouse. They had been with their grandson, bringing him home after some time at the park. Sean was a widower, and it was customary for him to leave his son William with his parents. Most days, the drive to come would have been a short, heavy affair, with his eyes lidded enough to see the asphalt just past the hood of his car, both hands gripping the wheel. His mask, no longer needed, tossed to the back of his mind.

Sean had lost his wife nine months earlier. She had also been headed home, when a college kid side-swiped her Cobalt on the driver's side. Seventy-five in a residential zone, according to the police report. Both motorists had died of their injuries. The kid, drunk and unbuckled, flew through the windshield, taken from this world before he ever knew the damage he'd caused; Sean's wife lingered in critical care for 39 hours. Brain swelling. Damaged liver from the gear shift. The medical bills and funeral had taken their toll, and

Sean's parents had welcomed him moving back in until he got back on his feet. He had found work at the weather station in February, and things were looking better for him and his son. The boy was sleeping better now, taking school seriously. This helped Sean sleep on some nights. Chemicals helped more.

Sean clocked out after exchanging pleasantries with the night staff and started down the metal stairs that led to the white gravel of the parking lot. When he reached his car, he took a moment to view the sky, horizon to horizon. Why? Something of that old, or young, weather-curious kid stirred in him. The boy who had seen *Twister,* and left the theater with a new soul, the younger man who had done an internship on Mt. Washington. Sunset was in an hour, and dinner was being prepared, so he had been told. He looked forward to it. He looked forward to pushing for an outdoors dinner. If he hurried, he could catch it…

The gloaming.

He got into the driver's seat and took the steering wheel in both hands. This had gotten easier. He just needed something to focus on. Tonight, it would be dinner outside, watching the blue hour. He could make the trip in fifteen minutes. Traffic was nonexistent in Hytop, so the only impediment to travel came from above. The roads were arrow-straight, flat, with no traffic lights — very easy to navigate… weather permitting. And weather was permitting.

Sean texted ahead, asking for a back porch dinner, and hit the ignition.

6:47 PM

The town of Hytop was the last vestige of civilization on Highway 79 as it shot northward and left Alabama to enter Tennessee. It stretched four miles north to south, and no more than a mile wide at any point. The other thoroughfare of note in town was Hytop Road, which criss-crossed 79 and linked the neighborhoods that straddled the highway. Beyond the edges of town on all sides lay miles of thick Alabama woodland, dotted here and there with crumbling cemeteries.

Highway 79 and Hytop Road ran north to south, both without guardrails, lined by home after home and shallow drainage ditches. Sean's office was a tall structure one might mistake for a water tower at the very northern tip.

As Sean drove, he marveled at the restfulness of the weather. The day had been the mildest of Spring days, which was not always the case for Alabama. Sean was old enough to remember the Piedmont Palm Sunday tornado of 1994. For that matter, much of the early Nineties was active for Alabama, but those days were a distant memory. Today was a day for a weatherman to catch up on other things. The temp topped at just under eighty degrees, not a cloud in the sky, and the air was dry and dead calm. It was one of the rare times on Earth when waterways had no waves and smoke rose straight up.

Twilight would not begin in earnest for half an hour, but Sean could see the pink behind the trees to the west. Sean never stopped watching the sky, but his gaze was magnetized to trees. A line of interlacing branches never failed to cause his mind to wonder… and wander.

"We all have to give account someday," his father had told him the night before. They had been watching *The First 48* on his father's new flatscreen, which prompted the comment. Sean thought the device looked out of place in the trailer's living room, set atop a cabinet for CDs and surrounded on all sides by wood paneling, stacks of *Reader's Digest,* and vases his mother had bought. Sean had barely been paying attention. He realized that his father spat out the remark as the announcer relayed that some murderer's accomplice was still at large. Sean had grunted in response.

Give account? No, not in this universe. There was no courtroom and no judge's bench awaiting the dead. Sean knew this deep in his gut. Gun to his head, if someone were to ask him where the dead went, where his wife was now, he would have said, "In the trees."

He stared at them, motionless. They would not show it today, but there was something in the way they moved when the wind blew. That is where he would go, Sean felt, when his heart stopped, after he had his last thought. That final roller coaster drop.

7:03 PM

He is still in here.

Sean came back to himself in his parents' driveway. There was that special bump of the drainpipe. There. Home.

Nausea stayed him. It hooked him to the seat. He knew this feeling, knew how to fight it. It came on strong, reminding him that the mother of his son was dead. That he, pathetic shit that he was, dared to try for a moment of contentment. And, he had to admit, it was right.

Your son will never have his mother back, and you're a man looking forward to a sunset.

Sean breathed deep but forgot to count the breaths. Let it pass. Or let the strong part pass, then fight back. Let it finish.

You worthless, pathetic piece of shit.

There, it was ebbing. Now, what was the chant? Yes, five things in the immediate environs.

"This seat is soft. It reminds me of old times, smells familiar. It smells like family," Sean said aloud. As he stared forward, he saw the front door of his parents' place swing open and his father step halfway out with a beckoning hand.

"C'mon, son! Don't let supper get cold. You okay?"

Sean exited the car, throwing an extra bit of grip on every handle he touched. That last part, about being okay, was so unnecessary. He gave one last deep breath and marched toward his father, mounting the wooden porch steps and following him into the smell of mothballs and shag carpet.

Supper, it turned out, was still in the process of cooking, but Sean let that go. William was helping his grandmother in the kitchenette when Sean squeezed between them to get a beer from the refrigerator. Sean saw his mother snatch up her soft pack of Camels from where she had left them atop the dishwasher and drop them without a word down the front of her apron. Sean let that go, too. There was no way William would touch a cigarette. Sean knew this, but there was something about them being casually left out in the open, near the boy, that bothered Sean on an instinctual level. To redirect his own attentions, Sean popped open a can of Snake Handler and asked, "What's for dinner?"

"Pork chops," William answered for his grandmother. He then went on to include sweet potatoes and other items — "And Ma said that I could have..." — but Sean had already started his exit.

"Bathroom," he announced, rounding the corner into the hallway.

Later. Later. Later. I'm not ready for human consumption. Not yet.

In the bathroom closet, behind the rolls of toilet paper on the top shelf, Sean kept a bottle of Wellbutrin. Why he bothered to hide it, he couldn't say. There were a lot of habits he had picked up over the past few months he could not explain. They *felt* right. It was Battle of the Red Flags; you give in to the little ones or the big ones. This felt like a little flag.

He opened the bottle and tumbled a single pill out onto his palm. It rested there for only an instant before he tossed it onto the back of his tongue and placed the bottle back where it came from. *Safe.* Sean sat on the toilet lid, rolling the pill against his palate and retrieved his beer from the floor.

He popped the cap on the Snake Handler, took a split second to stare down the oval hole as the smell hit him before washing down the pill.

"You taking your beer into the bathroom?" his father called from the living room. Sean stared at the can and took another swallow, a larger one. Then another. Pills had a bad habit of sticking in his throat. He felt a deep burp rising up from his stomach. He let it pass.

Outside, there was silence. The neighbors would be outside, walking dogs or tending to cars, but they were far enough that no sound carried. No one would be driving by. Truckers did not pass through Hytop, and everyone who left for work that day had returned. Within this silence, Sean, with his head in his hands, heard the fat frying around the pork chops down the hall, the buzzing TV and creaking recliner from his father's territory, William answered a question posed by his grandmother, accompanied by the sound of the stove door opening and shutting...

"Looks like!" Sean called out in response to his father's question, then added, "Still tastes the same!"

His voice was deafening in his ears.

Was I shouting?

Sean knelt back down to rest his head once more in his hands.

NO! No, do not do this. Get moving. Get up and get moving. Get up. Get up. Get up! Get UP! GET UP!

7: 34 PM

The Daytons' back porch gave a direct view of the treeline to the south and west that stood a half-mile past an open field. This field semi-circled and reached the brick home of their closest neighbors, a family named Walton. Sean could not get over the spot-on Rockwellian nature of this fact. They were in their eighties, a little older than Sean's parents, and Mr. Walton had died of a cardiac event around the time Sean's wife had had her accident.

Ms. Walton, Belinda by name, was able-bodied and sharp. She went into town to buy firewood and played Scrabble with a church group every Tuesday. In the months since her husband's passing, she had taken up the habit of bringing in her dog after hours, for company, Sean assumed. She had also, according to Diane, been making sporadic drives into Scottsboro to buy doggy treats.

Sean found himself thinking on Ms. Walton when his family ate dinners outside, but this time he was determined not to let it become an anchor to the past. As William helped his grandmother set the outside table, Sean could not help but notice the thin column of smoke rising from the Walton house. He cocked his head as the thought occurred to him.

Her arthritis is getting worse. The low tonight will only reach the upper 40's. William called to him, breaking him away from the reverie against reverie.

"Dad, and you don't have to answer right now. You can take your time. But, Dad, I was wondering if Ma and Pa could take me to Scottsboro this weekend… to Walmart."

He wanted Legos, Sean surmised. Or Pokémon cards.

"I don't mind at all," Sean said, taking a seat by his son. Sean looked over the spread — sure enough, there were pork chops, sweet potatoes in a casserole dish covered in some mysterious white material, rolls, butter —

"Let's bow our heads," Ralph Dayton announced, reaching out to take the hands of his wife and grandson. William reached for Sean, who completed the circle with Diane as the four bowed their heads and closed their eyes.

"Heavenly Father, we thank you for this bounty and bless it to our bodies' nourishment. We are thankful as well that…"

Sean began to drift but clinched his teeth and butt. In response, the wood of the chair rose in defiance against his flesh.

Good.

He hated being awake with his eyes closed. His mind had a bad habit of feeding him visions. These would stay with him until he drank them away, and that was not always feasible, such as tonight. Still, there was the Wellbutrin. He had trained himself to feel it, search it out, the subtle blanket it put around his mind. This, in turn, helped him keep that promise to hold it together. That the next minute would be better, and then the next.

"Amen."

Sean heard the word and looked up. It took him a moment to add, "Amen."

7: 58 PM

Twilight occurs in three stages. As the last of the solar orb dips below the Earth's horizon, its light bends into blue and other cool colors, ending the period of oranges, reds and pinks of sunset. This is *civil twilight.*

Civil twilight came to Hytop as the Daytons finished their meal. Ralph excused himself from the table to return to his recliner and television as William helped Diane clear the dishes and arrange them in the dishwasher. Sean, for his part, took another beer from the fridge and went back outside to watch the sky.

As he sat in his chair and leaned back, Sean heard the screen door behind him open and then found his son sitting across from him, holding an ice cream sandwich.

"Ma gave me some desert," he said, holding the unopened package up higher. "Is it okay if I…"

Can I sit with you, Dad?

"Don't mind at all, Rooster." Sean replied. Upon hearing his nickname, William opened the wrapper and began looking around, liable to speak again at any moment. Sean wondered if Ma would be joining them for a cigarette.

And, In truth, that wouldn't have bothered him either. Not in the least. Not as long as…

Ms. Walton's dogs began to bark. At nothing, so far as Sean could tell. This, in turn, triggered the same behavior from other neighbors' dogs even farther away. Sean was silently thankful his family had never wanted a dog, and then was shocked back to his appreciation of the blue hour when a murder of crows passed over them, headed south.

"Dad, is a flock of crows really called a murder?" William asked.

"Yes. That is actually true. But you know what animal group has a really weird name?"

"What's that?" William was shooting eyes back and forth from his father and the melting ice cream rivulets that raced to spill over the wrapper, ready to catch them with his tongue if need be.

"Ravens," said Sean. "They are called an 'unkindness.' And rooks — those are like a cousin to the ravens and the crows — are called a 'parliament.'"

"What about people?" asked William, not missing a beat, ice cream still under direct control. "I mean, humans."

"I know what you mean. There are lots of words — group, crowd, mob — it just depends on what you want to say about them."

"No, I mean, like," William thought and blinked before taking another bite. "What do scientists, biologists, call a group of humans. Is there a special term?"

"Oh, you know what?" Sean leaned back again and propped his feet onto the table as he put his beer in his lap, nestled between both hands. "That is a really good question. I have no idea, Rooster."

The temperature around father and son, the porch, the field, and the rest of Hytop sat at 64 degrees Fahrenheit. Wind picked up from the north, rose to a walking pace, and disturbed Ms. Walton's chimney smoke.

8:36 PM

Nautical twilight is reached as the sun slips further down. Within a perfectly cloudless sky, such as over Hytop, the blue hue of the sky starves into pale remnants of color. It is the time between, with no sunlight and no starlight.

This is when those outside notice streetlights buzz to life and the insects of the night come out of hiding.

Sean noticed this, but only as an aside. He had checked William's homework, two sheets of math review and a short essay on what, in William's opinion, had been the most interesting moment in Alabama history he had studied that year. William had chosen the flooding of the Capitol in Cahaba.

As Sean showed William how to break run-on sentences into shorter, narrative sentences, he heard his mother give into her craving and open the screen door to smoke on the porch. Five minutes later, she knocked on the doorjamb to get Sean's attention. When he walked up to her, he noticed she kept massaging her hands.

"What is it, Mom?"

"Sean… it's *chilly.*"

Sean did not know what she meant. Why was she telling him? It was not wonderment. Her face was pained, just slightly, a tug at the jowls and neck. And there, just for a moment, Sean, the son Sean, saw through his mother's mask. There, resting in the liquid of her eyes, fear.

8:49 PM

Sean had told his mother that he would go outside "to get a better idea of what was going on" once William had been showered, teeth brushed, put to bed and certain to stay there.

Now that he stood on the porch, he understood was she was talking about. It was chilly. More than that, it was *cold.*

Sean looked up to the moon as he considered what was happening. There it was, barely leaving its full phase and shining like a blade. Shifting his view, he saw, faint in the last of the light, Ms. Walton's smoke going strong, but no sound from her dogs. In fact…

There was no sound at all. No crickets. No owls. The field had developed a grey blanket of fog, pierced with the stem tops of dry Alabama grasses. This fog bank thickened into a low hanging soup at the forest's edge.

Sean took in a full breath. The chill felt … wet. The temp had neared the dew point, which meant upper forties. While not impossible, that was a monumental drop. Something that took a cold front hours to develop had happened in thirty minutes.

And there was no front.

9:09 PM

Astronomical twilight reveals the stars. It is, in essence, the birth of the night anew. Those outside see only the faintest of color from the world around them, if they can see at all. Shadows fill all available space, any place untouched by moonlight. One with healthy eyes can strain to see into such unlit spaces, but the image is unclear, and the mind can play tricks. The scientific name for this is *gloom.* Diurnal animals, those active during the day, know by instinct to avoid this time and seek shelter if they have not already.

In Hytop, astronomical twilight saw thick fog banks grow up from the ground, from roads and pastures, from forest floors. These billowed into behemoth towers miles high. Where these vapors alighted on glass and metal, they stuck and started the work of growing frost. This *hoar frost* resembled the white, aging hair that gave it its name and traced fractals of ice over each street light and window, doorknob and vehicle.

Sean had reassured his mother, detailing what a cold snap was. He then excused himself for his nightly routine — push ups and yoga followed by a quick shower. As he finished drying off and replacing the towel, he heard his father call from the living room.

Sean found Ralph with his program on pause, with the timer at the bottom of the screen showing it had been left on pause for ten minutes. Ralph was pointing out the window to his right, within arm's reach of his recliner. The glass was frosted opaque, a small, heavy square of pale church glass.

"What is this?" His father asked. Sean looked and shook his head.

"It's hoar frost, but…"

Sean walked, not quite a run, onto the porch. With his bare hand he smeared the fragile layer of ice off the family's outdoor thermometer. He looked at it in defiance, and then, again not quite running, returned to his father sitting in his recliner.

"Call Ms. Walton. In fact, call everyone on your tornado emergency list. Tell them to call everyone on theirs too. Tell them to get down to the church."

"Should we be worried, Son?"

"Us? No. No, we shouldn't be worried, but… just better to be safe than sorry."

"Sean, tell me. What did the thermometer say?"

"It said eighteen. Eighteen degrees," Sean waited for a minute before leaving to get his cell phone. He added, "And it was correct."

9:21 PM

A series of flashes, enormous strobes of sheet lightning, reached in to illuminate William's bedroom before Sean could flip the light switch. Flip it he did, and then knelt at the trundle bed, muddling how to phrase what he needed to tell his son.

When the thunder hit, it rattled the small window. Sean's head shot up, staring as more flashes lit the distant skyline, bright as stadium lights, piercing the thickness of frost on glass.

When Sean looked down again, his son was awake and looking at him with questioning eyes.

"Is it… there a tornado, Dad?" Sean shook his head and helped his son into a seated position and put clothes in his lap. "Do we need to go to the shelter?"

"Nope," Sean surprised himself with the brightness in his voice. "We are going to the station."

"Where you work?"

"Yep. With Ma and Pa. It's the safest place, and they are going to need me there anyway. Get dressed. All the layers you can. Meet downstairs in five, got it?"

William gave a salute and then a thumbs-up. He was in motion.

With William handled, Sean made his way out into the hall, phone in hand and his office number already ringing. There was a skeleton crew of one on duty tonight, a man named David Adkins. Sean and David worked well together. David was an affable, divorced Methodist who moved to Hytop from Florida. He also was not above cheating at cards, Sean recalled.

In the kitchenette, his parents were discussing the thunder. His mother was in denial, arguing it was construction work. He father was there, hands on her shoulders to lead her away from the windows.

"Ralph," Sean heard her say, regarding the windows. "I can't see a thing! Why won't this damn thing clear?"

He knew that anger. Not only in his mother, but in himself, and in a dozen others. When the world turns upside down, and even the small things refuse to play ball…

"Sean!" David's voice split Sean's ear as the line picked up. "I need you here, man! It's a dragon king. You hear me? I keep trying to get Huntsville on the line, but it's been spotty. I've contacted the firehouse, and they are busy getting people to the church. Just get here… yesterday!"

Sean reassured David, hung up and then paused. Behind him, William was fumbling through the process of dressing in layers. Ahead, his father had given up on coraling his mother away from the windows and had joined her in watching the thunder.

Both parents jumped as Sean's hands caught their shoulders.

"Dress in layers. We leave in five. I'll explain on the way."

Saying a silent prayer to God that his parents complied without question, Sean took his own advice and ransacked the closet for his thickest coat and socks.

9:28 PM

Sean was the first out the door, reminding himself that his ice scraper was in the glove box, that he could afford about three minutes to warm up the car before his parents and son—

The air hit him.

Holy shit.

His mind told him to say the words. They did not come. His skin felt a sea of acid splash over his face, invading his nose and finding his lungs before he could put up a defense. He coughed, and a white cloud, then another, erupted from him and floated out into the clear night sky.

Now with his hands covering his nose and mouth, Sean shot towards the car. He stayed, just for a moment, to watch his lung-clouds, intact and floating in the light of the streetlamps. In those handful of seconds, he could only marvel.

Wait. Just how cold is it?

He crushed that thought and started the car, giving God another silent thanks that it turned over. He reached over to the glove box, gritting his teeth against the tiniest hint of a cramp at his ribs, and … papers, more papers. A tire pressure gauge. A Wendy's straw, still in the wrapper. No ice scraper.

"God-*dammit!*"

Diane called to him from the door. "Sean, do you want me to boil some water?" He waved away the suggestion, running inside and retrieving a water bottle from the fridge. As he reentered the cold, he beckoned his family to join him.

"Be careful," he called back. He should have said more, but could not think of how to put it into words. The air was… indescribable. It would have been impossible to relate the feeling. This was *true cold.*

Sean took the cap from the bottle and used its rough edges to scrape the frost from as much of the windshield as he could. His parents were on the stairs. He heard his son telling Ma to watch her step, and Pa reiterating it.

Sean's phone rang in the distinct tone of the weather office.

He let it ring.

9:39 PM

From the road, one could see the totality of the event. Every inch of Hytop was lit between flashes of blue-white lightning and the sickly, dimming porch lights of occasional houses. The hoar frost had alighted on every available surface, not covering, but claiming. It cloyed at the edges of transformers, blanketed all metal and glass, and glazed each leaf and branch. Plastic toys in yards and chain link fences were adorned with small icicles. And, aside from the siren of a fire engine in the distance, the Daytons were the only vehicle on the road.

It was impossible not to watch. William pressed his face against his window and rubbed the glass with his sleeve for a better look. Sean's eyes followed fate and drifted up as he drove, and even his parents sat agog at the goings-on around them. Thunder was at the lip of the horizon on all sides. The night was clear as far as cloud cover, but the behemoth mists still curled and wafted among the trees. Occasionally, one would venture out and pass over the road ahead as the Daytons made their trek to the north of town.

The lightning was constant, a feature reserved for volcanic ash clouds and supercells. Yet, here it was, manifesting from thin air. The entire carload watched as a long bolt streaked overhead. Sean blinked and slowed the car, letting the stinging purple afterglow fade from his eyes.

"Everyone saw that one, didn't they? Whoa, what a spectacle! Right, Rooster?" His son nodded, no fear in his eyes, and Sean let himself breathe. His parents, however...

"We're in the eye of it," he added, just before the thunder hit, nesting in each person's chest like a burp.

No, Sean. A voice spoke to him, a voice he hoped he would never hear again. It was the voice that first spoke to him when he looked into the nurses' faces nine months ago. It spoke again that night and the next morning. It was the voice, clinical and dead, that admitted aloud what he could not.

No, Sean. It's not the eye. It's the middle. We are in the middle of it.

9:53 PM

As the car rolled to a stop along the gravel just before the stairs to the Weather Annex entrance, William spoke up.

"Dad. The gravel looks... fuzzy." Sean laughed. The rocks indeed looked fuzzy, with little hairdos of white.

"Alright, y'all brace yourselves. It's gonna be cold. I'll run up and key us in, but I want you guys following close behind. Just watch your step. The stairs will be slick."

It's gonna be cold. He was not wrong. Then again, he didn't feel it.

When Sean opened his door, he was hit with a new sensation, one he had not felt since his time on Mount Washington. There is a point when the human body cannot feel cold. When the temperature of the environs falls to such a level to be immediately dangerous to soft tissue, the body skips *cold* and goes straight to *pain.*

The air at Sean's face made the earlier sea of acid seem like a love tap. He grunted, unable to force his throat to open, his flesh refusing the hostile air. His eyes rebelled at the same time, squeezing themselves shut and refusing all commands to allow him sight once again. He reached out and forward, feeling for the railing.

Jesus... Jesus.

Behind him, he heard the others cry out as the air hit them. Unable to speak, Sean slapped the railing, causing the metal to ring out. He panted, full breaths impossible for him, and prayed they had the sense to follow the sound, and then began his ascent up the stairs. Each step was a gunshot in the hollow air, and it felt like minutes before Sean was standing at the door, grasping for his key card with both hands.

But his hands could not grasp. They shook like captive fish. The more he tried to steady them, the more violent their motions. His eyes, however, tearing now enough to work up a thin barrier against the air, squinted open just enough for him to see...

David opened the door.

"Jesus!" David summed up the experience. He had felt the blast of air for only thirty seconds as the Daytons entered, but that was enough. As everyone took seats in the employee lounge, David passed out small styrofoam cups and filled each with coffee.

"Just... *Jesus!*" David added. He was still squinting. Having provided everyone with warm liquids, he massaged his face.

"Oh, does anyone want cream or sugar"

No one did.

"Sean, I'm not going to tell you that your family can't be here," David was the first to speak when the two weathermen relocated into the radar room and sat at the array. "And I'm not going to tell you that you stink of beer, and you're probably fired if the cameras still work."

"You're *not* going to tell me?" Sean smiled.

"What I *am* gonna tell you is… remember when I said we have a dragon king?"

"Right… breaks all the rules that we know of. I kinda gathered," Sean hooked a thumb over his shoulder towards the direction of the outside door.

"Check this out," David pointed as he maximized the radar reading and let it play, starting at 7:00PM. In fifteen minute intervals, Sean watched as faint spots of green flashed throughout Hytop, with cloud cover materializing and disappearing within the spanse of an hour.

"What is that, virga?" Sean heard himself ask the question aloud, but that was a reflex. What he saw next, as his eyes trailed down to the temperature, illicited a string of "wait, wait, wait…" from his mouth. "Wait a minute, David. That can't — how?"

The temperature in Hytop, Alabama had dropped from 66 degrees Fahrenheit at nightfall to a full thirty below.

"I don't know, Sean. I have not the slightest clue. I've contacted—"

"That's like, Gobi-Desert-level—"

"Sean, I sent all the data to Huntsville. They were checking it last I spoke to them. They can't wrap their heads around it yet. Once they do, they will send emergency teams. In the meantime, I also called the fire department. I think I already told you."

Sean heard every word, but his eyes were still devouring the screen. Lightning readings were all around the town, forming a comet shape. Sean traced it with his finger.

"David, look at this. I think I just figured something out. All that heat, all that energy, has to go somewhere…"

"Sean," David interrupted again. "I don't need you on data right now. I need you on the horn. Do you know anyone with a radio? Cell phones are shit right now. And yes, it is because of the lightning. That being said, if you know someone who has a HAM—"

Outside, there was the sound of a transformer exploding, echoing on and on against the trees.

The lights flickered.

Died.

10:00 PM

Inside the Weather Annex, industrial generators kicked on and replenished the power. These were heavy-duty and regulated to every station in the Southeast after the Blizzard of 1993. They were insulated against temperatures as low as -40, and additives kept the diesel and lubricant from gelling. David and the Daytons enjoyed light and heat, unique among the residents of Hytop, with only a flicker every few minutes to remind them of what was waiting outside.

Hytop was struck blind and silent. Transformers and store-bought generators exploded or ground to a halt as their fuels and lubricants gelled. Those residents who attempted to flee found their vehicles dead. The lucky ones made it back inside with the first stages of frostbite, while the slower ones... did not.

Animals, obeying instinct, fled as best they could. Birds took wing and headed south. Mammals and reptiles buried themselves deep. Fish dove and hovered at just over the sludge at the bottoms of ponds. Domesticated animals in barns collapsed and died with white flecks adorning their eyelids and nostrils.

A softer blue glow began to spread among the trees as the air let loose more of its charge. This aura, St. Elmo's fire, crept over telephone poles and power lines. The steeple of the church at the southern edge of town shone like the sword at Eden. Those inside, should they have risked looking outside, may have taken it as a sign.

It was then that the cold began its onslaught in full force.

10:19 PM

William Dayton had a question. It was an important question, but he could not ask it. Instead, as he walked towards the room where his father was talking with the other man, he reached deep into his mind for something else to ask, something that would get his father to leave the room and come with him, if only for a few minutes.

Sean and David were glaring at their phones when he entered.

"Maybe we'd get better signal on the roof," Sean said with a smirk.

"You first," David replied without missing a beat, and then, "What can we do for you, Little Man?"

"Dad," William stepped forward. He had reached as deep as he could, but his imagination had given up zilch. "Can I ask you something? In private?"

His father joined him, and William took the older man's hand as if he had a private place in mind. Instead, he decided he could not wait, and turned to face his father as they stood in the hall.

"Everyone dies... Isn't that true?"

Sean took a full breath, then nodded as he answered. "Yes. Yes, Rooster. That is the truth."

William, Rooster, waited for the right time for his next question. "Isn't it better that we're all here?"

Sean waited a few breaths before answering that one.

Yes, Sean. Yes it is.

Sean saw his mother approach from the employee lounge down the hall and waved her over. She must have been a mind reader, because he went to William and took his hand.

"Sean, could I take Rooster for look around the place?" Before Sean could answer, William added.

"It's okay, Dad. I'm not scared."

Sean suspected that statement was layered, but let it go. All they had to do was last the night. He wasn't sure how he knew this, but it came to him, clear as a bell. He smiled and led his mother and son to the radar room, and then asked David to show them how everything worked. David fought a scowl and then motioned to Sean's chair for William to take a seat.

"Here, Little Man. Let me show you what's been going on."

Sean began rubbing his hands in anticipation of the next move. Checking fuel stores for the generators? Food? Another cup of coffee?

His mother leaned in and said to him in a soft voice meant only for his ears.

"Your father would like to talk to you."

10:31 PM

He found Ralph Dayton, his father, holding an open Bible. Not reading it. Shuffling the pages.

"Where did you get that?" Sean asked as he made a beeline to the coffee pot. "You want another cup? Or, if you're tired, there's a couch."

"I brought it with me… Sean, I appreciate you staying calm for your family. A man should do exactly that."

Sean pulled over a chair and sat before his father.

"But, Sean… I need you to level with me, man to man. How bad is this thing?"

"It's about as bad as northern weather," Sean rattled off, which was not untrue. "We can handle this. It's about like Alaska or Mount Washington."

"This isn't Mt. Washington." Ralph Dayton frowned, his entire face creasing with the effort. "It's worse. Listen. In the Navy I sailed all over. I've talked to a lot of people, and I read every history book I could get my hands on. Something like this has never happened before, not ever."

"What are you saying?"

"I'm saying it's not just a bad storm. Don't treat it like it is. No one has ever seen anything like this, so how do you know when it'll end? Or… will it end?"

"Dad, this isn't— we aren't talking about Aramgeddon here. It will be over by dawn."

"You know that? For certain?"

"Eighty percent," Sean said with a cock of his head. "And even still, Huntsville has our data. They're watching us with satellites. They are probably mobilizing crews right now as we speak."

Ralph closed his Bible and rose to put it on the table behind Sean. Turning back to his son, he said,

"I had a CO, and of course I'm talking about Nam here. We were talking politics, and I was mad as hell at being sent away from my country to die for nothing. And he said he had been thinking about that a lot and then asked me, 'How do you want to die?' It was such a weird question, and I think I said some dumb answer about sex. Later on, I thought about it, and here's what I think he meant. I think he meant it's not the situation you're in, it's you. The situation is where and when, but who are you when it happens? That's how you die."

Sean waited, searching for a gesture to show that he had heard, decided on an nod, and then left the room. His father watched him go.

10:58 PM

David and Sean explained all they could about radar maps, dewpoints, and diesel generators. They swapped storm stories, each trying to top the last. Dayton had been on duty in 2011 during the super outbreak; Sean could not resist mentioning Mount Washington. Then, David added he had been at sea when the ship he was on met with a rogue wave.

"What was that like?" asked William. David looked each member of his audience in the eyes.

"I have never been so *freakin'* — wait, is it okay if I curse?"

William laughed, and then yawned. Diane announced what everyone was thinking, and Sean volunteered to be the one to take the boy to lay down on the employee couch. He announced he would stay until William fell asleep, that he would then return, and to come get him if there were an emergency.

11:30 PM

Sean sat on the couch, a black leather relic from the Eighties, with his son laying prostrate beside him, his coat covering the boy's shoulders down to his hips. Sean's thigh was being commandeered as a pillow, and he wondered how he would return to the radar room without letting his son's head plop down to the hard leather of the couch.

He tussled his son's hair. Even without leaning, he smelled the tell-tale aroma a parent knows to be their own child's hair. Sean smiled, surprising himself. He wondered what gave God the idea to create that aroma.

For the first time in a year, he prayed out loud. Keeping his eyes open and pointed at the ceiling, he gave thanks that he and his family had arrived together and safely.

William murmured. Sean signed off with God and looked at his son. The boy had been talkative in his sleep off and on since his mother passed. Sometimes it was gibberish. Sometimes he narrated his dreams. Sometimes, he said things that needed comforting.

"What was that, Rooster?" Sean asked in the quietest voice he could manage. William answered, but Sean had to lean in. "One more time, Bud. Tell me one more time."

Then William said, "Cold Star. Cold Star. He's the one doing it."

Sean sat back up and smiled. His son was narrating his dreams again. Sean decided he could spare five more minutes.

Just five more minutes.

Midnight

Above the trees and buildings of Hytop, a new type of snow was forming. Collectives of carbon dioxide grew emboldened by the cold and netted together. They gathered others of their kind in pockets of cold air until they formed tiny white shards which hovered in the open air.

Below, trees swelled as their sap crystallized. One by one, they exploded like landmines.

Over the surfaces, of human-wrought material, of soil, of frozen flesh, lay the corpses of bacteria.

From the forest floor, moisture seeped into the waiting embrace of the cold, forming the behemoths anew and sending them wandering through the empty streets.

Wither

Roland got in his miles each morning. The pounding of the pavement had taken its toll as he neared his forties, prompting a switch from jogging to biking, but that was his only concession. Over the years, he had taken on the challenges of rain, heat, bone-chilling cold, and feral dogs, and gone back day after day, undeterred. It was a college habit that took root in his soul, and since his underclassman days he had logged over 6,000 miles.

Roland was proud of that.

It was early on a February morning, so when he coasted back into his driveway, the sun had started to brighten the heavens. Roland entered through the garage, hung up his bike and began the process of decompression— he removed his winterwear before going into the family gym to do his stretches.

He expected to hear his wife's feet on the floorboards as he went through sun salutations and transitioned to static stretches. He did his legs, then his neck and shoulders to relieve the tension built up by leaning into the handlebars. Still, not a sound from his wife. He finished with his lower back, wallowed in the aftermath of bones popping, and allowed himself five minutes of staring at the ceiling before going upstairs.

She was in the bedroom, surrounded by study materials. Her laptop was open on her side of the bed, and she had constructed a fort of pillows to prop up the assorted stationery items— stapler, highlighters, note packets, and envelopes. The morning routine of the first-year MBA student. Angelica, who went by Joni, had recently gone back to school, and thus all-nighters were not at all new.

They exchanged passing smiles as Roland made his way to the shower. Once in the seclusion of the bathroom, a feeling caught him, freezing him in place for a moment. He realized he was staring out the bathroom window, looking at the sunlight tracing the tree branches outside. They looked like veins, black against a sky that was well on its way to clear blue. But that was not what stayed him. The feeling was reminiscent of *deja vu*, but stronger, *darker.*

It wasn't that something like this situation had happened before, it was that something bad was about to happen. Something worse than bad. The kind of thing you don't come back from.

Aneurysm? The word shot into him. *Is this how it feels?* He shook his head. Then shook it harder. *No, this was not happening. Not now.* Something was wrong though. Undeniable.

Wait… What?

Is.

Happening?

Something red and deep and fragile in the back of Roland's mind shook loose. Shook loose, hovered for a second, and then slid down a deep, dark hole. In its place… a nebula of emptiness.

"Oh, no," Roland said, not even loud enough for his ears to catch. "No." This time he said it like a plea.

Give me that back. Make it come back. I need it. I need it. I need that back!

"Sweetie? Are you okay?" Joni's voice, coming through the flimsy white wood of the door. Roland nodded, then, catching himself, answered her, "Yeah. Yeah. Just fine."

"I didn't hear the water. I had to make sure you didn't stroke out in there."

Adopting his Coal Miner voice, he wheezed at her, "Dagnabbit, Woman, I ain't dat old!"

He turned on the water and decided to stand in the shower to feel this out. Whatever it was would fade. It had to. This could not be…

It is though. This is real. Admit it. It's real, and you're living it. You're living it in your actual life. Not a dream. Not a daydream. This is you now.

Roland entered the bedroom fresh and cologned. Joni caught the smell instantly.

"Going into the office today?" There was an edge to it. She was clearly disappointed.

"Yeah, I think that's best. Got a project that…" he shrugged to convey the rest of the answer.

"You know what I've been thinking about? Do you think me going back to school was my calling? I mean starting my businesses; is that my calling?"

Roland stopped where he was, reversed course and slid onto the bed, eliciting a landslide of paper he caught with seconds to spare. He sidled up to Joni, who was sucking on the insides of her cheeks.

"Is that the reason for the all-nighter?" She kamikazed her head into his shoulder and nodded. He put his hand on her back.

"Of course it's your calling. You breathe it. Back when we were seniors you were talking about finding secrets the markets couldn't. You'd bring it up during movies. You brought it up while we were watching *Dawn of the Dead*, you remember that?"

A muffled laugh sounded out somewhere near his armpit. She wasn't coming out of hiding yet. In fact, she might have fallen asleep. He hovered his hand over her, hesitating as to whether he should rub her back and tip her over onto the pillows or straighten her up to continue the talk.

Joni shot up suddenly. "But I mean, do you think it's my *calling-calling?*"

"Yes, of course!" Roland heard words after that, coming from his own mouth, but he had no idea what they were. They came from some kind of autopilot.

The next minute it seemed, Roland was in his car, watching a line of taillights ahead of him. He was comfortable, cognizant that something bad had happened this morning, but nothing pressing. No, *this* was pressing. He was working, married... sober. His third year clean was coming up.

You think that matters? Has the rat decided he loves the wheel now? Or maybe... you just don't want to start screaming right here in traffic.

The cars were like lines of ants, the more Roland looked at them, one line going to the picnic, the other coming back. A procession of duty. Or, for that matter, the thought of veins came to him, carrying little cells to their offices in a colossal body sprawled from horizon to horizon.

He caught the scream in his throat and bit it off with his back teeth. Driving on reflex, instinct, and sheer spite, found his way off at the next offramp and pulling into a gas station. Forehead on steering wheel, he took in a deep lungful of air. Swallowed. And then... a familiar demon crept in to join the fun.

You can't fight this thing... clearly. But you know what might? You don't have to deal with this right now. Joni doesn't expect you back for hours. Go inside and open those tall clear doors. Salvation. Release. Lies within.

Roland shook his head, not opening his eyes, the skin of his forehead skidded across the leather of the wheel. "No," he answered. "I hate beer, and I hate wine." He waited, letting his own words sink in. He added, "I'm a liquor man."

That settled the demon for the moment. But that band-aid would not hold for long. And he hadn't even hit on how to deal with … *It.*

"What is wrong with me?" Roland spoke out loud, just to do it, to force strength into his own voice. It sounded good. The voice of a healthy man. His fingers dialed as fast as they could.

His sponsor answered on the first ring. Before Roland could speak, Lewis, his sponsor for every day of the past three years said, "You need to get over here."

Roland had been to Lewis' house a handful of times. He was a bachelor, born to wealthy parents who bought him a house in the suburbs at the end of a dead-end road. He had a pool and back porch he never used, and spent most of his time in his kitchen, where he kept his widescreen, and his basement, where he had built a rec-room with a pool table, which, again, he never used.

Lewis' house had all-wood paneling, with large mirrors and numerous shelves in every room. In his rec room, he had a vinyl player, an electric guitar, and a poster of Sal Vulcano's "Employee of the Month" photo mounted on the wall. All four Jokers had signed it, but Lewis would tell anyone who would listen that they were forged.

Lewis was a conspiracy theorist of the "there must be *something* to it" variety. When he wasn't jamming, he was in his kitchen trading secrets with numerous sympathetic groups. Of all the mainstream social media outlets, he trusted Discord, and this was the page he had open when he welcomed Roland in from his back porch. Friends were only allowed to enter through the back porch.

"Take a look at this," he said before Roland had even shut the door. Roland, finding no other chair in the room, hovered over his sponsor's shoulder to see the familiar discord page, on general chat. No one had posted. Everyone was there, but with little moons by their icons, snoozing.

"Do you see what I see?" asked Lewis, running his cursor from the top of the list of members to the bottom.

"I mean, yeah. No one's talking," said Roland. "But what-"

"They're there. But no one's talking." Lewis spun around in his chair to face Roland. "That's like voting 'present.' No one is giving anyone anything to go on. All these people are local. Do you see what I mean now?"

Lewis jumped from his chair and went to his fridge. "Hang on. You need a Sprite. Or a Gatorade. Which do you prefer? You haven't fallen, have you? Please tell me you didn't break."

"Lewis, I swear. Please… start making sense."

Lewis left the fridge, a small blue Gatorade in his hand. He plugged it into Roland's chest as he walked past. "Outside. Porch. I have to show you. This will explain everything."

Once outside, Lewis positioned Roland so that the morning sun was to their left. "Keep your eyes on me," he said, examining his friend's face, staring into his eyes… "Has your mouth been dry?"

"No," Roland answered. Lewis turned and went back in without a word. "Goddammit, Lewis." Roland began, only to stop just short of running into his friend just past the door frame. It was much darker in Lewis' house, and for a moment he had been all but invisible.

"I know why you called me. Something been a little … *off* this morning?"

"You know what it is?" Roland was entertaining this now. Whatever Lewis was up to, he was onto something. He now had… *hope.* Maybe.

"You had a sense, didn't you, that something was… ?"Lewis prodded.

"Missing." Roland completed the thought. He needed to sit down. The thirst came back with a vengeance now, and all he wanted to do was collapse in a nice, soft chair. A sensation of cold from his hand reminded Roland he was still holding the Gatorade. He cracked the top and downed half the bottle. After that, he went into Lewis' kitchen, looked at his office chair for a second, and then planted himself on the linoleum. He propped his back against the stove and took another deep drink of the blue liquid. He liked how cold it was. It stung. He liked that. Needed it. That sting. "Missing," he said it again, looking at the ceiling.

"You want to know why I took you outside and kept looking at your face?"

"I was wondering that, Lewis, over and over."

"Your pupils, here, look at mine." Lewis knelt down in front of him. Sure enough, his pupils were pinpoints. "I've been craving like a dog all day, right after I did my gardening, but you know what? No dry mouth. Now tell me, has that ever happened to you? A craving and no dry mouth?"

"Wait a second," Roland was piecing it together. All the breadcrumbs, a nervous system not responding with the necessary reflexes, leading to… "Are you saying we have brain damage?"

"Sort of. We've been exposed to a nerve agent. These are all classic signs. Now, for some bad news—"

"Lewis, you have to say 'now for some bad news,' and then 'nerve agent.'"

"It's not just us. That's why all of them," he circled his hand at his laptop, "are all silent. That's why— wait, how's your wife? Joni? How was she this morning?"

"Fine. Her head was completely, you know. She had pulled an all-nighter."

"You sure? Women are better at hiding these things, man. Think. Why you and not her?"

"Whoa, whoa, whoa, I'm not even sold on this being a nerve— I'm not sure what is."

"You are a forty-year-old man sitting on my kitchen floor when you should be at work. You have the pupils of a smack-head, and you nearly fell off the wagon. So?"

"Stress. It's stress. They have us work from home, not work from home—"

"Oh? Then why is *it* missing? You been playing too much D&D? Fooling with a Ouija board or something?"

"Not funny, Lewis."

"Right. Right. I'm sorry. We don't have to talk about that part of it yet. Listen, I'm your sponsor. I'm here for you. All day if need be. I'll chain you like a goddamned werewolf if it stops you from drinking. But you need to think about your wife. Does she have any—"

"She didn't go outside!" Roland blurted, now locking eyes with Lewis again. "You gardened. I biked. Whoever did this must have sprayed it into the atmosphere. That's how they do it, right?"

Lewis nodded with a frown of a teacher shocked and impressed by his pupil. "He can be taught. Very astute. Unfortunately, there is more to it than that. What that means is that you and I got an early dose, but where do you think all that went? It hasn't rained. That shit, whatever it is, must be wafting through town like pollen. Maybe Joni wasn't affected this morning, but she *will* be."

"I can't help her like this. I wouldn't— what would I say… to someone? How do you even help someone with this?"

Lewis looked away for a moment.

"What was that?" asked Roland. "You were thinking something."

"I was just thinking of a few things," Lewis said. "It's so easy to forget a staple. Just to see them as a given. But it takes so much strength to be there, same as ever, always, every time. I'm sorry, that's not about you. Well, I mean, it's not just about you. But, it also applies to you with your wife, with what happened to us this morning, everything."

The pair sat in silence. Roland took another drink of Gatorade. He could feel the cement drying, fixing them both to the spot. He was not going home. He was not going to slip, either, but he was not going anywhere.

Lewis sat at the table and swiveled over to his laptop. He scrolled up and down, still no word from anyone. Roland, left alone, began letting his mind run.

No matter how long I sit here, it won't help. I can't wait this out. Five o'clock will come, and I'll still feel just as heavy. Joni will start calling. No change. I can't wait this out, and I can't move. And I can't hate myself enough to change that fact either.

Lewis spun back toward him, flicking him back into Outer World.

"Remember what I told you a while ago," said Lewis. "It's not about hope. It's about getting grounded."

Roland nodded but said nothing. "Alright," Lewis prodded him. "Your turn to spill."

"It was just my mind running. Has this thing got you doing that too?"

When Lewis nodded, Roland frowned before adding, "Some of the stuff going through my head. I, well one thing, a question. I don't even want to say."

"Do you remember that Beckett quote I sent you that you liked so much?"

"Fail better?"

"No, not that stupid Silicon Valley Corporate Drone bullshit. The one about 'obliterate the bastard'."

Roland laughed. "So, where are you slipping off to with this, Lewis. What about the quote?"

"Are you going to stay on my floor all day? Say it out loud."

"No."

"But you would if I let you, wouldn't you? You know it as well as I do. I'm too scared to let you out that door, because, as soon as I do, the Demon will get you. It'll wait until the right time, and it'll strike. But if YOU take yourself out that door. You see?"

"No. What's the difference?"

"The difference is *obliterate the bastard*. You don't have to let the thought in. That whole don't repress stuff, fuck that. Letting this thing eat you is what has you stuck to my floor. It has you wanting a drink. Then fuck it. Ignore it. Use what works, not what self-help says. Let it back in when you're ready and then *obliterate* it."

"When will this thing wear off, do you think?"

"I said, 'fuck it.' Doesn't matter. It will, that's the point. Was that the bad thing you were thinking?"

"No," said Roland, rising, lighter now. "But fuck it. I have work to do."

Roland snatched Lewis into a hug. He didn't say he was going home. He didn't have to.

Roland took a deep breath just outside Lewis' backdoor. He took another before getting into his car. After that, the wheels carried him forward, and it got easier. Momentum had been reattained.

Lewis hesitated before calling Roland that night. He had not wanted to disturb any conversation between husband and wife. To his delight, Roland answered on the first ring. They both asked the same question of each other at the same time.

"Better?" And each assured the other that the danger had passed. Whatever it was had left them.

"Hey, buddy," Lewis chanced, "I don't want to tread anywhere I shouldn't, but I wanted ask…"

"What was the big, bad question? Yeah, no. I don't mind. Okay, maybe it's nothing after all, but it sure was scary at the time. The thought that came to me was this: what does it mean that it could be turned off in the first place? What does that even mean?"

III

Opus Regulatum: Altschmerz

Just Taxes

My door opened with a slight excess of force, a little frustrated jerk and push. He was early.

"This is bordering on harassment." The first words out of my lawyer's mouth. It had been over a year since we had met in person. But this, this was harassment.

"I take it you are still set on Final Forfeiture?" he asked, not bothering to even look at me.

At least he had let himself in. It was an effort to get up at my age. I stayed in my chair, watching as he paced around the kitchenette. My kitchenette, with its half-wall separating it from the den, had become our agreed-upon demilitarized zone, with plenty of space for him to pace and act pissy.

I was determined ahead of time to be polite. I had had a nice conversation with myself about how this was going to go off without a hitch, without us degenerating into argument and shouting. Then again, that's what I told myself before every one of our meetings going back a decade, for all the good it did.

In the past year, he had done nothing in the way of research. I had been the one keeping files and certificates up to date. I was the one always reaching out to him. Unable to really think of a way to address his question while maintaining my cool, I stared at him in silence.

"What is this?" he asked, taking my silence as a ploy. "Negotiating? Is that what this silent treatment is about? Negotiating?"

No, son, not a ploy. Just rage that goes beyond this feeble body's capabilities.

I got up and went over to the kitchenette for a little coffee. And I sure did get right up in his personal space.

Fucking snowflake.

That's what we used to call such people.

In response, he sidestepped me and crossed my den to lean against the sliding glass door. It always made me nervous when people did that, but...

"Yes, goddammit!" I called from the kitchenette. "I am still wanting Final Forfeiture!"

That put me out of breath, and sent my heartbeat to my ears. Thump, thump, thump. The world faded out for a second. *Dammit.* I set my hands wide and steadied myself against the countertop, focusing my eyes on the coffee. The dizziness would fade. I just needed to wait it out. Yes, just breathe. Just. Breathe. Nice.

And.

Slow.

There. Back in business. My head cleared in time to hear his squawking.

"... but if we are to do that, we have to establish some things. First, this theatrical behavior, the histrionics, this sense of entitlement ... It has to stop."

The varied ingredients of this moment distract me. I begin thinking about how I hate this person, and yet I rely on him for the one and only thing I want in this whole world. I teeter on the edge of exploring how that is not, but might as well be, a Biblical-style curse, and then I command my brain to snap back to the business at hand.

"I am not trying to cross boundaries here," he continues. Dear God, he won't let me even think. Am I slowing down? I stare slack-jawed at the coffee machine while he steamrolls on. "But I have informed you, kindly and politely, that court training is done by paralegals. It is not in my job description to perform human interactions."

I struggled to find what to tackle first in what he had just said. First, paralegals weren't human, so I wouldn't be *meeting* with anyone. Second, he was doing this pro bono, which was good because: Third, I wasn't qualified for any job, and the stigma of Final Forfeiture had caused all my relatives within six generations to change their names. And fourth, and most telling, this was no altruism on his part. Any lawyer that could take the only Final Forfeiture in forty years and win could write his own ticket.

"Mr. Morton, are you listening?" I nod. I set my hands back to the task of preparing coffee. I marvel for a moment how well I can dodge the painful no-no spots in my knuckles, my wrists, and manipulate the little pod into its place. I accomplish the whole process without dropping a single thing. I let out a sigh. Am I smiling right now? I think I am. It feels like the same face I make when I'm in pain, but I'm not in pain. I am lifting the sides of my face— so heavy— but I feel good. Yes, I did something good, so this must be a smile. How quaint. I should do something to treat myself later tonight. Maybe ice cream?

Do I have ice cream? I can't remember. There's the path to the fridge and the path back to my chair. Also, there's the coffee to consider. I will have to come back here to get the coffee once it brews. Okay, fine. I decide I'll have to let it be a surprise whether or not I have ice cream waiting for me. Taking a breath, I set my hips into motion and propel my body back towards my chair.

And he is still talking.

"… which you don't seem to fully grasp. In fact, can I be real with you a bit? What you're… what you've been telling me these past few years, has taken a mental and emotional toll on me. It's disturbing. You realize that.

I'm sure you realize that. What you're talking about is… dea—" He makes a sound like a hiccup.

Fucking snowflake can't even say the word.

"Have you ever stopped to consider how this is affecting me? My family? My professional standing? My social standing?"

I have almost made it to my chair. I leave him hanging until I reach it, then I turn around and calculate how to let myself fall, then, angling my hips and bracing for the creak of bone on bone, then the impact, I sit.

"No," I turn to look him in the eye, forcing his face away. "No, I haven't." My hands are on the armrests now, and I press my fingertips as hard as I can into their soft fabric. This. This is so soothing. As I look down, the sunlight coming in from my patio doors reveal clouds of dust disturbed by my little scratchings. I snort.

Dust. That stuff used to be trash, dead skin and mites. Now, I wonder how many smart meds are in it. Are there even any mites left? Smart meds. Damn. Here comes another thought train. Okay, brain, give it to me.

Smart meds in filters, air and water. Smart meds in food. Smart meds in the bots hiding in your walls. They have to be in your walls. That's part of being "up to code."

"I… I…" my lawyer is close to tears now. "I … find it very hard to 'zealously' represent your interests when you exhibit such hostility."

It shoots back into my head the reason I beckoned him here. I have court tomorrow.

"Run me through it," I say. No preamble. No acknowledgement of his diatribe. He stares for a moment, paces, pinches the bridge of his nose, wipes his tears. I watch him, waiting. I can do that better than anyone. I wait as he collects himself, not moving a muscle. I concentrate on my breath. Good. Nice and easy. I am going to have a good night.

No heart trouble. I conjure the thought and absorb it. It's true, I tell myself.

No heart trouble, I manifest it again. I let another breath out. Yes, that was a good one, a home run. I am going to have a good night tonight.

I notice he has now gathered his strength and is facing me. The smell of coffee hits me. Good. I make a note to have that as a reward after my performance with him.

"Do you remember rule number one?" He shoots at me, face now blank with a jaw set tight. "There is no way to avoid cross-examination with this one. Final Forfeiture requires the petitioner to take the stand—"

"I remember. I have to outlawyer a lawyer who has all of society behind him." Okay. Good heart and lungs. Good heart and lungs. I have the power in me to speak. I do. Now is the time. Do it, body. Do it.

"Shall we begin?"

I nod, and he begins without missing a beat, adopting his practiced Prosecutor voice.

"Let's begin, Sir, with this: do you realize what you are asking for? If so, would you please describe it in your own words?"

"I'm seeking Final—"

"Everyone present knows the term, Mr. Morton. I asked you to describe in your own words what Final Forfeiture is, and *why* you are petitioning for it."

I struggle. I really did pay attention during the etiquette classes – and the law crash courses, the philosophy course, all the courses he threw at me – but on the spot I cannot ignore what my core is telling me.

I want to ... no, wait. I can't say it that way....

I feel deep down, after more than 200 years on this planet, that I have accomplished...

No, that won't work either. They'll ask how I reached this feeling, and back me into a philosophical corner, forcing me to sound suicidal.

THIS IS NOT NATURAL! IT'S TORTURE! EVERYTHING PASSES ON! HAVEN'T YOU EVER HEARD THE SAYING "THE WAY OF ALL FLESH?"
No, wait. No one has said that since... What year is it?
Wait...

Somewhere in the recesses of my mind, something happens that has not happened in over a hundred years— a new idea. I was caught, silenced by the intensity of it. My brain was now giving me something that no one had given it first.

Oh, my God. This feels good. This feels so... satisfying! It's like an org—

"Mr. Morton. I need an answer for us to proceed." He was still using his Prosecutor voice, but now with his arms crossed. For a moment, I wish I could force him to see how ridiculous he looks trying to intimidate a man who has lived two-hundred-and-forty-some-odd years, and who actually *wants* to die. Go ahead and look stern, sonny. Just try to scare me.

"I apologize, your Excellency. I am seeking a grant of Final Forfeiture, which I understand opens my life to irreversible risk. I need this in order for me to conduct my experiment, which will hopefully answer the second part of your question. I wish to conduct an experiment in which I will deprive myself of all modern medicine and nutrition. I wish to do this to study the untreated lifestyle of the human animal."

"Mr. Morton, I still do not understand *why* you feel you need to do this."

"I am doing this for my own curiosity. I plan to document my experiences, and others can study my case for years to come."

"Then, you do not wish to die, Mr. Morton?"

"No, sir, I do not. How could any person say that and mean it? But, if I may speak freely, your Excellency."

"Tread carefully, but proceed."

"I do not feel the State has a right to stand in my way if I seek knowledge, enrichment, or enjoyment. Are these not the reasons we live? Are these not the tenets we hold sacred in our founding documents?"

"I do not follow."

"Risking life and limb, or even Final Forfeiture, is thrilling. It is thrilling to feel one is a part of Nature. To experience what men long ago experienced when they braved the wild, is a dream of mine. I am not celebrating life's end, rather, I am celebrating life! I realize and I respect that I must go through proper channels to do this, so I have laid my case at the mercy of the court."

My lawyer is caught off guard, and still plays devil's advocate for a bit. He loses steam, and finally warns me that, should we win, I better go through with my "Grand Adventure." Otherwise, both he and I will be guilty of perjury. That word doesn't scare me.

In truth, nothing does.

I know that, even if I win, even if I get every single part of this just how I want it, they will use me as an example… make it harder for others to follow in my footsteps. Maybe they'll make it impossible. Maybe I will be the very last man to die.

He promises to contact me tomorrow with news. With any luck, we'll have a court date in as little as nine years, maybe even eight. I bid him goodbye and sit back in my chair. Seems like I was thinking about food before. Was I? No. I'm not hungry. That settles it.

I am going to sleep in my chair tonight. I will not get up and shut the blinds. It's a full moon tonight, and I want to look outside. I want to hear the night animals and fantasize about what they are saying.

I try to think about that point in the visit when I came up with an idea. God! That felt good! I try to conjure that feeling again, but habit gets the better of me. Instead, I sit and I stare.

I think about my memories. I lose myself, traveling through their corridors. I wait. There really is nothing else to do.

I wait.

A Piñata That Does Not Break Is Broken

"Heaven and Earth are impartial;
they treat all of creation as straw dogs.
The Master doesn't take sides;
she treats everyone like a straw dog.

The space between Heaven and Earth is like a bellows;
it is empty, yet has not lost its power.
The more it is used, the more it produces;
the more you talk of it, the less you comprehend.

It is better not to speak of things you do not understand."

• Tao Te Ching

Snuff: Death on Film was the working title. And the tragic thing about giving up on it was that I had really wanted to write it. I was driven. I could visualize the whole book from title page to the final paragraph. It would be a coffee table book, one to turn heads— something that even the jaded Kindle generation would jump at the chance to own. I imagined it as something like *Eyewitness Books*, put forth with clinical and academic precision. It would have been the pinnacle of sick and beautiful.

One thing you must have in place before you even really cement a project is the research. Not just sources, but actual inside information. I think, if life were a movie, my wife would have taken me aside and asked me something like, "How far are you willing to go?" And then something about not being able to un-see things.

Yawn.

I didn't even feel it at first, but that whole thing about not being able to handle dark topics is real. It comes on subtly, like an illness more than a shock. About a week after I had learned about *Daisy's Destruction*, and was going over the logistics of interviewing Peter Sculley, I noticed it.

I was tapped. Tapped in or tapped out, I don't know. Disconnected.

It was like every sensation was being filtered through gauze. My wife didn't notice. Even if she did, I doubt she would have said anything. I've learned not to push too hard with her. Any excuse to use again. The year prior, she had fallen off the wagon, and then there was at least one other time since we'd been married. As for when we were dating— we have settled on a truce that said time in our lives doesn't matter. I'm pretty sure I believe that. I don't think I've ever allowed myself to hate her for her past, and I try my best with the mantras she uses as defense mechanisms, but sometimes I wonder how I let someone like her be part of my life.

If you've ever spent time with a junkie, you know how annoying they can be. But let me tell you, they can't hold a candle to the monumental wounded ego of the recovered junkie.

The biggest fight of this period happened out of the blue. The best fights do. She was saying something about people having to own their own choices and cutting others out of your life if they don't change. Then she added, "Time doesn't matter. No matter how long you know someone…"

That set me off. She always mentions topics as broadly as possible, so it takes a lot of prompting to get her to admit who she is talking about. I had assumed she had been talking about me. And why not?

I judge you.

I hedge you in, making the decision for you, even though you're strong enough. What's one slip?

I will leave you first if you give me the chance.

I could practically smell the subtext. But no, apparently a friend from work had spoken in a way that reminded her of the party scene she was trying to avoid, and she was considering dropping this person. After informing me of this, she went on a long rant of what she could be capable of in the way of self-destruction. The shame-pride she is able to conjure in these moments makes me want to vomit in my hands, right there in front of her, and then frantically slap her with it. Instead, I sit with my hand on my chin, freezing my face into a psychologist's calm while I swallow my anger

Finally, she summed it up with a pitiful, mewing guess-you-should-leave-me speech, and then she went into total silent mode.

I was able to beg and cajole her out of it. Despite the bad taste these kinds of fights leave in my mouth, it had given me a new idea for a book. Forget snuff films. There was something just as deep, dark, and meaty that could satisfy my curiosity with society's underbelly, and I could explore it without losing my soul.

Homeless people. In short, I decided to collect the stories of the local homeless and do whatever it is when you sell such stories. Is it altruistic? I convinced myself it was, and I carried that notion well into the second interview.

The first went well. I talked with a man who was quite willing and open. He found work by selling paper flowers to people outside restaurants. But, as it turned out, he wasn't homeless. He was a vet, a recovering addict, and he lived with his brother. He had done time, and then was unable to find work. He had lost his apartment, and eventually settled in with his brother. Not what I was looking for.

The next guy brought friends. After I introduced myself and explained my project, he shouted to some people across the street, invited them to join our conversation, and then started interviewing *me*. Where did I live? What made me want to do this? How many people had I talked to? And last but not least…

"Now are you going to forget all your friends if you make money on this thing?"

I was too smart to fall for that one. They quickly started trying to relocate the conversation, and by the time I had excused myself from their group, I knew in my heart that this was another dead end.

By now I was running out of time. In the world of writers, your editor is Dad, and your agent is Mom. Dad is always mad at you, pushing you to do more and do it better. Meanwhile, Mom is telling you everything you want to hear, making sure your fragile artist's ego can stay on task and actually put words on paper. Therefore, I wasn't surprised that Dad wasn't too happy I was changing direction for a third time. Then, when I spoke to Mom the following day, she gave me "the speech".

"Do you know how many manuscripts I get every day?" she asked me. "Actually give me a guess."

"I don't want to guess. I know what you're going to say." I didn't want to be rude to the woman who would practically take a bullet for me, but I still felt the sting of almost being robbed and gang-raped by the homeless, and on top of that my wife was yelling from the other room that the toilet was making a noise.

"Eighty," she went on. "On average I skim through about a thousand manuscripts a year. One thousand different writers, a thousand different voices. And do you know how many of them have talent?"

"I know the drill. I've been given talent and I'm squandering it. Don't worry. I have a direction—"

"They *all* have talent, Honey. That's what I'm trying to tell you. Talent isn't what is going to keep you afloat. You have to *produce*. And you have to work harder than all those kids I turn down on a daily basis because people don't want what you're selling."

"They will want it if I can package it and show them … that fascination"

"The market is going and going fast. It's just libraries and New York intellectuals, and well-to-do Manhattanites don't want morbid curiosities and introspective brooding. They want slice-of-life pieces. They want to know what it's like to be Black or gay, or join the army, or live as a missionary. They want escapism. From their money and their... lives. Books are getaways now; no one opens a book to be challenged or shamed."

She waited a few moments, listening to me breathe.

"Think about what I told you," she prodded. "Remember Bartleby?"

I smiled. I guess she couldn't resist a lit reference. It was the spoonful of sugar. Of course I remembered Bartleby. Bartleby was that Melville character who lost his mind one day at work and simply refused to do any task put to him, even though it meant plunging into poverty. He just kept repeating "I would prefer not to." Melville seemed to specialize in these allegories – Bartleby, Billy Budd, and Ahab – all were men who self-destructed despite repeated warnings that they were inflicting real harm on themselves. Oh, yeah. I remembered that Bartleby was a scrivener, a man who was paid to put words on paper. That made her comment sting a little extra.

"Yeah, don't worry. I'll pull through." But how? I kept brainstorming that night while I searched YouTube for an hour looking for toilet repair tutorials.

I learned of the Visser brothers from an acquaintance who shared my interest in such topics. I had promised myself I would never write about serial killers. It had been done to death. It would be like establishing myself as a horror novelist and then trying my hand at vampire fiction. It had not been so long ago, around the time I was considering the homelessness theme. They had piqued my curiosity enough that I had even tracked them down. The older brother, the mastermind, had died of heart disease in 1997. However, the younger brother, the helper, was still alive under hospital care— committed to an asylum, that is— about three hours' drive from my house.

To my knowledge, no one had ever done a piece on them, not even a magazine article. There were blurbs, things mentioned in conjunction with other obscure killers like Joe Ball, but nothing really substantial. And then there was the advantage of proximity. I would never do a serial killer book, but ...

I'd been up since 5 AM to compare notes and establish rapport with another author. She had published a true crime series in the late nineties on serial killers, and was one of the few people who had read the ME notes and arrest reports on the Visser case. She was British, so I volunteered to accommodate her by Skyping at noon her time. I found her enthusiastic and charming, and there was none of the boring small talk that two people slip into when they try to force a connection. She had been retired for ten years, and seemed relieved that someone had taken such an interest in her earlier work. At the end of our session, I asked her,

"Why didn't you go more in-depth with the Visser case?"

"Well, there were a few reasons," she said, as if she had been waiting years for the question. "Now, I don't want to set your own journey off on the wrong foot, understand; what I'm about to say is just my own proclivities." She was being polite. I bid her continue. "Some individuals beg detailed analysis. Berkowitz was boring for me. Zodiac was not. They both committed basically the same crimes, but the Zodiac case has so much there, so much to explore for the author and the reader. But I had it easy when it came to those two. You see, others had already done the research. If I were to delve into the Vissers, I'd have to make it its own volume, and I would have to do all the work. I didn't have time.

"The other thing is this: The Vissers disgusted me. Pure and simple. I put in Fish and Chikatilo and Kurten, all the while gritting my teeth. In the end, I guess I was just full-up-to-the-gills with the grittier ones."

"Believe it or not, I know what you're talking about. I call it being tapped."

She laughed. "I can so see that. You're a barrel in the pub, and all the lovely patrons are enjoying your frothy output, but one day— pop!— you're tapped! Well, good luck to you. If there is anything else I can provide, you can always contact me."

I shut my laptop and sat in the living room, just staring. My wife's footsteps registered in my ears, and instantly I snapped back to attention.

"So, what are you working on?" It seemed to be one of those mornings. I was recognizable to her, a welcome stranger as opposed to the alternative. She sat a little closer than normal, and something in the way she held her face told me she would at least hear me out.

"To be honest I'm doing a book on a pair of serial killers. And I know—"

"I thought you said you'd never do one on serial killers."

"That's exactly what I was about to say, if you had let me finish." She sighed at that. A little eye roll. I was losing her, but I decided to press on.

"It's just two guys, two brothers," she was already looking off. "They worked as a team. It's actually pretty unique. I mean, it's exciting stuff." The word salad just kept spilling out. She had shown interest, and who knew where this could lead, but I was reluctant to get into the details. She hated criminals, and serial killers in general. I didn't want to hear any disparaging of my topic, but I also didn't want to hear her *announce* that she would kindly change the subject for my benefit.

I know this is your third topic, and I just ... don't want to hurt your feelings but ... maybe you should just talk about this with someone else, because ... I just don't want to say.

That irked me. Saying that you're not saying, that's saying. That's playing it safe while still trying to adopt the role of the righteous— pandering in reverse. To my surprise, she kept it going.

"So what happened?" she asked. "Did they turn on each other? Those usually don't work well in teams." Now that was, I think, genuine interest.

"Actually, no. They were caught, and the police just put it all together. The younger one kept asking if his brother was mad at him, and Peter, the eldest, kept telling the cops to ask him if they needed anything, to leave his little brother alone.

"How many did they kill?"

"Three or four. Not many. They attacked a lot more, but you know ... it's hard to kill people, it turns out."

"Women?"

"Yeah," I hesitated before answering that. One thing that had soured my wife from the whole true crime genre was the overwhelming prevalence of violence against women. I decided to shift the focus.

"But the thing— well two thing— that drew me to the case was that first, no one has ever covered it in-depth, so this won't just be some hack work for me. And also, this whole thing is a freak show. Well, I shouldn't say that, because the older one, Peter, was deformed, but I mean there's like this Tim Burton and *Batman Returns* appeal—"

"Eww!" she made a face. "You know I hate that movie!" With that, I had lost her. Oh well, it was mediocre while it lasted.

"Anyway, I got some great contacts from Myra this morning, and I'm setting up an interview with Ian's doctor this week. Ian is the younger one. Believe it or not, he's local, so I'm going to rope his doctor into having coffee with me, and then I'll pick his brain. I bet he'll also have access to the ME reports and court statements."

"That's good. Who's Myra?"

"She's an author." I tried to prepare a proper defense. "She's a British author. She's like sixty. She did a series. It was like those series that Time-Life used to do. She did it back in the nineties. It was on serial killers and spree killers and bizarre crimes. Locked door mysteries and such. I learned most of what I know about them from her. Her and Donald Rumbelow. Anyway. Whatever. I was lucky to get to talk to her. She gave me her sources. I wouldn't be able to move forward on the book if it weren't for her. Also," I took a breath and smiled, "Really took my mind off your Hep-C."

I was able to get the interview that Thursday, and all the pieces were falling into place. With the hospital so close by, I could vastly speed up the process. Two interviews could be squeezed into this week with the doctor, one Harold Cavanaugh, and then a weekend to go over my notes along with the ME reports and court testimony. Then, next week could be spent with Ian himself for a little insight into home life and firsthand anecdotes. After that, I could have a rough draft up and running in time to push for a deadline extension. And that was that. It was as good as done.

We met for coffee as planned, but immediately trouble came into paradise.

"I didn't want to turn you down over the phone," Dr. Cavanaugh told me. "But I have a problem with the ethics here. Doing this. It does not sit well with me, understand? I thought I should tell you that to your face. I'll allow you to see documentation. If I don't, you'll just go through another source for that, but full access and interviews—" He shook his head and held my gaze.

Dr. Cavanaugh was pushing eighty. He had been Ian's doctor since the arrest. He had flown in to testify at their trial, worked to have Ian declared mentally incompetent, and had enjoyed custody of Ian ever since. Not in the way of traditional guardianship, but in the unique circumstance of the criminally insane, the person's doctor might as well be their owner. Without Cavanaugh's sanction, there was no book.

"Now, I don't want you to be upset. It wasn't my intention, as I said, to waste your time. So, let's enjoy our coffee, and you get out your recorder— your phone, or whatever you prefer— and I'll give you some details you can work with.

"Peter was the eldest. But the story actually started with Mrs. Visser. She was having an affair, you see. Her husband was in sales, traveled, and she was lonely. I guess it's the kind of thing you see all the time now, but back then it was an awful scandal, having a woman betray her husband while he was away. Even worse was when a child came of it, which is what happened.

"Ms. Visser realized she was pregnant rather early on, so she did what any sensible woman would do and seduced her husband the instant he came back home. Once he was away again, she set about planning the miscarriage, and here is where I actually come into the story."

"You?" He smiled. All old men love telling stories, but I don't think I've ever seen a wider smile, even on a child.

"Didn't see that one coming? Don't worry. I'm not the other man. Maybe once you write your book, and you sell it to Hollywood they'll change my name and make me the murderer's father, make it a whole failed redemption story or the like. Anyway, the other man was known to me. He was a doctor, something of a friend of mine. He happened to mention the dilemma to me, because as I said this was a big deal in those days. It's a shame, but you know I can't remember what I told him to do. Isn't that something?

"I want to say I gave him some prudent advice, something that would minimize the damage to him and the young lady, but..."

"Go on. What did he end up doing?"

Cavanaugh raised his eyebrows and exhaled a long breath. "He got some Methotrexate, pills instead of the injection, and then gave them to her and left. I heard he went to Canada, and lived out the rest of his days there. I'm not sure. Anyway, Methotrexate has many uses, and it can be used to terminate a pregnancy. Note that I said *can be.* To this day I don't know why he chose to just leave her with some pills.

"So, she takes the pills, and waits to enact a miscarriage for her husband, but it doesn't work. She carries the child to term, now terrified and apparently convinced she is being punished by God. At this point, I lost touch with the story until I was contacted twenty years later about the murders. And, I couldn't believe it. I can't really describe the sensation it gave me. I won't say responsibility, and I can't say it was mere curiosity, but I knew I had to be the one to evaluate Peter and Ian. So, I flew there, and the rest is history."

"You said the pills didn't work? Is that why Peter was—?"

"Oh, yes. *Severely.* Methotrexate is a teratogen. It acts much like Thalidomide. Almost total reduction of the limbs, sometimes problems with the spine. Peter was lucky, in a way, to live as long as he did. Actually, I did remember to bring his mugshot."

With this, he produced a photo from his breast pocket, and just like that I was looking into the face of my white whale.

We spend years telling children not to judge on appearances, and we as a society find a way to worm the same song and dance into political movements and women's issues. It's a necessary evil, because we don't want unqualified people doing it. However, students of human behavior do it all the time— the cop on the street, the woman walking through the parking lot— of course you can read a person. Authors and journalists also develop this skill, and I was getting all sorts of signals from the man staring back at me.

He had been a smoker and a drinker; the effects hung around the softer features of his face. His eyes were focused, not blurred or distracted. He was used to being in charge. He had a bad temper, and let it run wild more often than not. This gave him his confidence. He had a jealous gaze. It obsessed over others, finding out what they took for granted that he could never have. I let my eyes drift down to his neck. Beside it was the number 60 on the height chart.

Wait. Over five feet tall with no legs? "Hey, this may seem like an odd question— "

"He's on a stool. Funny story. It would take two officers to lift him onto the thing, and they kept dropping him because he would bite them."

We adjourned, and I asked if he might be free Friday. He excused himself and said that he would not, but that I might contact him the coming week. That set my writing schedule back, but what choice did I have? I left him with my contact info in the good faith that he would provide the reports we discussed. He kept the mugshot, though.

I was dreading the whole drive home. Not because the fight was still going on. In reality, there had been no fight after my comment. A relationship is a weird material that can be broken and still function. We had reached that point where we couldn't hurt each other, so insults were just ways of showing disappointment or disengaging. After I mentioned Hepatitis, she had gotten up from the table with infuriating calm and just walked out of the room. Then, she probably spent the rest of the day going online and looking at nursery accessories she would never get to buy. But the reason I dreaded going back was that there was still a certain emptiness when we were at odds with each other. At least when we had a truce, there was *civility*.

As it happened, she was gone, so I made myself at home in a way not usually available to me. I laid out my notes and prepped to do some writing. Seeing as how I wouldn't have anyone to stop me, I cracked open some vodka. I knew this would mean more work revising in the morning, but it was worth it to at least enjoy my time alone while it lasted.

Vodka inevitably leads to repeated bathroom visits, but despite these repeated, brief interruptions I was able to construct a skeleton for the book, key details for each chapter and reminders to myself of pictures to include for emphasis. All was going well until I caught a glimpse of something in the mirror while leaving the bathroom.

I guess everyone must have that moment when they realize they have aged. But this was more than that. I knew, or at least part of me knew, that I was no longer a beaming 28-year-old man with his first published work and the world on a string. I knew those days were behind me, but there was something beyond the simple addition of years on this face. I began to see myself as a character.

Who was this man, with his drooping, listless eyes, and tucked chin? After wringing details from a thousand persons about their most intimate details, why did he still hang his head like a shy child? I began to feel an intense temptation to run, to turn off the light, to leave the mirror behind and focus back on the book. Instead, I kept looking. Who was this man? What would I expect from him if I saw him on the street? Was he a father? Hardly. This man warranted no authority. No power at all. All this man knew of power was in quiet defiance he showed in imaginary worlds of his own creation. And if he were a father, he would be that pathetic soul who copied his kids' fashion and musical choices, ever eager to impress them into accepting him.

I began to taste the lack of dignity I had been carrying through my everyday life. Even through the haze of vodka, the noise of hatred for all those people and things I considered beneath me, I finally felt the disgust rising to the surface. The shame of it, of choosing to build this man bit by bit from all the years of my life, all I could do was look away.

What have I done?

I said it out loud. And again.

No one answered me, which was good. If somehow some god or angel had appeared to review my life with me, I would have died of shock. Instead, I let that be the closure of the evening, a small voice and a rhetorical question, barely audible over a hissing toilet.

The ensuing days passed in a haze. I put down all I could in the way of structure, but otherwise the time was uneventful, at least on the surface. In the back of my mind, I felt a new idea brewing. I started thinking about what exactly my book was saying. I picked the topic because it was interesting, which echoed the same sentiment I remembered reading from Myra's introduction years ago. Was I worried about treading over the same old ground? Maybe, but it seemed like more than that. Myra wrote her series twenty years ago. Serial killers were a novel topic back then. Things had changed. Now they were practically a literary and historical stock character.

So why was I cataloging the crimes of two unknowns? What was there to explore in the first place? Did it matter that these two had slipped through the cracks? For a moment, I thought the hook in it lay with the fact that one of them was disabled, that I had fallen into the P. T. Barnum gutter—whatever sells, and if you can make it smuttier, do it.

There is a skill you perfect in adulthood wherein any problem not immediately threatening to one's finances can be postponed indefinitely. As such, I had still not really unraveled the mystery of my interest in the project by the time I found myself sitting in front of Dr. Cavanaugh again.

"I think I see what you were talking about earlier, with this being an ethical issue," I told him as soon as we had sat down with our coffees. Even though this was only our second meeting, it seemed like we both knew the ropes. We found a table without hesitation and there was no small talk. We got down to business. "Those girls were just teenagers. Runaways. Sure some of them were suspected of turning tricks, but... Jesus."

To my surprise, he smiled. "No. No, you're looking at this all wrong. Weren't you listening to me at all last week?"

I just shook my head, which prompted him to stretch his smile into a condescending grin. After holding it for a second and shaking his head, he said, "I just don't think it's *ethical* for me to reveal the secrets of a family I've been so involved with for so long. Do you understand?"

I stared at him. Was I hearing this? He continued. "Can you honestly say that you uncovered anything here? Did you discover anything? Anything at all? This has been my life's work. I've been closely involved and I've shown you the legwork I was able to collect. Now, I ask you, do you really think it's *ethical* for me to give all of that over to you without hesitation?"

Behind every P. T. Barnum, there's elephant shit, I guess.

"Co-writing credit?" I asked. He cocked his head to the side. *No? Time to switch gears.* "Have you ever been published?" I asked him.

"Does that even matter anymore? I would only legitimize your freak show by including my name on the cover page." He laughed at his own observation.

"The only question, son, is whether you're going to tell me it will happen or not."

"Yes."

He nodded and stuck out his lip. I whipped out my phone and made the introductions to my agent right then and there. It was surprisingly easy. They exchanged numbers and information, and at the end of the conversation he was excited enough to invite me to stay for a second cup of coffee. While we enjoyed our victory drink, he decided to excite me with some juicier details.

"All these girls, you know, hitched and crashed wherever they could— kindness of strangers and all— and Ian was tall and clean-cut. He really spoke and acted like a trustworthy young man. Back then you could find an Ian in every mechanic shop or grocery mart. Eager, helpful. I doubt you know the type. Hell, you can't even imagine what the world was like when these girls were out on the streets. A young man with a good haircut was a good man, and if he didn't drink or smoke, he was a saint.

"Actually, neither brother smoked or drank— Well, Peter did… later— their mother would not allow it. She really, truly believed God was punishing her, for her affair, for the cover-up, for trying to abort her firstborn. I guess it does look pretty Biblical from her perspective. Unfortunately, she lived in the real world, so after she confessed to her husband, he left her … after ten years. She apparently waited until the birth of their second son to come clean. It was at this point that she started to really go off the deep end.

"You can imagine the pressure of defending a deformed child in the '60s. Now add to that the guilt and financial hardship of divorce. She soldiered through it alone, living in churches and petitioning charity for most of her earnings. Ian was sent to live with relatives, or to foster families, but no one would take Peter. He was her burden, and she started to hate him.

"One thing led to another, and on the day Peter showed defiance and told his mother that he had put two and two together. Dad left because … you know. Ms. Visser had a psychotic break at this point. She knocked three teeth out of his mouth with her shoe, and made him swear to be righteous or something. She had a saying. If Peter were alive, he could tell you better. He had the whole thing memorized. If your agent pulls through and you get to interview Ian, maybe he can tell you.

"Anyway, there are several ways to manipulate a child, and some really bad ones if you have zero scruples. Peter was just then approaching puberty, so maybe it was a coincidence that Ms. Visser decided to target his testicles. Peter's arms weren't long enough to reach his own groin, and even if he crossed his legs, there was a pretty wide gap, wide enough that... well, anyway she would grab him and squeeze him there when he disappointed her. Eventually she decided she needed to castrate her son, or so he claimed when I interviewed him. The rest of what I told you I find believable, but that part I think is a little farfetched. Peter would apparently hide from her until she left for work. Once again, I must say that I'm not sure I believe that."

I held up my hand. I would need this for my notes, and I could decide later whether or not to put it in the book. In the meantime, I just needed an intermission. When the doctor asked if I were bothered by these details, I couldn't hold back.

"No! No, I'm not bothered. I'm bothered by the fact that there's nothing new! So, what happened exactly? A crazy mother in poverty who abused her son in like, hilariously bizarre ways? And of course, that means he had to go and kill half a dozen *other* women, all the while worshipping her? I'm sure. Fucking Christ, I've heard this story before."

"There's no need for that kind of language." The doctor was frowning now. "Oh, wait. I see what you're doing. No, trust me. You still need my information. I know you. I know your type. You will not be able to walk away from a real, live interview with one of the Vissers in the flesh. Now, let me tell you something funny. You know how they got caught? Most of the girls survived, I'm sure you knew that. None of them talked to the authorities at first, because they knew no one would believe it. But here's the thing; so many of their victims lived because the Vissers learned everything from the movies! They tried pillows and hand strangulation. Both brothers truly, truly believed that once a person lost consciousness, they were as good as dead."

I got home and killed a pint of vodka typing up my notes. That is to say, our notes. Far be it from me to forget the contribution of my partner. Last but not least, I had set up an interview date with Ian after listening to the rest of the colorful forensics.

My wife's footsteps woke me. Wherever she had been, she didn't mention it. She settled back into the usual routine, announcing to me when she would be leaving to and from work. She relayed that she was taking the last of something from the fridge, although I couldn't make out exactly what. Then, she was gone, leaving me with the task of shaking the slight heaviness that vodka leaves in your head and climbing out of bed. There was a long day ahead of me, proofreading and correcting the inebriated freestyling I had done the night before.

I had made headway by the time she came back.

"I read it. While you were sleeping this morning. I really like it. It's got something to it. I didn't think I would, but you need to finish it. This is a good book."

"I'm glad you see something in it." I really was. I was grateful for the slightest bit of encouragement. I told her about the doctor worming his way in, and the gruesome details he had mentioned. I told her how fed up I was with the project, but that out of sheer professionalism, I was determined to finish it. She looked at me with an intensity I never would have thought still survived at this point in our lives. Then she said the last thing I expected.

"You need to tell their story. I can't believe how much they loved each other."

"Who?" There was an obvious answer, but my mind rejected that outright.

"The brothers. I mean, that's why you chose this, didn't you? In all that isolation and pain, the devotion the younger one showed taking care of his brother, trying to make up for their mother... "

I got up from the table and left the house. On the way, I half shouted something about needing to clear my head with a jog. That night I had a nightmare. I was on trial for my book. Women's rights groups and disability groups were debating over the facts, and I had to convince the court that rape was worse than being handicapped or I wouldn't be able to label my book "true crime." My lawyer, who had no face, took me aside and told me that if I lost, I could be dismembered as poetic justice.

Again, the marvelous talent of thirtysomething procrastination allowed time to ooze rapidly and without incident until the date of Ian's interview, then I found myself stepping into the brightest, blankest hospital wing I could imagine.

When I saw him, I was unprepared. He was seated among his peers, a collection of motionless bodies, overweight and slouched. He was bald with large facial bones. Behind the excess flesh, I could see the younger man that would have charmed a young, stupid girl. To me he looked like a fat caveman: big brow, big hands, small mouth with lips too red.

I focused on that mouth.

I imagined that mouth, slack with lithium or whatever chemical made him safe for mass consumption, back in the days of twentysomething vigor.

I thought of the doctor and me.

I thought of his fat hands holding a fifteen-year-old's arms.

I thought of my wife and a multitude of sympathetic women protesting his execution. I thought of my faceless dream-lawyer telling me I had better not mock Peter for his disability.

Then that mouth. That safe little mouth, waiting to tell me all the details the doctor left out, waiting to smile at me.

Then, I was walking. I was stiff-legged, but I was walking. Cavanaugh appeared at my side and asked me with a threatening air if I was going to interview Ian, because chances like this are not easy to arrange and something else I couldn't make out. I spouted profanity and kept moving.

I drove home, the three hours a total blank. All of it passed as if I was dreaming, until I saw the stairs. Taking a deep breath, I mounted each one, and dropped everything at the top. The lights were out.

There was no one home.

The Orm

"Those who fear the Unknown have not studied enough of the Known."

Day I, Morning

"I'm not saying I want to *be* an Anglo; I just find them— their culture— interesting." It was rare for Elard to look at someone when deep in conversation, but for this he caught Spears and turned to face his friend. Others in the hallway, cadets mostly, slowed their steps to eavesdrop, but made little currents on either side of the men.

"Anglo was the language of the whole world," continued Elard. "They were the first culture to touch every single continent."

"They conquered the world," Spears scoffed. "They committed more genocide than any other culture… by a lot."

"I am not fawning over their politics," Elard resumed their walk. A polite political disagreement was not worth being late. "I'm not insane. I find their discoveries interesting. Their cultural practices. Little quirks, you know? I wouldn't want to live like an ant either, but ants are undeniably interesting."

"We aren't talking about ants." Spears was trepidatious. This was veering into some dark territory.

"No, but we are talking about the Dead. There's no helping the Dead. We might as well learn from them."

The two men continued down the hall, a gullet of gray, lit at each of its four corners with careful, safe autumnal colors. Soon, they would come to a door, and, once having crossed its threshold, this conversation would end.

In an attempt to lighten the mood as they neared the door, Spears asked his friend, "I've heard you studied Anglo, the language I mean. How is it?"

"Like trying to solve a Rubik's cube that fights back."

There was no time to reflect on that. They reached the door, and Elard volunteered to be the one to card them in, then signaled his friend to enter first. They passed through, entering the cabin of the observation deck, and dropped into "government mode."

The cabin was never empty, although its safety features allowed it to run with minimal personnel. It was the perfect vantage point for card-carriers. Scientists could study the skies, assessing all the assorted phenomena that occurred between the stars this far out, while enlisted men appreciated it because it overlooked the colony. In the event of an accident, the commanders, or CO's could assess the emergency with their own eyes. The cabin had windows from mid-knee height all the way to the ceiling, and these took up most of the cabin's eight walls. No other building in the colony had such a view.

The settlement was a small one. Its population hovered around 300 souls, and this waxed or waned depending on research demands and budget constraints... or fatigue. That last one was the kicker. Fatigue plagued humankind in any and all such habitats. It happened in the extremes of the stations on either pole on Earth, and everywhere else. Those of the Moon and Mars still suffered from the disconnect. There were stations, and then there were stations. This one, which counted among the farthest out, graced the surface of Ceres, the lady dwarf planet, she who hovered among the asteroids. Assignments were government-issue only, and lasted for a maximum of 18 months by law. It was, however, deemed safe for both civilian contractors and even child cadets, provided at least one parent was present on base.

Spears and Elard had been on the same charter flight to start the new personnel shift. Spears was an instruments overseer. Elard was a physicist. The two men were the same age, and were unique among the new crew in that they were accompanying their wives and children to the colony. This became the icebreaker, and the pair became fast work friends.

Spears was to oversee the instruments, and this meant replacing the old techie, who was overdue for a change of the guard, as well as teach the cadets informatics and general upkeep.

Elard was to apply and test a new material for the base's shielding. Domes and enclosed walkways were the norm, which gave them the common term of "Gerbilvilles." Among civilians, "Hamstertowns" was also common. These domes consisted of layers of reinforced material, and between them pumped a cocktail of protective chemicals to supplement the protection of an upper atmosphere. This kept out harmful UV rays and the tiny rocks that rained down on the base every few hours. Elard was testing a thin, solid coating to replace this cocktail. In theory, this would be more effective, as a single puncture would not lead to a leak. Repairs and replacement would also be easier.

This morning, however, Elard had been called off his assignment and sent to accompany Spears to the observation deck. Clearance regulations had prevented either man from knowing why until they arrived. A casual comment during the walk down the hall – a comparison of these deeper space colonies to the twentieth-century research stations in Antarctica – had led to the political discussion, but this was forgotten by both men as they took in the scene around the cabin.

Two cadets, both showing signs of pulling a red-eyed double shift, were examining reports. Nothing about this was unusual at first, until both men saw the general size of the readouts. There were printed hard copies, something normally only needed for historical or forensic evidence, on stacks on the floor and a few spare chairs. The youths stood to attention as the two men entered, polished boots clicking the floor in unison. They saluted Spears and waited. The reports, it seemed, would speak for themselves.

"At ease, cadets." Spears told them, and then motioned to Elard. "I want to introduce Dr. Elard. He will be lending his expertise today as the astrophysicist-in-residence. Now, what have you got for me?"

The two handed over the latest report. When cadets were this quiet, it meant they did not want to volunteer to be questioned. That meant something totally left field had happened, and that, Spears sighed to himself, meant for a long day. He handed the extra copy to Elard and announced to the room, "Let's see what we have got here."

The two men looked over the reports, and then the reports before them. Then they asked for the ones before that.

A half-hour later, they called the base captain.

The captain-in-residence, Laron by name, answered Spears' call with a warmth the junior officer did not expect.

"The cadets reported last night there was some ongoing confusion with the instruments. What are we talking here, Officer? A few weeks' research lost?"

"Sir, I don't think so. The Reads can't find anything wrong with the instruments. At most, I think just a hard reset and a new test to recalibrate, Sir."

The call ended with the captain advising Spears to keep him posted, and that he would be visiting the cabin later that day or the next.

Now in the relative privacy of the cabin, save that all conversation was recorded into an official observation log, the two began to discuss the readings in detail. What the instruments had captured was a complete mystery. It was all wrong.

All celestial bodies spin, and any given spot can only be observed by snapshot. And, because such long distances in space also signify length of time into the past, cameras could be adjusted to restructure the entire occurrence of an event.

But that was the damnable kernel of it all. In a singular section of the sky, 200 million kilometers distant, stars were showing changes in color, and even partial lensing, with no other disturbance apparent. The changes in color could be any of several things. They could be changes in temperature, but that was not even worth considering. There was another possibility, that it was their *light* that was being shifted. Something heavy enough could stretch or squeeze the light, changing its wavelength and thereby causing a change in color. This would also account for the lensing. Very heavy objects bent spacetime itself, and commanded light to go around them rather than block it.

The problem was that there was *nothing there.* A heavy object, even a black hole, follows a trajectory. But this was different. These snapshots were a mess. The distortions were all over the place, with no pattern. It was more like an abstract painting. Yet here it was, showing itself in reality, with the AI's reporting that nothing was wrong with the instruments.

Day I, Midmorning

The two friends met in the cafeteria as was their habit. They liked to get there before the school children had lunch. It was better that way. No sticky tables, and the place was still well-stocked. The size of the cafe made it a cozy spot, less imposing than most buildings on base. There was also the nostalgia of it, the folding tables with their lily pad chairs of dull red and orange, the smell of the wet rags the staff used to wipe them down after each meal. It was also better for privacy's sake. No one bothered to bug the place. The ambient noise made it a fool's errand. For this meeting, the two men took seats away from the others, cadets and contractors on break, and sat in the corner, near the restrooms.

"So," began Elard, placing his tablet on the table, out to the side. If anyone contacted him, he would see it, but he kept Spears right in front. "What do you think the big reveal will be with Apple-Head?"

Spears gave a quiet nose-laugh. "Apple-Head?"

"Our anomaly," said Elard. "The name just came to me. Like that painting where the man's face is hidden because there's an apple floating in the way. You can't see his face, his identity... but it makes no sense why. What is an apple doing just floating there?"

"I get it. I like that. Yeah, I think you're with me that this isn't instrument failure. There's just too much to it. I've seen ghosts and bugs, glitches, the whole nine yards. This is too detailed. Whatever this is, it's real... Here's a pitch: how about a family of rogue black holes? They wouldn't have an x-ray signature unless they're eating, so they could cause the distortions and be otherwise invisible."

"True, but I don't buy it," said Elard "It's a great premise, except that that many black holes would be affecting *each other.* But it's not a bad place to start. I didn't see any measurements for gravity waves in the reports. I'm guessing that's not standard?"

"Right," said Spears. "Our array doesn't do that as standard. But they will, as soon as I rule out instrument error. It might take a while, so goodbye sleep. But, yes, as soon as I can get the captain to sign off on it, I'll run an LSGA/USE. And, before you ask, that's Long-Range Gravitational Array and Unidentified Spatial Event. It requires a high-ranking officer."

"Why?"

"Well, the short answer is: because government. The long answer is, they don't want sensors accidentally picking up experimental spacecraft and waste time explaining them away."

"That just put a wild idea in my head," Elard said, "What if Apple-Head turns out to be first contact? Remember the old saying that goes 'One of two things is true: we are alone in the universe … or we are not. Either answer is terrifying."

"And you see, I don't agree with that." added Spears. "I say, either answer is *interesting.*"

"Yes, exactly!" Elard beamed and held up his arms like the scales of Libra, balancing the two options. "And you know what? The man who said that was the same one who invented satellite-based navigation, but that's not the weirdest thing about him. He was not an engineer; he was a novelist."

"What's that?"

"A storyteller. He made his living inventing stories to entertain… or to stoke curiosity… or- "

"So, he made money doing what I do to get my son to go to bed?"

"Well, you know, 'from humble beginnings do we not all grow' as Lazarus said once. Look at mathematics. The man who discovered the hypotenuse did that by counting beans."

"Ah, yes. Or did he hate beans?"

"I forget. The point is that he worked with beans. That is about as humble as you can get compared to where we are now. But I'm getting off-topic.

Want a coffee? I'm buying." Elard rose from the table. No matter what his friend would say, he was going for a cup.

"Yeah, I think I better," answered Spears. He had his tablet out in a wink, and was checking it, scrolling, sucking his lips into a frown.

"Somebody let you down?" asked Elard, stopping when he saw the other man's expression.

"It's just a bunch of tangled wires around here," answered Spears, not looking up. "The hard reset will take long enough by itself. First, the Reads have to run their checks. They'll go over the code. Every line of it. And then they will reassess the images and the measurements after they've eliminated any possible errors. After *that*, the cadets and I get to follow their tracks and make sure they made no errors. But anyway, let me get to the part you want to know—I can't access the LSGA without a password and confirmation codes from both the head of IO and a CO. I can get the CO's, but no one has switched out the IO code from the last guy to me, and he's gone. No one seems to know where I can get a surrogate code to bypass … It's just a whole thing." Spears paused. "Yes, to the coffee, by the way. I don't know if I answered you or not."

Day I, Evening

One thing Elard had noticed at this base more than any other was the little touches. As the evening shift ended, and the night shift arrived, the walls dimmed the lights at the seams of the ceiling and floor, draining the sprites of peach and soft mauve and letting them run into corners here and there. Then came the harsh, dull orange light. It greeted the night shift cadets as they milled through the halls. Those orange lights would last just long enough, and then die down, allowing the walls to show their natural coat, assorted shades of gray plaster. Last, the night lights came on, arrays of deep indigo with a piercing white spot which served as moonlight. It made him smile, and he found himself looking for reasons to be out in the halls to watch these dawns and dusks.

Elard counted himself fortunate that his family's apartment was in the next building over from the cafeteria, which itself was nestled in the shadow of the observation deck. As such, he was able to walk home and observe the lights' change in their entirety. As he watched the lights change, warm to cool, cool to cooler, and then intersperced with shocks of artificial starlight, it hit him.

Eureka.

He had it. Or at least, a version of it. The digestible morsel of an answer. All he needed was for Spears to unlock the LSGA, and then he could build his model. From there, it was, as physicists were fond of saying, "just math."

Elard knew what to expect once he reached home. Michael and Nolan, his wife and son, would be at the kitchen table, reviewing the day's homework. Michael, who was an enlisted officer, oversaw biology and health sciences for the colony's elementary-age children. Their son, being five, got a thorough debriefing of his day's lessons every night after dinner. Then, once Nolan bedded down, Michael liked to wind down with an hour on the treadmill while Elard worked equations on his glass board.

Tonight, his brain would be hungry. Apple-Head was just out of reach, so he needed to steer it onto something tasty and challenging. His go-to was The Busy Beavers Project. Millions of mathematicians, physicists, and hobbyists from every walk of life worked on it. It was an ongoing quest to define certain types of Turing machines, deemed "Busy Beavers." Four had been found, but the fifth remained elusive. In fact, it might not be possible to find within the remaining time in the universe. And yet, the project persisted. Participants kept each other abreast of their work via forums, servers, and file sharing sites. Elard had not delved into his teams' latest updates since landing on Ceres, and this was a perfect opportunity.

As expected, Michael and Nolan were at the table. He slid by them, took some orange juice from the refrigerator, and asked how homework was going. They both answered him, but try as he might, their words melted into bright spots on a background of stars, with terms like "trajectory" and "wavelength" getting in the way, robbing them of any coherence. Michael gave him a look. She could tell he was caught up in his own kind of reverie, trying to be dutiful, but not making the cut.

He downed his orange juice, left his mug in the sink, and left the kitchen before he could do any more damage. While trying not to seem like he was retreating, he found his way into the living room and sat in a sectional that fit into the corner. There, he fired up his tablet and began looking for available programs to build his model. Once Spears got access to that LSGA, Elard would need to work fast. That was no problem. He was hungry for this. It beat the hell out of installing and testing panels. He did not go to space to be a glorified roofer.

Roofer. He smiled at that while watching his downloads. Apple-Head was going to be his— unmasked, studied, *discovered.* It was so close he could taste it.

"What in the world did they show you in that observation deck?" Michael snapped him back into reality. Her hair was now tied up in a bun, and she had changed, now decked shoulders to ankles in sweats. "Yes, he's in bed," she said, anticipating his next question. "Sound asleep. Long day."

"Sorry," said Elard. "I wanted to at least read to him and say goodnight."

"I know that look," Michael said on the heels of his apology. "Even if you tried, you would get distracted. Your Math-Brain is driving right now." She sat beside him and pulled out her own tablet, sighing, "And I'm just going to have to be okay with it."

Elard let the silence grow for a little while. "We both know I can't talk about my work. They didn't say it was classified per se, but by tomorrow we both know it will be. So, how are things at the school?"

"Is this all that we do?" she said, turning to look at him. "We just do the same things over and over. I teach the same lessons, struggle with the same developmental or behavioral problems, rinse and repeat, rinse and repeat. Don't you ever feel like that? Remember those posters in college, or even the stock images in our lessons? Those explorers, those scientists. They all look off as if they're seeing a bright future coming right at them. They look *powerful.* And that… that's what I wanted with you. But I don't feel powerful. I feel like I'm just spinning. Please, please tell me you know what I'm talking about."

"Have you spoken to the chaplain about this?"

"No. Don't do that. I can practically see the gears… just you doing what it is you do. You panic at anything at all emotional. I can see you opening the files in your head, searching procedures… what solves emotion? What solves emotion? Oh, she's questioning her purpose! Aha! Ergo: philosophy; *ergo:* religion! Who is expert? Opening file. Expert is: Chaplain. Eureka! Throw her, and her problem, to the chaplain."

"That's not how I meant it. I mean, if he or she told you something, and it isn't helping, then I could…"

"See? You don't even know who the chaplain is!"

"I'm not religious. Why would I? And why is that a big deal now?"

"No, no, no. The big deal here is that I need you to not run away at the first sign of me talking about something real." Her shoulders slumped. "It's been a long day, for both of us. I know it must have been for you. I didn't mean for all this to come out this way, but… it's not going away. We will have to talk about this. But, I'm calling it a night. Goodnight."

"Can you give me two days?"

Her curiosity perked. "Two days?"

"Give me two days to get this observation deck problem solved. After that, you get me, no distractions. I'll be dialed in. Promise."

"I won't be holding my breath. Let's see what happens in two days." She left him with that and walked down the hall to their bedroom, stopping once to check if Nolan had kicked his blankets off. By the time she left their son's room, she heard Elard filling his thermos with coffee. Once done, he slipped out of the apartment, silent as a shade.

Day I to Day II, overnight

When Elard carded himself into the observation cabin, the scene was exactly as he expected. The same two cadets were in the middle of filter inspection and cleaning. Meanwhile, Spears sat off to the side. He was leaning back in his chair, looking at the ceiling. He was playing with a children's toy; his son's most likely. Elard was familiar with these, a collapsing ball that gave the vague impression of a sea urchin when closed, but when opened, its assorted lattices and hinges blossomed it into the shape of a buckyball.

Spears continued tossing it to the ceiling and catching it as Elard sat down.

"You didn't have to come," he said, keeping his eyes on the ball. "Couldn't sleep?"

"Nope."

"What's the coffee for then?" asked Spears, giving the thermos a look.

"That's for you, if you need it."

"Don't need it," Spears said, and rose to put the buckyball toy back in his locker. "My own sense of duty is enough." He retook his seat. "But I might have a cup later."

"Still no news on the password?"

"No, which I expected, but that's okay. I already have a workaround. That's really why I'm pulling this all-nighter. I'm going to give it a few more hours, and then I'm going to escalate use of the LSGA to a safety protocol. At that point, the station's safety code can be used as an override with the written consent and direct supervision of the Instruments Overseer." He emphasized the point by pointing both thumbs at himself. Both cadets looked at him. He smiled back.

"Well, hot damn!" said Elard. "Why didn't you do that earlier?"

"Because earlier today, we were just looking at blotches. Not anymore." Spears handed Elard a stack of new images. "The latest of these was taken just four hours ago. We still don't have a proper trajectory... or, hell, any kind of identity... but one thing is now very clear. Our friend Apple-Head is headed into our neighborhood. That means a super-heavy event is passing within one astronomical unit of us. That qualifies it as an emergency. And now I have the photographic evidence."

"It's still blurry. How long will the LSGA take?"

"It'll be morning when we have the data cleaned up enough for anything useful."

"Okay, what about this? Forget making it coherent. Can you send me the raw data? I have an idea of what to do with it."

"What to do with it?"

"Yeah, I think I know how to knock away the apple... make this guy show us his face." Elard heard his tablet receive a text. Checking, he saw it was from Michael.

"Be home to see Nolan before school?" it read. He gave it a thumbs-up.

"Need to go?" asked Spears.

"Nope… what if you started that array now?"

"I don't see it making much of a difference. As soon as those two—" he motioned to the cadets, both still elbow-deep in the vents— "finish, then we can go ahead and fire it up."

Work stretched into the small hours, with Elard looking up from his tablet or pacing to break the monotony. With each break, he looked out through the observation deck windows. That scene! Windows were scarce on base, and those that were present were small and translucent, either blurred, heavy glass or smoked-out. Having spent the past day in the observation deck, he understood why. A day on Ceres was nine hours long. Nine. The sun, Jupiter, the countless neighboring asteroids, moved in real time. It gave a sense of vertigo if one watched for too long. Worse than that, it made you feel like a tiny bug in a cold, dark room that went on spinning forever.

He allowed it to wash over him — the faint whine of fear, the humbling grandeur— before pushing himself back into work mode. This dance ate through the night, and the others killed time by swapping stories. Elard heard these, but did not join in. He learned the entire life stories of both cadets, and the entire childhood of Spears's firstborn during his overnight tenure, and yet, by the time he stumbled home to see his own son off to school, he found he could not recall a word of it. He did remember their names, Darcie and Eric, which he counted as a small victory.

When he neared his door, his legs had regained life, and the lights were shuffling off their indigo hues to make way for the peach and mauve of daybreak.

Day II, Morning - Midmorning

Elard had wanted his brain to be satiated. He had made an unspoken deal as he poured the coffee into the thermos seven hours prior. *If I do this for you, you will stay quiet while I spend a morning with my son.*

When he entered, he saw that a new pot of coffee had been brewed, and Michael was standing next to the stove.

"I could use a hand with breakfast," she managed to sound cheerful, and Elard stole a sip straight from the pot before asking, "How about I tackle the sausages?"

For a little while, it was like college again. They were in a little one-room flat, working close as a tango, anticipating each step, each reach. Elard forgot the mystery in the sky, forgot that he had skipped an entire night of sleep, and for a second he was a young man, dumb and hot with love.

The table was set, and Elard leaned into the hall, calling Nolan to make sure he was brushing his teeth and not just letting the sink run.

"I am, Dad!" came the answer. When Nolan joined them, he saw his mother at one end of the table with an untouched breakfast plate and wearing her wannabe smile – the smile that was meant for the situation, but she didn't really feel. His father was at the other end, an untouched mug of coffee between his hands, his knees bouncing like springs. He got this way when he was thinking a lot about math. Nolan knew this, and he believed he understood it. More than once he had gotten lost watching videos or making up his own stories, and wound up still wide awake at 2AM. It must be like that with his father and numbers.

"Dad, can I ask you a question?" Nolan said upon sitting.

"First," said his mother. "Let's say what we are thankful for."

"Okay. I am thankful for the hands that made the food. I am thankful that we can— our family can— be fortunate and be able to come live out here in the stars. And I'm grateful my dad will get to sleep soon." Elard chuckled and held the smile afterward, and Nolan gave himself a secret congratulation. *Score! Joke landed. Dad laughed.*

"Dad," Nolan pressed again. "Can I ask you a question?" When his dad nodded, Nolan shot his shot, "Does math make everyone crazy? Not crazy, but where they can't think about anything else? Because, if it does, then I don't think I should be studying it. You know, for safety. I'm just a kid."

Elard smiled wider. "No, Nolander, math doesn't make you crazy. The thing is, I'm a physicist. I use math to solve mysteries. That means I have to use my creativity and my math— that logical, making-sense-of-things side— both at the same time. But that's not everyone. Everyone uses math, and it doesn't make them crazy. A lot of people can do math in their heads, like your mom."

"So," pressed Nolan. "You're saying I shouldn't become a physicist?" Elard laughed at that, too. Michael did not, for reasons she chose not say.

After breakfast, and after bidding his family a good day at work and school, Elard did plan to lay down in earnest to steal at least two hours' worth of a power nap. Instead, he decided to set up the preliminary steps of his project to discover the nature of Apple-Head. Preliminary, that's all. He had set his foot down.

Five hours later, he contacted Spears.

"You still up?"

"Just got up. Did you rest?" Came the reply.

"Better, I have something to show you. Can you come here? I'll explain."

Spears sent a thumbs up and arrived at Elard's door almost fifteen minutes later to the second.

"Don't tell me you've cracked it," said Spears by way of a greeting as he stepped over the threshold. "By the way, is that offer for coffee still good? I'm still shrugging off sleep."

Later, with coffee in hand, Spears sat in Elard's now-dimmed kitchen as the physicist wheeled in and booted up his wife's holographic projector. Elard began his explanation.

"With the gravitational wave data, I was able to get a better scope, a better frame of reference. I took the data, cleaned it, checked it, and then converted it into a 3D animation. Check it out. This is our friend, Apple-Head, from start to finish."

Elard played the loop, and, as the two men circled the open stage of the projector, they saw a patch of sky, replete with familiar stars. Immediately, at the top of one corner, a bright object appeared and began floating forward. It neared the middle of the stage at a slight downward angle, now sending out a wake of light, resembling heat rising off a road. These waves continued outward, shifting starlight blue or red depending on where the two men stood. Spears stepped in front of the thing and marveled. It was creating the same distorted ring of light from the photos.

"Pretty realistic, right?" Elard said, smiling. "Now watch." Just as he indicated, the lighted object disappeared as, off to the middle of the stage another appeared, wide and rounded. It floated, threatening to fall off the side of the stage, then veered back toward the center. Just as the first had done, it sent waves of distortion as it moved. As it neared the center, it too vanished, and made way for a third. This third light shot out like a bullet as soon as it appeared, beginning at stage right and ending its meteoric flight offscreen.

"That is what we have. Apple-Head seems to be three dense objects – A, B, and C. Each with separate trajectories, starting and ending points, and densities."

Spears watched the sequence two more times, until the newness wore off. Then, he caught his friend's eye. "What happened to A and B? Where did they go? For that matter, where did they even come from?"

"Right!" said Elard. "That's the question that gets stuck in your teeth, isn't it? No object can just manifest out of nothing. Or disappear into nothingness. Equally impossible. I don't have a complete answer, but I did notice something interesting."

"What's that?"

"Objects A, B, and C, *all have the same mass!* Which means… they could all be the same object."

"They can't be. How could they skip around like that? Also, what about the different speeds and densities?"

"Occam's razor. Either one object is moving in ways that are hard to explain, or we have three supermassive objects that appeared out of nowhere, and two of them vanished from the known universe."

Spears took a drink of coffee. He was kicking himself for not expecting this to get weird. This, however, was getting weird fast.

"Still not buying it," Spears said after taking some time to enjoy the coffee. Elard was a coffee snob, and this brew was one of his best. Spears continued. "Something has to be up with the instruments, or it's some type of object we've never seen before."

"It *is* something we've never seen before!" replied Elard, his eyes dancing. "What we are looking at is something we've been theorizing about for over a hundred years, but we've never seen in the wild."

Spears' mood dropped like a stone, and he stepped forward to cut Elard off. "Careful what you say next. This is dangerous. Even us having this conversation is dangerous. Don't talk about this to anyone. As far as anyone on this station is concerned, *those things* are theoretical, nothing more."

"Understood, Sir." Elard said after thinking on it. That frantic energy was gone from his eyes. Duty was back in control. Yes, the station. We must remember why we are here. "But may I speak freely?" Elard asked. Spears nodded his assent.

"I've read the literature," Elard continued. "For something that is entirely theoretical, there sure are enough post-impact damage studies."

Spears stared at his friend's face, searching for anything – signs of lying or exaggeration – that might calm him out of this moment. "Post-*impact?*" he asked. Elard nodded.

"Stop," said Spears in a lower, deeper tone now. "We can't continue this here. Grab all your research, wipe that machine, and meet me on the deck in one hour."

When Spears exited Elard's apartment and marched full speed into the hallway, he was still holding the coffee mug.

Day II, Afternoon

Spears had messaged Elard that he was setting up a conference with Captain Laron. Darcie and Eric would also be there. The plan was to have the crew give their reports, including Elard's animation. Then, they would assess the latest observations, and decide where to go from there.

Even with this warning, Elard was still hard pressed to contain himself. The conference was held in an office annex connected to the observation deck. Spears had set up his own projector, and a star map was on display, loud and bright and spanning the entire room. Captain Laron was seated at the far end, a frown etched to the corners of his face, and even the cadets held the predatory air of stubborn authority. Elard expected the phrase, "Excuse me. I'm sorry, but what exactly am I looking at here?" to come out of someone's mouth at any moment.

"… We are using the codename "Johnny" for the time being, Sir," Spears had finished saying. "This"— he zoomed in to show the ringed distortion— "is Johnny at a distance of 1,000,000 kilometers. Instruments estimate—"

"What is the object's speed, Officer?" interjected the captain.

"Sir, 732 meters per second, Sir," answered Spears. The captain accepted paperwork from the cadets, who nodded to confirm what Spears had just said. Laron began flipping through the readouts, while Spears took this as a signal to continue.

"Sir, Johnny's trajectory is hard to pin down. Our team, Dr. Elard, Darcie, Eric and I—" Laron cut him off, filling the room with a loud whistle.

"Seven hundred and thirty-two," said Laron, eyes planted firmly in the pages. "Seven hundred… thirty-two. Quite the speed demon, our little Johnny, isn't he?" With that, he handed the report back to the cadets. "This is precisely why we are out here in the boondocks, gentlemen. Excellent work. Continue monitoring. Notify me of any changes… Officer Spears, I understand you ran these tests using the LSGA under emergency protocol. Given the nature of the measurements, and their proximity, I commend you. That being said, as this incident is now a strictly scientific investigation, I expect the next readings to be recorded under your own authorization code."

"Sir, yes sir," replied Spears, his voice as even and measured as his face.

"Captain," Elard spoke up and stepped forward. "May I have a word in private?"

"Yes, doctor," said Laron, a tiny smile spreading like a wound among the lines of his lower jaw. "Everyone, dismissed."

Once Spears and the cadets had exited, the captain motioned to the chair at his left, bid Elard sit. He crossed his hands and leaned forward as Elard straightened, almost leaning back. "I hear you have been working on fumes, Doctor, so for both our sakes I will make this expedient. If you are wondering about publishing, there are certain protocols that will need to be followed, but it's still very early in the process for all that. Until then, the information you gather is to remain on base, kept encrypted under Spears' code, and is not to be discussed with anyone outside the project. Is that understood?"

"Yes, Captain. I understand that compl—"

"Spears also relayed you are concerned about safety, is that right? Don't be. As I just said, it's still very early on. Would you not agree that at this time there is no reason to think that Johnny is heading toward us, is there?" Elard was reluctant, but agreed.

"Sir… Captain, what is the lifeboat situation on the station?" asked Elard. The captain leaned back in his chair, regarding him, studying him. In his smirk was an air of … disappointment?

"80 percent capacity, Doctor Elard… well above the industry standard. Are you saying that you believe, against all scientific evidence, that Johnny is dangerous?"

"Captain, speaking from what we know for sure – Johnny is a *heavily* massive anomaly moving at breakneck speed with an unpredictable flight pattern. Hell yes, I'd say he's dangerous."

"All the more reason to watch him closely, Doctor," said the captain. He rose from his chair and strode from the room, casting back, "Excuse me."

Elard sat for a while in the empty room, the wiry connective tissue in his neck and upper back was starting to twist.

"Miles to go before I sleep," he said to no one. When he juiced himself back onto his feet and out the door, he found Spears waiting for him.

"Johnny? It's Johnny now?" Elard was confused more than offended at the name change. Spears smiled.

"*Johnny,* as in 'Appleseed.' See what I did there?"

Elard fought the coming smile… valiantly. Spears waved him forward and put a finger to his lips signaling they both must stay silent. He produced a piece of paper with a screen capture on it. It was from the Reads' relays, the messages they sent at regular intervals to high-ranking officers and black box logs.

It read:

ALERT: User ID [SPEARS-342A] Queried Error 502. Vocal.

ACTION: User flagged for monitoring.

ACTION: Report sent to ADMIN-CONSOLE [GovSec-1].

Elard took Spears by the arm and the two started walking. Once in the cafeteria, Elard blurted out, "What the hell does that mean?"

"I found it on a routine check. Five minutes before the conference. Nearly shat myself. So, if I was a little off in there, that's why. I got flagged by the Reads when we were talking about our friend out there, probably when we discussed the damage reports. I couldn't see what they sent in the reports. It's encrypted. Still, that means you were right. These things are way more than hypothetical. That's the good news. You get to say 'I told you so.' The bad news is… I don't think I'll be staying for much longer. Expect me to be transferred within the week."

Elard rubbed his temples. "God, I'm sorry. That's such *bullshit.*"

"Hey, it is what it is. Until then, I'm going to get you all the data you can handle. I'm going home. I need real sleep. I suggest you do the same. And do I have to say…?"

"No, you don't have to warn me. The captain made it loud and clear. See you bright and early. And hey, maybe they won't …" Spears walked away, waving his hand.

"I don't mean to be rude, Bud, but I'm handling this as best as I can, and I don't need platitudes." With that, he left Elard, still seated, in the café.

Day II, Evening

Elard waited in the empty cafeteria, running down the clock. When he was certain that everyone back home was asleep, he left and made his way there on foot. To his surprise, Michael was biking when he came in.

"Don't run off. I want to talk to you," she said. She caught her breath before adding, "I didn't mean that the way it sounded. I mean, I haven't talked to you in forever… wait, what's wrong?"

"I can't talk about it," said Elard, sitting on the floor before the sofa and leaning back against the cushions. He arched his back and neck, hoping for a pop. Nothing. "I literally *am* sworn to secrecy."

"You're not used to that, are you?"

"Well, it's not that. Or maybe it is that, exactly that. But it's combined with how they are running this thing… I don't know what I'm saying."

"No, you do know what you're saying," she dismounted and began to stretch on the floor beside him. "Everything you said makes sense. It's just the sleep-dep. Keep going. Maybe you could tell me … I don't know … something, without telling me anything? You need rest, Lardy, and I know you aren't going to get it while this thing is eating at you."

"Okay," he said, after a silent moment that consumed the rest of her stretching time. She slid up beside him by the time he had found his voice again. "Let me tell you about a boy named Johnny."

"Johnny!" she laughed. "I can't wait. Go ahead and tell me about Johnny." She wrapped her arms around one of his and made his shoulder her pillow. He smiled. For a glowing split second, he was floating and the neck-wires loosened.

"Johnny runs track," he heard himself say. "Johnny skips here and there. Johnny might go anywhere. Johnny is faster than anyone on the team. Johnny is faster than anyone's ever seen."

Michael laughed again. "Okay, so what's wrong with Johnny? Why are you still tensing your arm?" She squeezed his bicep for emphasis.

"Because Johnny…" Elard paused, his mouth still open. Dry. He turned and faced her with his whole body. His gaze threatened to wander, but he locked it into the eyes of his wife.

"Johnny is an Orm."

That did not get a laugh from Michael. Instead, she shook her head, opening her mouth for the inevitable question. Elard squeezed her hands.

"Johnny… an Orm is a wormhole… a wormhole that moves. A good comparison would be… imagine a portal to Nowhere, if Nowhere were a place."

"Hmm, that sounds like one of those things like contemplating the edge of the universe. You can't really. You get lost in your own head trying to imagine it… And you get to study one?"

"Well, yes, but… I mean…"

"Elard… what does Johnny look like? What would it be like to meet

Johnny?"

Elard, the physicist, the admirer of storytellers, considered that question for so long that Michael thought he might have fallen asleep with his eyes open. Then, he spoke.

"Imagine you're back at the house where you grew up. It's nighttime, and it's a full moon. You are lying on a mattress outside… in the road. But this mattress is a special mattress. It's magical, like a flying carpet. As you lie back and look up, watching the moon, watching the stars, it starts to lift off the ground. Before you know it, you are above the trees. You feel scared for a moment, but there is something about your magical mattress that lets you know you are safe. It will not let you fall.

You look here and there, only turning your head – you're still not brave enough to sit up. On either side, you see the tree tops. They are almost black, but you can still see the faintest hint of green allowed by the moonlight. You look back up at the sky and take deep breaths. You realize that you are still rising up. Up, up, and up, until you look outward again and see you are even with the great, black towers with blinking red lights.

Now, you look back at the sky. The moon is naked, white as a lily, and so stark in the dark heavens that it hurts your eyes. And as your eyes wander out from the moon, away from that pain, you see stars like sand on a table. For the first time, you see what is really out there, living in the great ocean of the sky.

It finally registers in your mind how cold it is this high up. You get goosebumps in places you never knew could get goosebumps, and you wish you had brought a blanket on this journey. You contemplate grabbing the corners of your mattress and wrapping them around you. You even try for a little bit, but it won't budge. You take a deep breath and let it out, watching the long trail of steam wisp away from your nose and mouth, off to join the night air.

Just then, something attracts your attention. It's subtle. You look up, and you see some stars, little glowing grains of sand… *bloop* outward in a ring, like God dabbed some water on that table. It's a bright ring of white and silver, and, as you watch, it spills out wider. More stars get caught at the edge. They dissolve and join the ring. And in the middle – nothing. Blacker than black, a great big dab of water on that table of sand.

You get distracted, because at the edges of your vision, there is an orange glow. It's like the sun is trying to rise, but it's rising at every single point on the horizon, everywhere. And, as you look here and there, left, right, upward, you see that orange glow is waving in trails. It's an aurora. Wondering if there's a connection, you look back at that big black dot, and you see it's almost grown large enough to touch the Moon.

Just as you have that thought, it *does* take the moon. It takes it into that blinding ring of silver and white. Sound distorts. The same motion you committed to before, looking left and looking right, now seems to take forever, or happen at the same time. You can't tell. You feel drugged. As you watch, the edges of the horizon burn bright blue, and long arcs of lightning begin to jet across the edges of the world. Above you, the orange haze has deepened into a nice, clean red. And that perfectly round black thing is so big… you feel like the world is fake and you are hanging over *it*. Instead of lying on your mattress, you are clinging to it. The world is not the bottom now, and the sky is not the top.

Everything is upside down!

And that, *that* is the last thought you ever have."

Elard realized his gaze had wandered from his wife's as he had been speaking. This came as a shock when she kissed his forehead.

"You are so talented," she told him, locking his eyes back into hers. She told him something after that, and it was calm. Calm and calming. He could not understand it. Sleep was taking him. He was falling backward into it, whether he wanted to or not.

Day III, Early Morning

Just as Michael's voice was the last sound he had heard before dreamless sleep, Elard awoke to his wife's voice and hands on his shoulders. She baptized him back into the world, lifting his head off the floor and onto her shoulder before sitting him upright and giving him a light slap.

She is speaking. Elard thought. *She was already saying something, wasn't she?* His mind fed him, now with more clarity of the situation.

"… and they are saying it's an emergency, Elard. Wake *up!*"

Elard took a deep breath, and, as soon as he exhaled it, he saw his son start to totter down the far hall. Just as soon, he found himself rushing out the door.

Yes. Emergency. He broke into a sprint, tablet tucked under his right arm. As he bounded from weightless to wobbling during his sprint, his wife's words from minutes before began to take on coherence. Spears had called. The captain was with him. They had been calling from the observation deck, and he needed to join them.

Something was wrong.

Elard slid his card three times when he reached the observation deck, all to no effect. He was spinning out ideas as to whether any and all access to the deck had been restricted when the doors opened and Darcie and Eric reached out in unison and pulled him inside.

Captain Laron handed him a cup of coffee and pulled him into the center of the room.

"How are the probes maintaining?" Laron jawed at the cadets. They responded, but as Elard's brain was busy converting their numbers into real satellites and real positions, the captain filled his field of vision.

"We have to deflect your friend, Johnny, Doctor."

"Johnny changed course… again." Spears called over his shoulder, his tone friendly. Elard smiled at that. Wait, a smile? Wait… *Johnny is headed this way?*

"… such as black holes can be deflected by placing objects with enough mass in their paths. We have nuclear…" that voice was coming from somewhere, but it did not matter to Elard.

In that moment, his son getting ready for school… lunchroom tables with lily pad chairs… a thousand moments spent with the only woman he had shared a bed with… scientists in textbooks looking powerful… taking words and making them numbers… getting excited about it… wakefulness…

sleepiness…

He just…

Hiccupped.

The captain asked him what he had just said, and he made the same sound. It was not a hiccup, he realized. He apologized, but he did not know why. He was not sorry. He walked away, and out into the hallway, once again causing currents of cadets to part around him. It was not a hiccup, the thought hit him again.

Elard bent at the waist and laughed like he had never laughed in his life. It hurt. He tasted blood. He gasped beyond gasping, swallowing air in chunks. Then… he jerked back against the wall, the laughs coming up from him, vibrating him. Some of the cadets stopped, ready to give medical assistance. The captain was there now, hovering over him, debating whether to deliver a swift blow or shake him with a friendly invitation back into authority's embrace.

Yet, he could not. Elard hugged himself hard enough to bruise his own ribs. Lungs full, he let loose again.

He could not stop laughing.

IV

Opus Sectile: Ellipsism

Blackberry Winter

Vaclav spent that morning practicing in the mirror. He didn't hear the words, focusing instead on his voice and face. Delivery. He was aiming for perfect delivery.

"I'm dying," he said. *No, no good. I'm nodding at "dying." I shouldn't sound like I need her to believe me. I should sound like... exactly what it is. The truth.*

"I'm dying. I have..."

That's better. More casual. But that's its flaw. This isn't casual. This needs to carry weight.

Time to go.

The trees are moving as we pass by. I used to love watching this during a drive, especially while being a passenger. Clouds. Yes, also the clouds. Okay, maybe I'll get that back. It's just blunted, but I'll have it back after I get into meditation or hypnosis... something like that.

Trees. Plantlife. Foliage. It reminds me I've been smoking that gas station weed quite a bit since the diagnosis.

The library isn't far.

We meet in the sunroom. Tiny table, just big enough for notebooks and one laptop. Three white wicker chairs surrounded on three sides by glass walls. In short, perfect.

...

She knows me. Not just from the writer's get-togethers each month. She jokes. Do you read Vaclav Mraz? I make the same joke. Do you read Suzie Kewpie? I say that this has to be a pseudonym.

No. No. Not a pseudonym. It's more of a pen name. And you haven't read my work unless you've been sneaking into my room. Or you're one hell of a hacker.

Really? I thought you only wrote in a notebook.

No, I write on a laptop. I don't leave my room without it anymore.

There's a story there, I say. What is it?

When I was living with my mom we stayed at this trailer park that was like a commune. Imagine a cul-de-sac, but with trailers, and it was out in the middle of BFE. My mom got behind on the rent, and our landlord wanted her to pay him in sex. She told him where to go; so, he broke into our place in the middle of the day while she was at work. I was at school, thank God. Anyway, I had left my laptop on the kitchen table. He thought it was hers, so he took it and burned it. I should mention that there were these steel drums, like oil drums, that everyone used to burn trash. He tossed it in there and poured gas on it. Lit it up. It was still burning when I got home from school. I think I was about a sophomore then. I was 15, I think. I cried my fucking eyes out for a month. I also spent the whole time we lived there trying to come up with a way to kill him and make it look like an accident. I'm bad about procrastinating though, so I never did it. But I learned my lesson. I keep my shit with me at all times, and I have back-ups.

I nod. What's BFE?

Bum-Fuck Egypt. You've never been to Bum-Fuck Egypt?

And with that we become fast friends.

...

She takes the news well. I have maybe one good year left. After that, my health, my upkeep, will be a full-time job. I want to know my stories will find their endings. You see, I am also bad with procrastination. I mean for that to land better, but I am not sure it does. Anyhoo, I say, biting off the awkward moment with a smile, I have dozens of stories that have endings in my head, but I haven't discovered the pathways to get them there. And some just don't have anywhere to go at all. That is what I need from you, I tell her. Your style, your humor, your ability to be gruesome, and yes, there is something about you that tells me I can trust you. If you say you will do this, I know that you will. So... I never beg, but...

She agrees.

...

There are two stories from the anthology that stick out, she says.

I think they are your best ideas. You are at your best when you try to be Rod Serling.

"He Would Know What to Do" is a good one, but I don't think you or me has the tech know-how to give it... well, no, I think there might be a way to do it. Okay, so, let me get it straight. This game designer makes an AI to test like a real-life opponent. I think you mention he wants to use it to make harder video game bosses, right? So, he imprisons it in a VPN and let's it attack anything on that VPN. It can fuck up the hard drive. It can fuck up the ... whatever. Anyway, it escapes, gets onto his computer, then escapes to the Internet, where it begins engaging people in life-or-death games, taking over planes in flight, things like that. All good. One thing I would change is the thing's name – The Ouroborus. That's not what a gamer or a computer guy would call it. That's something a mythology guy would come up with. I'm sorry, but that's not knowing your character, and putting in a self-insert. He should come up with something that sounded like Edgar Rice Burroughs, a name like "The Wieroo," or "The Dar-Thak" because I bet that is what he's familiar with, comic books and things like that. Okay, so the Dar-Thak escapes and begins wreaking havoc. We have the conflict, but what's the crisis? We need a crisis before we can have a resolution. Is the gamer the main character, or do we want to leave him behind and focus on a random victim that the Dar-Thak targets, maybe someone elderly, in the hospital, or how about a group of forest rangers in the middle of a wildfire?

I smile. She's doing it. She's writing. She's helping my stories find their paths.

...

If you wrote an autobiography or your memoirs, what would the title be?

I consider it for a moment. "Chasing Sensation," I tell her. By the way, I was thinking of a funny story that I wanted to tell you, but I'm not sure if we could include it in the book.

I always used to joke to my wife that wasps don't bother me because I am one.

She smiles. That makes me feel good.

It's the truth, I continue. For years, they would just avoid me. There were several times I was even in the car with one, and it would just mind its own business. I would roll down the window, and eventually it would fly out.

Cut to – I think it was last year – I finally got stung. It was right in the middle of a spousal argument, one of those dumb ones. It was about how my daughter likes her bacon cooked, whether I was allowed to use the microwave. I said yes, and my wife was saying I had to use the stove or it wouldn't cook right. I sat down at the kitchen table – and then instantly I hopped back up. I didn't even know what was happening to me. Has that ever happened to you, where you know you're being hurt, but you don't even know what's doing it? I jump up and twist around, trying to see what the hell is causing this burning, stabbing sensation, and my wife just watches. A little aside, she thinks that it's unmanly when a man shows that he's in pain, so she gets stoic when she sees it.

It turns out that not only had I sat on a wasp, but somehow it had gotten inside my goddamn shorts. It got me two good times, then flew up my shirt and got me a third time on the stomach before we parted ways. I didn't kill it, by the way. I caught it in a paper towel and let it go outside.

She has been laughing this whole time.

I don't mean to laugh at your expense, but it's just funny to picture you walking around with a sting on your butt like a cartoon.

Oh, if only it had been my butt!

Don't tell me. Not the eggplant!

Twice! I hold up two fingers. Twice. And I don't blame the poor thing. Can you imagine? You're lost, wandering around, minding your own business, and then out of nowhere you get tea-bagged by this giant!

...

There is only one way I would believe a compliment— if someone said it, about me, to someone else. That's it. There's no way I could convince myself they're lying.

I know exactly how she feels.

...

I stabbed him as hard as I could. Both hands. I don't even know if—I couldn't tell if I even drew blood. I was looking at his shirt when he hit me. And he just kept hitting me. He broke my cheekbone, right here. He dislocated my jaw. After that, he kept me. We had a room in the trailer, my side of the trailer, that we didn't use. He put me in there. Wouldn't let me leave. He wouldn't let me eat anything. I remember he gave me these three plates of meat. He said the baby was in one of them, but he wouldn't tell me which one. But, anyway, after some days, I don't know if it was a week, we made so much noise the neighbors called the cops.

She has a certain way, in her openness, of being vulnerable and strong in equal measure, never giving quarter, never losing ground.

...

I used to have OCD. I still do, but I've gotten a lot better. Meditation was what helped me, but back when I was a teen, I took Anafranil. Weirdly enough, my mom told my psychiatrist, the guy who prescribed me the Anafranil, that I had recently become an atheist, and he witnessed to me for the better part of an hour during one of our meetings. He was the first person to lay that whole "as long as the Resurrection is real" horseshit on me.

Did your mom ever make you watch one of those atheist-finds-the-Lord movies?

Bwah. That's funny. No, those came out a bit late for me. I was already in my thirties when they started making those. But, yeah, I binge-watched quite a few. For laughs, I guess. The firefighter who finds God. The reporter who interviews God. The brave college kid who proves God. I can't get over the actresses in the supporting roles. I find it funny that so many of them are girls who did skin-flick cop shows back in the 90's, the ones that USA used to show after prime time. So, if you want a bit of taboo, guilty pleasure, you can watch a starlet pout her way through finding Jesus and then go back in time and watch her strangled in a bikini. Or mastermind a diamond heist only to be betrayed by her male model partner ... and then get strangled in a bikini.

Is that your fifty shades? She asks with a smirk.

I fucking lose it on that one. I laugh so hard I taste blood.

...

V, I'm sorry but I can't do this. Please know this decision doesn't come easy. I feel like shit, but this is how it has to be. I can't watch you go away. The more we talk, the more I get to know you. It's selfish, I know. I will keep my promises. I will finish your work, but no more meeting in person. You can write to me if you want. I'll respond each Saturday, and that's it. I think that's fair. Also, I won't be going to the writer's group anymore. Don't contact anyone there and try to get them to change my mind. I don't think you would do that anyway, but I had to say it.

There is more to it, but that is as much as I can bear to read.

...

It's a Saturday and I am sitting on my couch, staring at my laptop. I'm trying to get back into the headspace for one of my favorite stories. I call it "Brumous Seraphinus." It came from a line from the movie "The Prophecy," where someone talks about a war in Heaven between rival factions of angels. If the war doesn't end, the character says, "...then ash from a burning Heaven will cover the Earth." In my tale, a man wanders around a wasteland, perhaps all that remains of the whole world. Ash falls from the sky like snow. He begins seeing a figure with more and more frequency, a dark, gray angelic figure which he intuitively, maybe even via some psychic power, knows to be the "Brumous Seraphim." He doesn't know what it wants, but he finds himself drawn to it, and it to him. That's as deep as I got. I never could come up with a second act that did any justice to the setup.

"The ash did not fall evenly. It chose its memories. It drifted past clean porcelain and cold metal, leaving them shown, the ribs of the world. You aren't fighting your way out of this one. It, the ash, loved door frames and heirlooms. Broken windows. It loved the glass, loved it for its cluttered, frozen dance on the floors. It clung there. It found its way to corpses, but it chose decoration over burial. When the wind picked up, you could look at a corpse and lose yourself. Did people once dance at night in beautiful buildings? Was it haunted by soft, orange lights? Did that happen in real life?

When you wander, you think. I wander, so I think. A lot."

Not a bad beginning. I didn't realize it would become so prophetic, though. I keep staring at the words. I used to see that ash coming down, covering the world, so easily. Not anymore. Now, when I close my eyes, I see snow. I see frost. And the world isn't dead, it's still green. The only problem is that I realize what that means. Me and the world switched places.

My phone gets a text. It's her. She says she's at the library and wonders if I'm busy. She also asks if I am mad at her. No, I say. I am not.

I fly off the couch.

...

She brings up "The Human Abstract," which is one I actually did finish.

Okay, so you set it up beautifully, if a bit rushed, with a great idea. The cartels are executing people, and they have this technique where they remove the DMT from their brains so they can't see the light and the tunnel and all that, and then they burn the poor guy alive, right? They spread the rumor that this makes the victim feel like they burning forever, and bing, bang, boom, people believe in it. It's like going to hell. Ultimate weapon, ultimate torture, I get it. Then you have this magician, this Penn Jillette type, who wants to undergo the first part of the process and then get drowned and brought back to prove that you don't feel the moment of pain forever. So, he gets his brain sucked dry of DMT, they drown him, and then you end it with him still in a coma. That's bullshit. That's a bad story. There is no payoff. That's not even a downer ending. It's a cock-tease with no reason to it. There has to be a reason, you know what I'm saying? The story has to tell you something. If it doesn't, then why am I reading it?

Fair point, I must admit. And it brings something to mind. Do you ever wonder how deep it can go? Like, as soon as you hear the premise of a story, you've already told yourself pretty much the whole thing?

...

My wife is asleep in the other room with my daughter. They avoid me at night. Night hits me hard. In your forties you can expect, as a man, to wake up for a bathroom break at around 3 or 4. With me lately, I don't know where I am, and I scream. One time, when I realized I was still here, I looked at my face in the bathroom mirror and broke down sobbing. My wife took to sleeping in our daughter's room after that. She says it's because I scared the little one. I admit that is probably half of it.

Tonight, though, I'm thinking about "The Human Abstract." Suzie was right in everything she said, but that is not why it's on my mind.

"One thing my mentor taught me was that magic happens in the in-between, like shuffling cards, like when I'm talking to you, asking what you do for a living. You get that into your head, and you start catching things other people don't notice.

Case in point, one of the news reports. They were talking about the cartels and their method. People liked to call it their "damnations" or "perditions." It had everyone freaked.

It was one of those blink-and-miss-it blips in a news reel — dirty streets, people milling about, as the talking heads droned on about the bastards expanding their territory and the police being powerless or complicit. I saw some graffiti on an alley wall behind a taco cart. It read, "They told me the pain was real because it had a name."

That was it, the seed. That one line of relinquishment just started burning me up until I had to do something. A week later, I had decided – I was going to debunk those jack-asses. I was going to clip their wings.

In short, I was going to dare damnation."

...

How can I tell her? How could I? It's like I have been holding my breath my entire life, and now I can breathe. I'm being eaten alive by flesh turned against me, but I don't care. I want more. I want it. I want more. Just one more day, one more hour. Just talk with me one more time. One more memory. I've already sold myself the lie that it's enough. Please. There is no such thing as "should" in this whole sorry mess, but could ... Goddammit. No, I can't say that. Fuck me. Fucking fuck me. So, where now and what now?

I know what you meant now, Janis.

Maybe I'll have that as my epitaph. And maybe she will wonder what I meant... until she hears that song. I'd give all my tomorrows for just one more yesterday. And freedom is just another word for nothing left to lose. Nothing, nothing, baby, if it ain't free.

What Goes Around

All that I did to find the organization called Yggdrasil is not what I want to talk about here. In fact, right here and right now I'm not sure exactly what I want to talk about. I just know that I have the need to talk about what happened to me, and everything else.

…

A good friend once told me: you're not an alcoholic if you know when the liquor store closes. But if you know what time it opens…

…

Citra.

…

First an introduction to what Yggdrasil actually is. If you've seen the movie *Armageddon* there's a scene when Bruce Willis' character, an oil rigger, is approached by NASA to drill a bomb into an approaching asteroid to prevent an extinction level event. Nonplussed, he asks the recruiter,

"Is this your best idea? You guys are NASA. I bet you have a big room where you just have a bunch of guys thinking things up. And this is your best plan?"

That was 1998. Come the 21st century and the advent of cyber-attacks and global economic events moving faster than the slow wheels of legislation, and that idea of a room of brainstormers became more than a good idea. It became essential.

Yggdrasil is the place that trains the people who sit in a room and think shit up. They are a non-profit, multinational organization which has mastered the techniques of filling the human mind with information and teaching it how to use said information. They make Sherlock Holmes. Insider information told of only three graduates, bestowed with code names— Nike, Pallas, and Nemesis.

That was the scuttlebutt. It was half-true.

Nemesis was the one who clued me in to it. I didn't know why at the time. I chalked it up to one of those male excuses people like me tell themselves, something like "It was her nature to be mysterious." But can you blame me? There was no trail of breadcrumbs. She told me, announced she would break contact and disappear, and promptly did just that. After a long search, I walked into the Yggdrasil office.

Amidst a forest of ferns and decidedly Indian furnishings, I saw a middle-aged man sitting in lotus on a pillow.

...

My favorite joke: Back in the Nineties, David Letterman would read viewer mail and give advice with a twist to those who wrote in. After he was done, Dave would flick the letter behind him at a fake New York nightscape, accompanied by the sound of breaking glass.

One letter asked, "David, I'm really hoping you can help me with something, because it's really embarrassing, but I need an honest answer. David...

Is it wrong to watch horses do it?"

Letterman looks into the camera with a serious face and quiets his audience's whooping and laughing.

"Listen now. Listen." He says, "This is a serious matter, and I'm glad you've had the bravery to address this topic. Is it wrong to watch horses 'do it'?"

He sighs. "No. There is nothing wrong with watching horses do it."

After that, David ponders a moment.

"*Paying* to watch horses do it, though— "

I laughed until I lost my voice. Today, I consider this not only my favorite joke, but also a good basis of my moral code.

…

We're all in this alone. How many times had I heard that? It always reminded me of those twenty-something's who are still in the throes of passion with Bukowski or Nietzsche or Carlin. To them it must seem empowering, catering to a sense of stubbornness and rebellion. Just imagine though, that the saying is true. Imagine that there is no such thing as human connection, just brief illusions when you share a moment with someone. You could build on that moment, expound on the commonality between you and the person, but you're just building a taller structure to topple. One day the betrayal will come, or the failing, or my personal favorite, when the person no longer recognizes you, and you wonder how two people could have drifted so far apart.

Then comes that magic moment. The phrase ekes back into your head, *we're all in this alone.* You struggle to reconnect. More than anything you want to feel warm again, but they just shrug and keep drifting. They are fine with it, of course.

Forget not the lesson of the wrasse and the blenny.

…

A friend once said to me, "My father was a proud… closeted… gay man." His eyes were moist with admiration and understanding. "He was good to my mother. The only time he cheated on her was with me."

Such is love.

…

DEMIURGE … the flowers had the look of flowers that are looked at. Ha ha ha ha. As above, so below. The deoxyribonucleic acids produced in the atmosphere of this Goldilocks planet followed suit of what the Cosmos had already done so long ago, and at the same time so omni-now, that the irony is sickening.

I found this in my journal. My journal is now any wall in my house between the hours of sunset and sunup apparently. Anyway, it seems at some point during my blackouts I had discovered the reality of God.

I had forgotten it by morning.

…

Math is truth, and truth is a strange thing. Truth can be an addiction. Mike Gentry showed me that. Mike was a specimen in my social circle from the early '00s, and he had an adherence to speaking his mind that was rather unique.

To convey how it was to be around Mike, it would first be necessary to describe him. Mike was just two inches shy of seven feet tall and hovered somewhere around 300 pounds most of his adult life. He had blonde hair and a round, boyish face with a flat nose. In a way, he was the most disciplined of us all – he joined an Aikido dojo at 16, freely admitting his inspiration came from watching Steven Seagal movies, and stayed with it until he had earned his brown belt. He believed in "discipline in everything" and thought that lying to spare someone's feelings was disrespectful.

One late night at Waffle House we were all discussing movies when Mike declared in his loud baritone, "… just like all Black people love *Training Day*."

Our entire group was white, and as I and a guy named Devin tried to shush Mike, he offered his rebuttal.

"No. No. No, Seriously. Angela— you remember her?— I worked with her. I was telling her how much I love *Training Day*, and she said, 'you want to know a secret? All Black people love that movie. Well, we just love anything with Denzel, to tell you the truth.' I'm not being racist; I'm just repeating what a Black friend told me. Well, she's not really a friend but— "

"Could you *please* stop saying 'Black' so much?" I hissed at him.

"What's wrong with Black?" He raised his voice then, getting up from the table. To our horror, he walked over to a pair of other patrons in an adjacent booth, both African-American. Mike kept eyes locked with us, freezing us in utter astonishment of what he was about to do.

"Excuse me." He turned to them. They had already been eyeing him from the instant he took a step in their direction, and I half expected there to be a quiet moment before anyone spoke. Not so.

"Excuse me." Mike led into his interrogation immediately. "Sir, I'm sorry, excuse me, but … you know that movie *Training Day…?*"

Oh my God. My breath caught in my throat.

The man nodded good naturedly. "Yeah. Yeah, I know it." I could see wheels turning behind his eyes. It's my understanding that every Black man's brain goes through a quick risk assessment when a White stranger asks him about artistic preferences. It goes something like *If I say to this person that we have something in common, what are the chances he will say "Mah-Nigga" and come in for a fist bump?*

"Okay, and so… what do you think of it?"

"It's alright."

At that, Mike spun back to us and motioned with both hands from the man in the booth to us and back again, as if physically shoveling proof of his argument to us.

…

I don't believe in Heaven, but I do believe in Hell. In one way or another, it's the driving force behind everything I do. I am so scared. I don't want to go to Hell.

…

I have always loved role-playing games— D&D and Vampire the Masquerade were my main go-to's— so I was doubly thrilled and amused when I found out how they got started. It's quite a tale in and of itself.

Back in the Edwardian era, a young man moved into a flat in New York. I don't remember the man's name, but for the sake of the story let's call him Hedwig.

The apartment Hedwig moved into was a newly converted warehouse, and outside the residents' rooms there was tremendous open space filled with unclaimed merchandise under sheets. One day, Hedwig decided to explore this space and uncovered a large aquarium. It covered the area of a large throw rug and housed a still-living shark, a Great White about ten feet long.

The shark introduced himself as John Haartman, and asked Hedwig if he would come visit again. Hedwig said he would and then left. The next time Hedwig visited, the shark asked him if he liked to play games, and Hedwig replied that he did.

"There is a game I made myself," said the shark, "that combines the pleasures of the campfire tale, the improv, the pantomime, and the luck of the draw. It begins as the player or players invent a character and then they and the host commence to tell a story together. When it comes to the part when a player's character is to act, the host relinquishes the narrative to him for that moment. To balance the game, dice are used to see if one's actions succeed or fail. Does this sound enjoyable to you?"

Hedwig agreed to try it out, and soon the two of them would spend Sunday evenings roleplaying.

It turned out, I later learned, that the shark hadn't invented role-playing games. Before he had been stationed in the upper floors of a warehouse in New York, the shark had belonged to a man in Holland. That man's name was *Jan* Haartman, and after he passed it was discovered among his papers that he had drawn up plans to entertain dinner guests by combining improv comedy and dice rolling.

...

I first met Nemesis at Citra's place. This would have been back when she had first moved out of her parents' house, and she and her boyfriend had a little trailer just outside of Austin.

...

"The thing is," the middle-aged Indian man said to me while I was staring at the course catalogue. "I always wanted to be that wise man, sitting under the tree or at the top of a mountain in a monastery. The thing is, though, that guy – being that guy is *hard*. But I can play the part well, I discovered. My patrons thought so, and so ... here I am."

"Uh-huh." I was frustrated. "You really expect me to believe this curriculum was tailor-made for me? How? How could you know what I wanted? I never wrote it down. I mean, I never mentioned it, never put it anywhere. Even if you were spying on me, you couldn't know."

"I don't design the courses. I just tell the initiates what they need to know."

"Oh, okay," I began reading the courses. "Euclidean geometry? Chess 1, 2, 3 – beginner to Grandmaster? Logic, also all the way to Masters level? Statistics and probability, and what is this? Introduction to calculation? What, why? Then only one Algebra course before Calculus?"

"It is a course designed to teach the human mind to understand numbers. Normally in academia, the student is asked to work with numbers and learn how they work with each other as the student does the work. That is folly. One must learn the relationship between them first. It makes it easier. The human mind deals most easily with duality. It's an easy concept to grasp, and it can make room for exception. For this reason, people excel at math that deals with 2s and 3s. Halves and thirds. But, if you introduce a 7 or a 9, or if you mix it all up – 2s and 3s and 5s and on and on – the mind reels and loses focus at the alien concepts. The calculation course teaches the student how to familiarize oneself with the relationship between each number, so that no combination is unfamiliar."

"Okay, but it lasts up until the Masters level. I wouldn't even be taking Math classes until I was already – "

"Yes, yes. After you master numbers, the rest is very elementary to you. You will be taking all your maths in the upper levels. By that point, it will be like art to you. You will be able to wrangle them and make them sing!"

"I wouldn't even begin Algebra until my fifth year!"

"Yes, I'm afraid that's perfunctory. But with all the Chess, Logic and Calculation training, it will, as I said, seem like an art to you by that point."

"In four years!?"

"The program you asked for takes ten in total. Did you think it would be simple? Like an injection? A Captain America experiment or some other super hero origin? No, it doesn't work that way. To be extraordinary, you must *become* extraordinary. You must build that new self, piece by piece. Now tell me, really, doesn't that make sense?"

He had me there. A decade though! I would be approaching forty. I looked back at the catalogue. The last four years sold me.

Doctoral Studies 1-2:
Advanced Quantum Mechanics
Meditation
Grandmaster Chess 2
Symphonic Studies

Humor
Applied Robotics
Doctoral Studies 3:
Quantum Studies: Manipulation of Fields
Meta-Ego Meditations
Doctoral Studies 4:
Four Forces Field Manipulation Mastery

...

I had a crush on Nemesis. It took hold instantaneously, impossible to resist. Citra and her beau had invited me to a game of Monopoly. They had hosted a get-together for about a dozen people, an average college hangout, a little booze and marijuana, a few couples and plus ones. People came and went. It was around midnight and things had dwindled down to those who were crashing out and those of us who were dedicated to staying up all night. Citra, for one, never went to sleep. Most women I've known have a nervous energy that robs them of sleep, but I'd never seen it like it was with Citra, so I knew I could count on not going back to my everyday life for hours. I was safe.

Citra loved Monopoly, and we usually ended up playing it around this time. The set up was always the same— Citra and her boyfriend, me, and one or two others would sit down and get halfway through a game. It would take us till dawn, and we would tear through an entire bottle of liquor, a few Adderall would change hands, and more than a few joints would be rolled and enjoyed.

I hadn't noticed her before. It was as if she had been summoned out of thin air. Citra asked me if I minded if "Nemesis" joined us, and I obligingly said no. It was the kind of etiquette question you answer a thousand times.

And just like that, she sat down beside me.

Citra had a gaming table stationed next to a window overlooking the lake outside. I remember the moon was full, and combined with the porch lights, it might as well have been day. It was that bright. I was sitting on a small, two-seat couch, and Nemesis sat beside me. She was in mid-conversation with someone else and sat down in a motion that struck me as ... *assertive.*

Her hip touched mine, and then I drank her in.

She was pale with thick, black hair in a cute pixie cut, no jewelry, no perfume. Her shirt was a size too large for her, draping over a hairless pair of slender arms as she propped her elbows on the table and continued her talk with Citra, who walked around cleaning while I was supposed to be setting up the board.

Citra's guy, whose name I cannot remember, sat down and began to talk to me, for which I was religiously grateful. I was desperate for distraction. The flesh of her hip, soft and yielding, was still there, pressing against my leg, stealing my thoughts. I felt the strap of her thong against my pocket.

I needed help.

Citra's guy talked to me for a few seconds, long enough for my breath and heart to calm down. I imagined I was a soldier, and this was it— time to default to my training. Name, rank, serial number. No, wait, not serial number. What the hell was it that soldiers say under interrogation?

A pair of feminine hands clasped around one of mine. And then, she had my hand in her lap, looking down into my palm. Not one word. She hadn't said one word to me. I couldn't move.

I didn't want to. Wherever this was going. Please, as a prayer to all that was holy, let it last.

She didn't explain why she did it. Nor did she ever introduce herself. The moment passed, Citra joined us, and then we started the game.

...

"Are you serious?" I asked the Indian man, whose name I later learned was Gerry. Also, he turned out not to be Indian at all. I wasn't trying to be rude, but the whole scene was too contrived. "Enrollment is free? And I learn magic. That's what you're selling me?"

"No," he said. "It's not magic. And you have to pay for materials..." He seemed to drift off for a moment. "Books."

"Okay," I said. "How do I sign up?"

"Be there when class starts. That's all."

"You know what this sounds like? It sounds like Scholomance. You ever heard of that? The college run by the Devil, and he keeps every tenth student's soul?"

"Ridiculous. No one can take your soul."

I just looked at him. He put such sincerity into the statement, my frustration faded, and I couldn't stop myself from smiling.

"After all," he added. "How could they? Magic?"

...

It turns out reality is more complicated than you think. It doesn't matter who you are, or where you approach it from. Just to be clear, I'm not talking about Life – that is a different matter entirely. Life is a more fluid thing and can be as simple or as complicated as it needs to be. I'm talking about Reality.

Assuming you are an intelligent, well-educated person, Reality is about three times more complicated than you think it is right now. Imagine that you had to start over, all of your learning, all the knowledge and intuition, all the piles and woven patterns of thought and memory that attuned you to the world around you. Begin all of that over again, layering it over the first like fresh paint.

And then, exhausted but feeling rather rewarded, you do it one more time. *Then* you begin to understand the way things are. It's the way it *flows*, now coming to you like second nature the way you understand the fundamental concepts you learned as a child. What is near, what is far. Hard and soft, motion and stillness. Sound and silence. Hot and cold. Speech and noise. Passing of Time.

Reality is an art form. And the greatest thing about it is that you are part of it. This is your story, and I'm telling it to you. And because you read my words, you are my story too.

Three and four are a pattern that creeps up over and over in the nature of things. It's not mystical; it's just what works best. Soft things come in threes, hard forms in fours. A good example is the chakras of the body. This flies in the face of me claiming it's not mystical, but it's the best example nonetheless.

There are three chakras that govern the non-physical, and they come in increasingly distant placement throughout the body. The highest one, the 1000-petal lotus, is not even contained within the body. It floats above you.

Still, it is an inseparable treasure, all yours. The lower four chakras are more mundane, and govern the workings of your physical body.

Color works this way as well. It is no happenstance that we as humans see color the way we do. It works best, just as I said before. In ROY G. BIV, you will notice that the colors of ROY and G. are very distinct from each other, whereas BIV – the "cool" colors – seem to mix. Royal blue can seem very much like purple, and purple is contained in Indigo. Some shades are unique to themselves, lilac and violet, but none are so different as Red is to Green.

But why is this essential? Why does it work best this way? Because of the way information is carried. Color is a wave, and shorter waves carry more information in a smaller area. Thus, waves with shorter wavelengths (higher frequency) carry more information but over a shorter distance. With longer (lower frequency) waves, it is the opposite. Color is not imaginary; it lies outside the realm of "a rose by any other name." Red can only be Red, it is unique to that wavelength. If you catch Red, and squeeze it, it becomes Yellow, as inevitably as water will become ice as it loses its energy. Cooler colors occur almost exclusively in the realm of the very small. Insects for instance use blues and even ultraviolet in their visual spectrum. We, however, being larger and seeing over vast distances, interact with a world of green plants and red fruit.

Nature is using this tapestry irrespective of us. One might argue that another animal might view another color reflected from leaves and fruit, but no. This is not so. The plants came before us. They evolved the colors of their tissue long before humans ever walked the earth. We followed their example and evolved retinas with cones that can detect these colors, and remember, these are very real wavelengths. Red is red and green is green. No other color, indeed, no other wavelength can do what color can do. Shorter wavelengths are too small for living tissue to absorb without harm— X-rays and gamma rays slice through DNA like microscopic shrapnel— while longer waves would require our eyes to be the size of satellite dishes and the images we rendered with them would be so distorted as to be useless. Therefore, we use visual light. We are tuned to the energy of the universe by our very cells.

...

Now go back to the beginning.

…

Life is growing. Reincarnation, whether in a spiritual sense or merely physical, is as plain as the food chain. You could call it recycling. Once again, you could just call it the food chain. But if you believe that a given person in front of you, moving around and having thoughts, interacting with you, was once someone else— if you were to look at your son as a child and wonder who he was before your wife birthed him— you will eventually come to a question.

Just how many souls are there? Are there new souls? If life continues ever onward through the lensing of endless minds and bodies, punctuated by deaths, then how are there more people now than before? And why?

That is a good question. I don't claim to know the answer, but I can apply Occam's razor here: there are in fact more people, therefore new people. Perhaps some of us are living more than one life at a time? Maybe some of us need to.

…

Perhaps you are thinking about what my name could be, and why I haven't mentioned it. Names are not necessary for an introduction. I think you know me well enough by now. If you don't, you will.

I don't have a name. If you like, you may give me one.

I think I'd quite like that. A gift.

…

"Don't you know what they call you?" she asked me. I tried to care, just for the sake of courtesy. In the deep recesses of my mind, I wanted to stoke the fires of respect I had once had for her. I mustered sympathy for her sex. Desperate, I conjured guilt from the Y chromosome I had inherited from birth. Still, nothing.

I just stared at her, my Genesis in all this. I wanted to move, to act. To do anything. I couldn't.

…

I watched my parents die from afar. It was easy by that point. Truth can be a drug. Anything can be a drug. That is true. So, meditation can be a drug. Anything can be unlocked inside of you, including altered states. I was well acquainted with the practice of medicating uncomfortable situations, so that's what I did, almost constantly. I was stoned, drunk, buzzed, and tripping on an hourly basis. Anything to put a handle on it.

I knew that if I was there in person, I would not be able to stop myself. I would look deep into them and try to watch them go, and then try to track them to wherever they went.

Thank God I didn't.

...

I met Citra in Sunday school. We were 11. One day, when class adjourned, she approached me and asked me about Mario World on SNES. I was flabbergasted – the idea that girls played video games was new to me.

I told her how the Koopa armies reminded me of mythology and that was it. We stole away and hid under a staircase, talking about video games in all the esoteric, English major ways our 11-year-old minds could conjure until services ended.

I was grounded for a week for that, and it was worth it.

Citra's parents were Christian doctors from Indonesia who moved to America in the hopes that it would be more accepting to their religious ideals. Results were mixed. They always treated me well, if a little strict. The best thing about hanging out with her was the space in her house. Her room was so far from the rest of her family we could play music as loud as we wanted. At 13 we were air-guitaring to Cherub Rock in her room.

It never occurred to me to ask her out.

The first time I seriously considered girls in a sexual way was when I saw the Smashing Pumpkins video for "Bullet with Butterfly Wings." At one point, there is a quick cut of Darcy bouncing to the beat as the song intensifies. Her breasts move ever so slightly under her skin-tight leotard, and the image refused to leave. My mind's eye fed the memory to me over and over. That night, I had my first nocturnal emission. My embarrassment in the morning was beyond description. I felt damned. Putting my moves on a girl was something as alien to me as becoming President.

Being raised as an Evangelical Christian had had a unique effect on me. I didn't even see a pornographic film until I was 18. It took two years after that before I even had a girlfriend. I wrote a love letter that won me a girl's affections at 17, but after a month of going steady, I reached the point of putting my hand on her hip and putting my tongue in her mouth. Shockingly, it didn't last.

But, back to Citra. We were thick as thieves throughout high school and into college. She met her guy at 18, and they were married at 21. He was good to her, I think. I liked him. After a year, they divorced, and she moved out to California. I lost contact, and I can only guess that's what she wanted.

...

Now it's time for me to describe the first time I saw it. The big IT. The grand revelation. Unfortunately, at the time that I'm writing this down, I'm not in the mood. Do you ever think about that? Have you ever been in the middle of a novel and thought, I wonder if the author was troubled by his divorce, or depression, or a bout of constipation on the day he put this to paper? It must happen. Do we just gloss over it, or is it noticeable?

Oh, never mind. I'll try.

The first thing I looked for was an electron, and it was precisely because of Heisenberg. I sat in the Yggdrasil lounge and settled into lotus, then peered out as far as I dared. I needed to reach an area without noise, a place where atoms are rare, perhaps a wandering hydrogen here and there. I went to outer space.

It was my first time going so deep. It's like deep diving, plunging into darker and colder, alien waters. Down, down, down, and down further, leaving the familiar behind, entering Fear, and then going right into the heart of that.

As you draw near their territory, your senses clear, and *it* makes itself known to you. The animations you'll find online, the ones that scientists make to illustrate their equations, all paint it across a flat grid on an endless black background. This is not at all how it looks in the flesh.

Close your eyes. If there is light around you, you will see either a warm space of reds, oranges and maybe some yellow mixed in, impossible to distinguish one from the other. And in-between, there is a kind of static. You cannot, no matter how hard you try, locate one dot from another.

What color are those dots? Could you say? They change so fast.

Squint now, squeeze your eyelids, and the color of the background changes to purple, with remnants of the warmth bleeding through each time you relax your eyelids in the slightest. Peer up through the middle of your brow, and the background moves away from you, appearing more distant.

Now you know what it is like, or as close as I can get to relating it. And into this soup I dove down to discover an electron. I was going to play with it.

Here's the problem: There is no such thing as an electron. Not as an object, anyway. To revive my analogy of chakras, the elementary particles are like chakras. A chakra is not an object. You cannot dissect a human body and find the heart chakra. Rather, they are locations where the energies of the body coalesce in specific ways. It is exactly the same with our friend the electron.

Let me just tell it to you straight— every particle is everywhere at all times. If you look, they're there. The only real questions are how many and for how long. An atom is a place in space and time that a minimum number of quarks and electrons show up together indefinitely. Now, if you were to ask me (or anyone else) *why* Nature acts this way, I would have no answer for you. It simply is.

Remembering my training, I soon switched from trying to find a single electron to trying to excite the electron *field*.

...

"What do you like to be?" Nemesis asked, holding all the player pieces out to me, giving me first choice.

"Top Hat, please."

"Top Hat to the Gent," she said, placing it at Go, and offering the others their choices. She chose the Shoe, and then we talked almost an hour before the dice hit the board. I think for brevity's sake I'll start calling Citra's boyfriend (future husband and ex-husband) Anatoly. Anatoly excused himself outside for a cigarette. Nemesis and I joined him, mainly for the sake of etiquette.

Citra never came outside when he smoked. She hated it.

Anatoly always got darkly philosophical when he smoked. It was like clockwork. He would bring up the darkest, most depressing things you could imagine, then, he would snub out his butt or flick it and be right as rain. On this particular night he mused about the illusion of choice and how happiness was so fleeting because of it.

"There's always a choice." I spoke up.

"Well, there's a Democrat," put in Nemesis, absently waving a hand my way. I ignored her. Anatoly didn't let me get far with that comment. He described the Iraqi torture techniques that had been everywhere on the news lately.

"You can't tell me that some poor schmo waiting to have his feet smacked with a 2X4 has any choice about his happiness." I thought about that for a moment.

"No, but that's the situation you're talking about. I mean, you're not wrong, but if all you think about is having your feet smacked and how they won't let you go no matter what you tell them then— well, that's an impossible situation. No lie. But I'll tell you this, I'd fuck with him. Whenever he'd come in and start his intimidation speech I'd be like, 'if only your mother could see you now.'"

"What if he doesn't speak English?"

"Oh, well, for shit's sake! I'm a 'Merkin! If you torture me, you got to learn my language! If you don't, I'll just get louder!"

Anatoly laughed and pointed his cigarette hand at me. We were all still feeling the alcohol, and maybe that explains what he said next. "You know what? I've always liked this about you. You are never not *you*. But you know how to be … I don't know what I'm saying or trying to say. Here, I'll put it this way. You're not John Paul."

I burst into a short laugh. "No one is John Paul but John Paul!"

"Who's John Paul?" asked Nemesis. I noticed she hadn't cracked a smile.

"He's Pre-Med," Anatoly and I said at the same time. Anatoly continued chuckling as he explained.

"Nemesis, John Paul— JP to his friends— is an Undeclared, but like every Undeclared he signs up for Biology and tells everyone he's Pre-Med."

"To impress people." I put in. That was stupid, I thought. Completely unnecessary, but I was hoping Nemesis would ask me her next question.

"It *does* impress people – Freshman girls in Nursing. You know he even bought a stethoscope? He keeps it in his bedroom. You know how I know this?"

"Oh my God, you banged him!" I said. "I'm sorry man. It happens to the best of us. Lobster dinner? Candlelight and a little Barry White? Deadly combination, man."

"Fuck you, dude. He posted it on MySpace." At that, Anatoly laughed out the last cloud of smoke, flicked his butt and turned to go back inside. Nemesis looked at me and cocked an eyebrow.

I shrugged. "He probably did"

Fate was smiling on Anatoly that night. About an hour into the game, he landed on Park Place after rolling doubles for the second time. He clasped the dice in his hands and looked at all of us playfully.

"Here it is, guys. I'm off to jail. I can *feel it.*" Sure enough, he was right. He rolled snake eyes, landing squarely on Boardwalk, which he promptly bought. My jaw dropped.

"What kind of Pre-Med shit is that?" I said. Citra erupted into laughter. Anatoly joined in.

"That is some straight-up Pre-Med shit!" Anatoly exulted. "Gimme my propertyyyy! I'm off to jail, kids!"

Pre-Med became the word of the night. I was feeling great. I noticed, among other things, that Nemesis had been smiling.

...

Now go back to the beginning.

...

One of the greatest minds since Einstein, and let me say that there are many, was Richard Feynman, known lovingly as "The Great Explainer" among physics students. He approached Carl Sagan in his ability to make the scientific world attainable, and he did it like all great orators, by putting himself in the shoes of his listeners. Looking much like Clint Eastwood in the 1970's, he would playfully taunt his audience in his thick Queens accent,

"There's a kind of *not-understand* that's 'I don't believe it. It's too crazy. It's just ... I'm not going to accept it.' ... well, I hope you'll come along with me. You'll have to accept it, because it's the way Nature works. If you want to know how Nature works, we looked at it, and that's the way it looks! You don't like it? Well, go live somewhere else! To another universe, where the rules are simpler!"

It's impossible to describe Feynman's contribution, standing on the shoulders of giants as they all did, without mentioning Dirac and the Double Slit Experiment. If you're not familiar, the Double Slit Experiment was the first mind-breaker in quantum physics. Energy was passed through two slits in an opaque barrier to be recorded on a light-sensitive sheet on the other side. The goal was to reduce the energy stream to such a degree as to see if Nature used particles or waves because a wave would pass through both slits, but a particle would have to pass through one or the other. Without explaining the whole thing, it showed that electrons (or photons) were both; any given "particle" was passing through both slits at the same time. Feynman supposedly, as a student, asked one of his professors about increasing the number of slits to see what effect that would have on the particle's "choice." He then expanded that to infinite slits, because— due to the equations of Heisenberg, Dirac and others— particles are taking an infinite number of paths (to our knowledge) and the real task is to narrow the parameter down to just a few that make sense.

I mention this because it gave me a revelation about my own abilities. Feynman drew up diagrams (called Feynman diagrams of course) to show the possible paths elementary particles can take. A lot can happen to them on their way between point A and point B – electrons can change into photons and back again, or run into positrons, annihilate each other and then reform, or multiple instances of both. Here's where that benefited me; an electron in flight *can* be a photon, which means if I want it to be, it *is.* And I can feel, touch and redirect photons.

As such, I didn't need to bombard an electron field with any new energy to control it, I just needed to clear my head and reach out to touch it.

And it worked.

Before I get lost in technical jargon, let me sum it up. With the four forces I could do three basic things: change any substance into any other substance, move anything weighing less than the Earth to anywhere, and control any type of energy. There were upper bounds to my influence, but there was so much I could do within those limits it hardly mattered. That was it in a nutshell.

Certain things were impossible. One was reversing time. This just cannot be done, which is weird, because there is no concrete reason this is so. But, anyway… Another was reaching past the event horizon of a black hole. I wouldn't go near those, not even to peek inside. And lastly, I wouldn't watch someone die. That was the major one. And by people, I don't only mean human beings. I averted my gaze from any animal suffering its last moments.

I'm not religious, not anymore, but I am superstitious. That may seem odd, but we all do it in one way or another. We avoid things that remind us of the frightening or grotesque aspects of life, even in effigy. We avoid even the idea of misfortune and reward ourselves for it. Mine was death. I could not shake the idea that I had trespassed into the territory of gods and was marked for it. They wouldn't let that stand. How could they, or He, or She? Death was how they would get me. I was still mortal, and I felt in my bones that should I watch the life ebbing from anything with breath, my mind would be pulled down with it. It was my Gorgon.

…

I attended Yggdrasil in Canada. Never you mind *where* in Canada. And it came to pass that during my junior year, none other than Mike Gentry sent me an invitation to his wedding. He lived in Philadelphia by that time, so I caught a flight, eager to see one of our old group again. Perhaps, I thought, Citra might show up there.

I had decided to stay at a hotel close to the airport. It seemed sensible, as I didn't have enough to rent a car, and didn't want to blow a large sum on taxis. Mike said he would pick me up, so I thought I was set.

I arrived at the local Sheraton at noon. The plane ride had been a breeze. I'd had a margarita in the air and was feeling nice. However, a surprise was waiting for me in the lobby.

There was no clerk at the desk, so I asked in an elevated tone, "Hey, is anyone back there?"

"I'm a-comin', hon," came an older woman's voice. She waddled out from the employee office and gave me a strained smile. She was approaching 60 and was about 100 pounds overweight with a severe limp. She had two moles on her left cheek, and skin so pale I could see individual capillaries in her face.

"I'm sorry, hon. It takes a bit for me to get movin', y'see. I hope you weren't waiting out here too long." She had left the door to the employee office open, and I could hear a television on at high volume. Steve Harvey's voice was telling us, "This is Family Feud!"

I apologized to her and said I hadn't been waiting long. I truly felt bad for her.

It took the woman, whose name was Fanny, fifteen minutes to check me in. She obviously had no experience with computers and would type by hitting a button with her index finger and then looking very closely at the screen before typing the next letter. She did this with each letter of my name, and every number of my credit card.

Joke's on them. I had no intention of paying off that card.

...

After graduation, I knew my next steps exactly. I had just turned 39, with my maturing years spent deep in academia, watching the world fully embrace the 24-hour news cycle, the advent of content creators, the MeToo movement, all of it. The last shreds of my youthful tethers were cut. It no longer felt like my world. I was a relic now. The songs of my youth were used to sell cars or fill time in grocery stores. But the wrath remained. My disappointment with humanity was as strong as ever, but cooler, more tempered. Tempered with the Fear, that clichéd fear of the aged that the young now have their hands on the wheel, and disaster looms. There was no time to waste on guilt for what needed to be done. My patrons were now a liability. If my plans were to succeed, they must be dealt with.

No more Yggdrasil. I erased it, all their records, their accounts, their funds. I reached out into their labs and shredded everything, every slide and every centrifuge, down to the last molecule. I wouldn't allow myself to murder any of them, so they might be able to rebuild, given enough time and resources. But they would not have that time. In the decade it would take for them to regain sufficient ground to provide anyone else with my power, I would be too well established. The world would be mine, and the idea of defying me a blasphemous pipe dream.

First, I moved to the North— Victoria Island to be exact, on the border between Nunavut and the Northwest Territories. There was a spot of land there I had been dreaming of since time out of mind. It was perfect for me, my nucleus, my nest. Victoria Island is entirely covered in tundra, a gray expanse larger than Britain and dotted with countless lakes. On one such lake in the middle of the island, there is yet another island, and on this island, there is a sizeable lake. Within this lake, there is yet another island. That is where I would make my home. Geologically, it is known as a sub-sub-sub-island, and it spoke to me like the fuzzy, vibrating nucleus of an atom.

I flew there, and naturally I don't mean on a plane. I had a way of cocooning myself in exactly the type of conditions to make my body comfortable, and then I would slide that whole mass to wherever I wanted, much like a chess piece. A moment's thought and it was done. There and then, I dredged up the frozen earth and rock and made my house. I went through several ideas. I'm not an architect. I do have some engineering training, but that is hardly a substitute. Eventually, I settled on something of a keep – a basic outer structure with several quasi-independent collections of rooms contained within. At first everything was very rudimentary, looking much like the crude mock housing one finds as decoration in an aquarium. There were no doors, windows were just holes in the walls. No pipes, no electricity. It was a shell, an earthen separation between my abode and the elements outside, a place I could build fires and lay my bedding.

I found I had no need for more. Niceties were beyond me. Not beneath, which I think is an important distinction, but simply beyond, outside my sphere. I no longer had any interest in experimenting with how a storm window operates, or even a sewer pipe. I did not need these things. Fire kept me warm day and night, and I could summon it at a moment's thought. My own waste could be buried miles into the crust if I wished, or even ejected into space. I was immune to the shackles of humanity at last. So, why bother myself with duplicating its compensations?

I didn't. Instead, I explored what my new life had to offer. After securing my home, I ascended into the heavens. I think it was at that moment I truly grew to appreciate my new state of being.

I went miles high. Not ten or twenty, but hundreds. Beyond the weather that you have come to know, beyond even ten times the distance of the highest cloud. How could I describe it? I was a deep-sea fish having arisen to the very surface of the ocean and able to view the sky in its entirety. When I turned my gaze in any direction, I saw immensity, and meaning. Upward, I saw our place in the cosmos, floating at the very surface of all that could be called "Earth." Turning downward, I saw the cradle of everyone that has ever been born and also their grave. I saw the playground of soldiers and doctors, of children, of ignorant bacteria and trees milling about without a single thought as to their purpose, all this and so much more lay miles beneath me.

Cities were yellow-white volcanoes with rivulets spilling out from their centers, connecting with others of their kind. This was night on Earth.

Day caught its true beauty. I could watch the landscape for what is truly was – magnificence made material. Earth was sculpted to earn the word "awesome," for I was in awe— *true awe*. There was nothing I could do but look upon it, the whole immense complexity of it. The water that seeped into clouds above the surface, only to be squeezed out in electrical fury over this place or that. The plants that slowly plotted to cover every square of the land. The liquid splendor of ocean that shown our personal star back to me. Nothing was ugly here. Nothing.

I wept. Right there in the air, my tears leaving my face and becoming steam.

Below me was Life, and I was finally able to appreciate it while remaining immune to its treachery.

There is weather in space. At the very top of the atmosphere hydrogen and helium bubble and jump like ocean waves. Their spray leaps halfway to the moon before raining back down in airy showers. As I hovered, orbiting the globe, I would feel them now and then, a sudden cool rush all around me. Below me, near the poles, green auroras snaked out their paths. I spent most of my waking moments there. When I grew tired, or needed to meditate, I would descend back to my house, tend to the upkeep there, and then ascend again as soon as I was able.

…

I had toyed with the idea of making the world a better place – whatever that truly meant. There were many targets I could think of. Dictators, mob bosses, and corrupt politicians came to mind. The problem was this – you can't save humanity from itself. Corrupted people are like weeds. Making a vacancy only invited successors, sometimes worse than their predecessors. No, a hermit's life it was to be.

At first.

When I wiped Yggdrasil off the map, I mostly wanted to ensure no one would follow in my footsteps and come seek me out to overthrow me. Human beings are like that. They can't stand anyone with real power, so they seek and destroy it. A great example of this would be their constant battle with Nature.

In the end, I couldn't stay away forever. Ted Kaczynski I was not. Eventually, the solitude became a weight on my soul, and I craved social interaction. To this end, I began flying to Yellowknife, and then to Vancouver. I would scrounge up money, buy groceries, catch a movie or go to a bar. That last idea wasn't the brightest, considering my low opinion of humanity in general, but oddly enough it never gave me any problems. I only met welcoming, congenial people in the watering holes of Canada.

It was in a gas station in Vancouver where my temper got the best of me.

…

A riddle for you real quick: when two time travelers fight, who wins? Funny. Why, it's the one who leaves first.

…

I had needed the restroom for some time. My bladder was screaming at me, so with that one thing on my mind I made a beeline straight to the men's room and locked the door. No sooner had I started to relieve myself than someone started banging on the door.

"There are other people waiting out here, buddy!" said a voice.

He pounded two more times before I could finish. Once I exited, I apologized to him as he passed me and then put it out of my mind. For whatever stupid reason, I decided to keep shopping. The thought entered my head that I hadn't had any coffee in ages, so I found myself frozen in option paralysis in front of the assorted cappuccinos and exotic brews when the man from the bathroom walked up to me.

To this day, I don't know why he did it. Some people truly go out looking for a fight. Maybe it was that I was smaller than him, which I was by half a foot. Maybe it was my look. My hair and beard had grown out for some time. Or maybe it was just his nature. No one can say.

"Hey," he said, standing well within my personal space. "Why don't you come outside? I want to show you something. Come on. Come outside." He was young, with broad shoulders and a shaven head. From his nose and scarred brow, I could tell this one had seen his fair share of violence.

"Oh, yeah? Show me what?"

"Just a little something. It won't take long. Come on." He smiled, more of a grimace.

"I tell you what. Why don't we just call it a day?"

"'I tell you what,'" he repeated my words in an effeminate voice. "How about I curb stomp your bitch-ass? How about that?"

That was it. I couldn't even tell it was happening. Before I could think about what I was saying, I heard words come out of my mouth as my voice dropped an octave.

"You listen to me. If you don't quit hassling me, there won't be enough left of you to bury."

I took the air out of his lungs and wrapped him in folded space while I said it. To hammer the point home, I microwaved him a little. Then, I turned on my heel and left. For some stupid reason, I thought that would be the end of it.

I felt him coming at me full speed out in the parking lot. He was running up from behind me, knife in hand. This time, I felt, I had no choice.

I squeezed him down to the size of a basketball, then burned the whole messy heap to charcoal. After that, I left society for a long while and took to writing on my walls and other unhealthy behaviors.

My trips to the upper atmosphere lost their splendor. Nothing helped. I felt lonely but also tainted. I was now a murderer.

I spent months going over the incident, wishing I had just looked the other way, pushed him down, or only hurt him a little. I could have done so many things differently. Yet, I didn't, and now I was stuck. I was in a prison of my own making. My life was now dirty. His face was imprinted perfectly in my memory, along with his smell and the sound of his voice. It was as if by taking his life, I had made it a permanent part of my own. Now he lived inside of me, a bully, a reprobate, the type of person I hate. But I did not hate him. I pitied him. I felt a strange love for him, some mother's son, and because of me his life ended in pain and anger, and futility.

And now, there was nothing, absolutely nothing I could do about it. I had found yet another thing I could not do.

...

Hawthorne's work speaks to the psyche of a person in the deepest of contemplation over their choices. Each of his better stories— *The Scarlet Letter*, "Young Goodman Brown," "Rappaccini's Daughter," "The Birth-Mark," "The Maypole at Merry-Mount"— force the question: what do you want, and what are you willing to pay for it? However, Hawthorne diverges from his contemporaries, especially among the Romantics, in that he casts Circumstance in the role of God. He excelled at showing that, while choice is linked to consequence, oftentimes the choice one makes was never much of a choice at all.

...

I can't believe I am where I am now. I never thought starting over would feel like this.

...

"Don't you even know what Nemesis means?"

…

She is my yesterday, and I am her tomorrow. She will keep trying. To outsmart me. To exhaust me. To trap me for good. That is what she is for, and I am everything to her. I like that.

Will she, though?

Catch me?

I think you know me better than that.

Now go back to the beginning.

Eschatology

I want to tell you a story. It is not *my* story, per se, nor is it fiction. It is all true, to the best of my knowledge. This story, which I want you to hear and remember well, is your story.

You are old, older than you can possibly imagine. If you could experience living one thousand years, and truly encapsulate that in your mind, you would be nowhere close. Imagine, if you can, a thousand times that number— rather than a millennium, a collection of one thousand millennia— and yet, still you are nowhere close to imagining your actual age. I am talking about one thousand times greater still, a life of one billion years. You are at least that old.

You were carried to term in the womb of a nameless star. She gave birth, losing her life in the process, and tiny pieces of you were born and sent on their way. Her sisters, too many to count, lent their hands and lives, adding to the tiny parts that would journey through those billions of years to arrive together in you. All that and more was necessary to get the shine in your eyes just right.

Think on that number: billion. That is the number of your birth.

Finally, the time came for your mother to give you consciousness. The star-born pieces which are arranged into what you call "you," began a process. Of course, I am speaking of atoms, but you are not made of atoms, not exactly. You, the real you, are merely a funnel for atoms. You take them from the

Earth with every breath. And, as you exhale, you lose them again. The mere act of reading these words has cost you a little calcium, salt, and other things, lost back to the world. You will replace them. On your journey, as you take in your meals, you will borrow them and conjure them into your movements, your body, and your thoughts. And then the day will come when you will lose consciousness for good. You will no longer borrow, but you will be borrowed from. You will go back into that dark, the same darkness that nursed you in that time long ago. Still, your journey has scarcely begun.

Now, for the next number, one trillion. That number is the impossible number, which I will explain. To say that it is one thousand times greater than one billion – the number of your birth – would be accurate, but this is a pathetically inadequate definition. You could, if you set your mind to it, count to one billion. Beginning right now, avoiding sleep and food, tapping out the numbers with your foot or hand if you run out of breath, you would finish in a little over thirty years. However, you cannot count to one trillion. Not even if your descendants continued where you left off, continuing for generations and generations. By the time your successor reached the number one trillion, they would not be speaking the same language. It is even possible that this hypothetical person would not even be your same species.

After you spend your brief time with consciousness, you will continue on, almost as if you are counting to a trillion. At this time you will be different. Everything you ever touched or borrowed will in turn be claimed and borrowed by others. There will be nothing to distinguish you from the dirt or air. You will have joined countless others and been a part of multiple minds.

Still, you will be counting. But you will not be counting in digits, you will be counting in years. In one trillion years, the universe, so familiar it seems eternal, will have changed. The dried skin of your planet will cease to float across the molten rock beneath. There will be no more earthquakes, nor any more mountains. The yellow sphere of light you found guiding your eyes and warming your skin all the days you could feel it will grow larger, its light deepening into the color of blood. This giver of light and life will become a monster. It will swallow the world, and you with it. You will become part of it, wafting across its angry surface as it begins its death throes.

All of this will happen. I must remind you that this is a true story. It is as inevitable as your next breath. And we have not even scratched the surface of one trillion years. The red monster upon which you dwell will die and shed its skin. This shedding will carry you with it out into the depth of space, back to where you came from before there was a Sun or an Earth, a mother, or even a single consciousness.

Only now has your journey begun.

Think on that number: trillion. It is the number of your death.

The time comes when the stars begin to die. There will be no more borrowing and rebirth, no new stars. Their time has passed. You are spread far and wide, all of your pieces, everything you ever touched. The remnants of your hands, your eyes, and every spark of thought or memory, will be adrift in the currents of the night sky. Another trillion years will pass, and the night will grow. Pale remnants of stars will add their lights to the darkness. Trillions of more years will pass until the last star dims and goes out. There will never be another day. No more suns to rise or set. Nothing for them to rise or set upon.

A trillion trillion years, or perhaps longer, will pass. The time will finally come when something happens. It is something miraculous, an event that has never happened before. All of your borrowings, the tiny pieces which made the "you" which you came to know, will begin to grow tired. They will lose their boundless energy, not so boundless after all. They will slow, crease, and crack at the edges. Finally, they will dissolve into space itself, indistinguishable from the vacuum.

Now you are gone.

www.ingramcontent.com/pod-product-compliance
Lightning Source LLC
Chambersburg PA
CBHW051108300726
48981CB00001B/52